**weeks on end because you have a deal to
complete! That's a crime!'**

'Incendiary words, Miss Brennan.'

Lucas leaned over and placed both hands on either side
of her chair, caging her in so that she automatically
cringed back. The power of his personality was so
suffocating that she had to make an effort to remember
how to breathe.

'I won't be kidnapping you. Far from it. You can walk
out of here, but you know the consequences if you do.
I am an extremely powerful man, for my sins. Please
do us both a favour by not crossing me.'

'Arrogant!' Katy's green eyes narrowed in a display of
bravado she was inwardly far from feeling. 'That's what
you are, Mr Cipriani! You're an arrogant, domineering
bully!' She collided with eyes that burned with the heat
of molten lava.

Lucas's eyes drifted to her full lips and for a second he
was overwhelmed by a powerful, crazy urge to crush
them under his mouth. He drew back, straightened and
resumed his seat behind his desk.

'I can't just be *kept under watch* for *two weeks*. How is
it going to work?'

'It's simple.' He leaned forward, the very essence of
practicality. 'You will be accommodated, without benefit
of your phone or personal computer, for a fortnight. You
can consider it a pleasant holiday without the nuisance
of having your time interrupted by gadgets.'

'A *pleasant holiday*?' Her breathing was ragged and her
imagination, released to run wild, was coming up with
all sorts of giddying scenarios…

Cathy Williams can remember reading Mills & Boon books as a teenager, and now that she is writing them she remains an avid fan. For her, there is nothing like creating romantic stories and engaging plots, and each and every book is a new adventure. Cathy lives in London. Her three daughters—Charlotte, Olivia and Emma—have always been, and continue to be, the greatest inspirations in her life.

Books by Cathy Williams

Mills & Boon Modern Romance

The Secret Sanchez Heir
Bought to Wear the Billionaire's Ring
Snowbound with His Innocent Temptation
A Virgin for Vasquez
Seduced into Her Boss's Service
The Wedding Night Debt
A Pawn in the Playboy's Game
At Her Boss's Pleasure
The Real Romero
The Uncompromising Italian
The Argentinian's Demand
Secrets of a Ruthless Tycoon

The Italian Titans

Wearing the De Angelis Ring
The Surprise De Angelis Baby

One Night With Consequences

Bound by the Billionaire's Baby

Seven Sexy Sins

To Sin with the Tycoon

Visit the Author Profile page
at millsandboon.co.uk for more titles.

CIPRIANI'S INNOCENT CAPTIVE

BY
CATHY WILLIAMS

MILLS & BOON

First Published in Great Britain 2017
By Mills & Boon, an imprint of HarperCollins*Publishers*
1 London Bridge Street, London, SE1 9GF

© 2017 Cathy Williams

ISBN: 978-0-263-92464-0

Printed and bound in Spain
by CPI, Barcelona

CIPRIANI'S INNOCENT CAPTIVE

CHAPTER ONE

'MR CIPRIANI IS ready for you now.'

Katy Brennan looked up at the middle-aged, angular woman who had earlier met her in the foyer of Cipriani Head Office and ushered her to the directors' floor, where she had now been waiting for over twenty minutes.

She didn't want to feel nervous but she did. She had been summoned from her office in Shoreditch, where she worked as an IT specialist in a small team of four, and informed that Lucas Cipriani, the ultimate god to whom everyone answered, requested her presence.

She had no idea why he might want to talk to her, but she suspected that it concerned the complex job she was currently working on and, whilst she told herself that he probably only wanted to go through some of the finer details with her, she was still...*nervous*.

Katy stood up, wishing that she had had some kind of advance warning of this meeting, because if she had she would have dressed in something more in keeping with the über-plush surroundings in which she now found herself.

As it was, she was in her usual casual uniform of jeans and a tee-shirt, with her backpack and a lightweight bomber jacket, perfect for the cool spring weather, but utterly inappropriate for this high-tech, eight-storey glasshouse.

She took a deep breath and looked neither left nor right as she followed his PA along the carpeted corridor, past the hushed offices of executives and the many boardrooms where deals worth millions were closed, until the corridor ballooned out into a seating area. At the back of this was a closed eight-foot wooden door which was enough to send a chill through any person who had been arbitrarily summoned by the head of her company—a man whose ability to make deals and turn straw into gold was legendary.

Katy took a deep breath and stood back as his PA pushed open the door.

Staring absently through the floor-to-ceiling pane of reinforced glass that separated him from the streets below, Lucas Cipriani thought that this meeting was the last thing he needed to kick off the day.

But it could not be avoided. Security had been breached on the deal he had been working on for the past eight months, and this woman was going to have to take the consequences—pure and simple.

This was the deal of a lifetime and there was no way he was going to allow it to be jeopardised.

As his PA knocked and entered his office, Lucas slowly turned round, hand in trouser pocket, and looked at the woman whose job was a thing of the past, if only she knew it.

Eyes narrowed, it hit him that he really should catch up on the people who actually worked for him, because he hadn't expected this. He'd expected a nerd with heavy spectacles and an earnest manner, whilst the girl in front of him looked less like a computer whizz-kid and more like a hippy. Her clothes were generic: faded jeans and a tee-shirt with the name of a band he had never heard of. Her shoes were masculine black boots, suitable for heavy-duty construction work. She had a backpack slung over her shoulder, and stuffed into the top of it was some kind of jacket, which she had clearly just removed. Her entire dress code contradicted every single thing he associated with a woman, but she had the sort of multi-coloured coppery hair that would have had artists queuing up to commit it to canvas, and an elfin face with enormous bright-green eyes that held his gaze for reasons he couldn't begin to fathom.

'Miss Brennan.' He strolled towards his desk as Vicky, his secretary, clicked the heavy door to his office shut behind her. 'Sit, please.'

At the sound of that deep, dark, velvety voice, Katy started and realised that she had been holding her breath. When she had entered the office she'd thought that she more or less knew what to expect. She vaguely knew what her boss looked like because she had seen pictures of him in the company magazines that occasionally landed on her desk in Shoreditch, far away from the cutting-edge glass building that housed the great and the good in the company: from Lucas Cipriani, who sat at the very top like a god atop Mount Olympus, to his team of powerful executives who made sure that his empire ran without a hitch.

Those were people whose names appeared on letterheads and whose voices were occasionally heard down the end of phone lines, but who were never, ever seen. At least, not in Shoreditch, which was reserved for the small cogs in the machine.

But she still hadn't expected *this*. Lucas Cipriani was, simply put, beautiful. There was no other word to describe him. It wasn't just the arrangement of perfect features, or the burnished bronze of his skin, or even the dramatic masculinity of his physique: Lucas Cipriani's good looks went far beyond the physical. He exuded a certain power and charisma that made the breath catch in your throat and scrambled your ability to think in straight lines.

Which was why Katy was here now, in his office, drawing a blank where her thoughts should be and with her mouth so dry that she wouldn't have been able to say a word if she'd wanted to.

She vaguely recalled him saying something about sitting down, which she badly wanted to do, and she shuffled her way to the enormous leather chair that faced his desk and sank into it with some relief.

'You've been working on the Chinese deal,' Lucas stated without preamble.

'Yes.' She could talk about work, she could answer any question he might have, but she was unsettled by a dark, brooding, in-your-face sensuality she hadn't expected, and when she spoke her voice was jerky and nervous. 'I've been working on the legal side of the deal, dedicating all the details to a programme that will enable instant access to whatever is required, without having to sift through reams of documentation. I hope there isn't a problem. I'm running ahead of schedule, in actual fact. I'll be honest with you,

Mr Cipriani, it's one of the most exciting projects I've ever worked on. Complex, but really challenging.'

She cleared her throat and hazarded a smile, which was met with stony silence, and her already frayed nerves took a further battering. Stunning dark eyes, fringed with inky black, luxuriant lashes, pierced through the thin veneer of her self-confidence, leaving her breathless and red-faced.

Lucas positioned himself at his desk, an enormous chrome-and-glass affair that housed a computer with an over-sized screen, a metallic lamp and a small, very artfully designed bank of clocks that made sure he knew, at any given moment, what time it was in all the major cities in which his companies were located.

He lowered his eyes now and, saying nothing, swivelled his computer so that it was facing her.

'Recognise that man?'

Katy blanched. Her mouth fell open as she found herself staring at Duncan Powell, the guy she had fallen for three years previously. Floppy blond hair, blue eyes that crinkled when he grinned and boyish charm had combined to hook an innocent young girl barely out of her teens.

She had not expected this. Not in a million years. Confused, flustered and with a thousand alarm bells suddenly ringing in her head, Katy fixed bewildered green eyes on Lucas.

'I don't understand…'

'I'm not asking you to understand. I'm asking you whether you know this man.'

'Y-yes,' she stammered. 'I… Well, I knew him a few years ago…'

'And it would seem that you bypassed certain security systems and discovered that he is, these days, employed by the Chinese company I am in the process of finalising a deal with. Correct? No, don't bother answering that. I have a series of alerts on my computer and what I'm saying does not require verification.'

She felt dazed. Katy's thoughts had zoomed back in time to her disastrous relationship with Duncan.

She'd met him shortly after she had returned home to her parents' house in Yorkshire. Torn between staying where she was and facing the big, brave world of London, where the lights were bright and the job prospects were decidedly better, she had taken up a temporary post as an assistant teacher at one of the local schools to give herself some thinking time and to plan a strategy.

Duncan had worked at the bank on the high street, a stone's throw from the primary school.

In fairness, it had not been love at first sight. She had always liked a quirky guy; Duncan had been just the opposite. A snappy dresser, he had homed in on her with the single-minded focus of a heat-seeking missile with a pre-set target. Before she'd even decided whether she liked him or not, they had had coffee, then a meal, and then they were going out.

He'd been persistent and funny, and she'd started rethinking her London agenda when the whole thing had fallen apart because she'd discovered that the man who had stolen her heart wasn't the honest, sincere, single guy he had made himself out to be.

Nor had he even been a permanent resident in the little village where her parents lived. He'd been there on a one-year secondment, which was a minor detail he had cleverly kept under wraps. He had a wife and twin daughters keeping the fires warm in the house in Milton Keynes he shared with them.

She had been a diversion and, once she had discovered the truth about him, he had shrugged and held his hands up in rueful surrender and she had known, in a flash of pure gut instinct, that he had done that because she had refused to sleep with him. Duncan Powell had planned to have fun on his year out and, whilst he had been content to chase her for a few months, he hadn't been prepared to take the chase to a church and up an aisle, because he had been a fully committed family man.

'I don't understand.' Katy looked away from the reminder of her steep learning curve staring out at her from Lucas's computer screen. 'So Duncan works for their company. I honestly didn't go hunting for that information.' Although, she *had* done some basic background checks, just out of sheer curiosity, to see whether it was the same creep once she'd stumbled upon him. A couple of clicks of a button was all it had taken to confirm her suspicion.

Lucas leaned forward, his body language darkly, dangerously menacing. 'That's as may be,' he told her, 'but it does present certain problems.'

With cool, clear precision he presented those *certain problems* to her and she listened to him in ever-increasing alarm. A deal done in complete secrecy…a family company rooted in strong values of tradition… a variable stock market that hinged on nothing being leaked and the threat her connection to Duncan posed at a delicate time in the negotiations.

Katy was brilliant with computers, but the mysteries of high finance were lost on her. The race for money had never interested her. From an early age, her parents had impressed upon her the importance of recognising value in the things that money couldn't buy. Her father was a parish priest and both her parents lived a life that was rooted in the fundamental importance of putting the needs of other people first. Katy didn't care who earned what or how much money anyone had. She had been brought up with a different set of values. For better or for worse, she occasionally thought.

'I don't care about any of that,' she said unevenly, when there was a brief lull in his cold tabulation of her transgressions. It seemed a good moment to set him straight because she was beginning to have a nasty feeling that he was circling her like a predator, preparing to attack.

Was he going to sack her? She would survive. The bottom line was that that was the very worst he could do. He wasn't some kind of mediaeval war lord who could have her hung, drawn and quartered because she'd disobeyed him.

'Whether you care about a deal that isn't going to impact on you or not is immaterial. Either by design or incompetence, you're now in possession of information that could unravel nearly a year and a half of intense negotiation.'

'To start with, I'm obviously very sorry about what happened. It's been a very complex job and, if I accidentally happened upon information I shouldn't have, then I apologise. I didn't mean to. In fact, I'm not at all interested in your deal, Mr Cipriani. You gave me a job to do and I was doing it to the best of my ability.'

'Which clearly wasn't up to the promised standard, because an error of the magnitude of the one you made is inexcusable.'

'But that's not fair!'

'Remind me to give you a life lesson about what's fair and what isn't. I'm not interested in your excuses, Miss Brennan. I'm interested in working out a solution to bypass the headache you created.'

Katy's mind had stung at his criticism of her ability. She was good at what she did. Brilliant, even. To have her competence called into question attacked the very heart of her.

'If you look at the quality of what I've done, sir, you'll find that I've done an excellent job. I realise that I may have stumbled upon information that should have not been available to me, but you have my word that anything I've uncovered stays right here with me.'

'And I'm to believe you because…?'

'Because I'm telling you the truth!'

'I'm sorry to drag you into the world of reality, Miss Brennan, but taking things at face value, including other people's *sincerely meant promises*, is something I don't do.' He leaned back into his chair and looked at her.

Without trying, Lucas was capable of exuding the sort of lethal cool that made grown men quake in their shoes. A chit of a girl who was destined for the scrapheap should have been a breeze but for some reason he was finding some of his formidable focus diluted by her arresting good looks.

He went for tall, career-driven brunettes who were rarely seen without their armour of high-end designer suits and killer heels. He enjoyed the back and forth of intellectual repartee and had oftentimes found himself embroiled in heated debates about work-related issues.

His women knew the difference between a bear market and a bull market and would have sneered at anyone who didn't.

They were alpha females and that was the way he liked it.

He had seen the damage caused to rich men by airheads and bimbos. His fun-loving, amiable father had had ten good years of marriage to Lucas's mother and then, when Annabel Cipriani had died, he had promptly lost himself in a succession of stunningly sexy blondes, intelligence not a prerequisite.

He had been taken to the cleaners three times and it was a miracle that any family money, of which there had been a considerable sum at the starting block, had been left in the coffers.

But far worse than the nuisance of having his bank accounts bled by rapacious gold-diggers was the *hope* his father stupidly had always invested in the women he ended up marrying. Hope that they would be there for him, would somehow give him the emotional support he had had with his first wife. He had been looking for love and that weakness had opened him up to being used over and over again.

Lucas had absorbed all this from the side lines and had learned the necessary lessons: avoid emotional investment and you'd never end up getting hurt. Indeed, bimbos he could handle, though they repulsed him. At least they were a known quantity. What he really didn't do were women who demanded anything from him he knew he was incapable of giving, which was why he always went for women as emotionally and financially independent as him. They obeyed the same rules that he did and were as dismissive of emotional, overblown scenes as he was.

The fact was that, if you didn't let anyone in, then you were protected from disappointment, and not just the superficial disappointment of discovering that some replaceable woman was more interested in your bank account than she was in *you*.

He had learned more valuable lessons about the sort of weaknesses that could permanently scar and so he had locked his heart away and thrown away the key and, in truth, he had never had a moment's doubt that he had done the right thing.

'Are you still in contact with the man?' he murmured, watching her like a hawk.

'No! I am *not*!' Heated colour made her face burn. She found that she was gripping the arms of the chair for dear life, her whole body rigid with affront that he would even ask her such a personal question. 'Are you going to sack me, Mr Cipriani? Because, if you are, then perhaps you could just get on with it.'

Her temples were beginning to throb painfully. Of course she was going to be sacked. This wasn't going to be a ticking off before being dismissed back to Shoreditch to resume her duties as normal, nor was she simply going to be removed from the task at which inadvertently she had blundered.

She had been hauled in here like a common criminal so that she could be fired. No one-month's notice, no final warning, and there was no way that she could even consider a plea of unfair dismissal. She would be left without her main source of income and that was something she would just have to deal with.

And the guy sitting in front of her having fun being judge, jury and executioner didn't give a hoot as to whether she was telling the truth or not, or whether her life would be affected by an abrupt sacking or not.

'Regrettably, it's not quite so straightforward—'

'Why not?' Katy interrupted feverishly. 'You obviously don't believe a word I've told you and I know I certainly wouldn't be allowed anywhere near the project again. If you just wanted me off it, you would have probably told Tim, my manager, and let him pass the message on to me. The fact that I've been summoned here tells me that you're going to give me the boot, but not before you make sure I know why. Will you at the very least give me a reference, Mr Cipriani? I've worked extremely hard for your company for the past year and a half and I've had nothing but glowing reports on the work I've done. I think I deserve some credit for that.'

Lucas marvelled that she could think, for a minute, that he had so much time on his hands that he would personally call her in just to sack her. She was looking at him with an urgent expression, her green eyes defiant.

Again distracted, he found himself saying, 'I noticed on your file that you only work two days a week for my company. Why is that?'

'Sorry?' Katy's eyes narrowed suspiciously.

'It's unusual for someone of your age to be a part-time employee. That's generally the domain of women with children of school age who want to earn a little money but can't afford the demands of a full-time job.'

'I… I have another job,' she admitted, wondering where this was heading and whether she needed to be on her guard. 'I work as an IT teacher at one of the secondary schools near where I live.'

Lucas was reluctantly fascinated by the ebb and flow of colour that stained her cheeks. Her face was as transparent as glass and that in itself was an unusual enough quality to hold his attention. The tough career women he dated knew how to school their expressions because, the higher up the ladder they climbed, the faster they learned that blushing like virginal maidens did nothing when it came to career advancement.

'Can't pay well,' he murmured.

'That's not the point!'

Lucas had turned his attention to his computer and was very quickly pulling up the file he had on her, which he had only briefly scanned before he had scheduled his meeting with her. The list of favourable references was impressively long.

'So,' he mused, sitting back and giving her his undivided attention. 'You work for me for the pay and you work as a teacher for the enjoyment.'

'That's right.' She was disconcerted at how quickly he had reached the right conclusions.

'So the loss of your job at my company would presumably have a serious impact on your finances.'

'I would find another job to take its place.'

'Look around the market, Miss Brennan. Well paid part-time work is thin on the ground. I make it my duty to pay my employees over the odds. I find that tends to engender commitment and loyalty to the company. You'd be hard pressed to find the equivalent anywhere in London.'

Lucas had planned on a simple solution to this unexpected problem. Now, he was pressed to find out a bit more about her. As a part-time worker, it seemed she contributed beyond the call of duty, and both the people she answered to within the company and external clients couldn't praise her enough. She'd pleaded her innocence, and he wasn't gullible enough to wipe the slate clean, but a more detailed hearing might be in order. His initial impressions weren't of a thief who might be attracted to the lure of insider trading but, on the other hand, someone with a part-time job might find it irresistible to take advantage of an unexpected opportunity, and Duncan Powell represented that unexpected opportunity.

'Money doesn't mean that much to me, Mr Cipriani.' Katy was confused as to how a man whose values were so different from hers could make her go hot and cold and draw her attention in a way that left her feeling helpless and exposed. She was finding it hard to string simple sentences together. 'I have a place to myself but, if I had to share with other people, then it wouldn't be the end of the world.'

The thought of sharing space with a bunch of strangers was only slightly less appalling to Lucas than incarceration with the key thrown away.

Besides, how much did she mean that? he wondered with grim practicality, dark eyes drifting over her full, stubborn mouth and challenging angle of her head. What had been behind that situation with Powell, a married man? It wasn't often that Lucas found himself questioning his own judgements but in this instance he did wonder whether it was just a simple tale of a woman who had been prepared to overlook the fact that her lover was a married man because of the financial benefits he could bring to the table. Although, he'd seen enough of that to know that it was the oldest story in the world.

Maybe he would test the waters and see what came out in the wash. If this had been a case of hire and fire, then she would have been clearing out her desk eighteen hours ago, but it wasn't, because he couldn't sack her just yet, and it paid to know your quarry. He would not allow any misjudgements to wreck his deal.

'You never thought about packing in the teaching and taking up the job at my company full time?'

'No.' The silence stretched between them while Katy frantically tried to work out where this sudden interest was leading. 'Some people aren't motivated by money.' She finally broke the silence because she was beginning to perspire with discomfort. 'I wasn't raised to put any value on material things.'

'Interesting. Unique.'

'Maybe in *your* world, Mr Cipriani.'

'Money, Miss Brennan, is the engine that makes everything go, and not just in my world. In everyone's world. The best things in life are not, as rumour would have it, free.'

'Maybe not for you,' Katy said with frank disapproval. She knew that she was treading on thin ice. She sensed that Lucas Cipriani was not a man who enjoyed other people airing too many contradictory opinions. He'd hauled her in to sack her and was now subjecting her to the Spanish Inquisition because he was cold, arrogant and because *he could*.

But what was the point of tiptoeing around him when she was on her way out for a crime she hadn't committed?

'That's why you don't believe what I'm saying,'

she expanded. 'That's why you don't trust me. You probably don't trust anyone, which is sad, when you think about it. I'd hate to go through life never knowing my friends from my enemies. When your whole world is about money, then you lose sight of the things that really matter.'

Lucas's lips thinned disapprovingly at her directness. She was right when she said that he didn't trust anyone but that was exactly the way he liked it.

'Let me be perfectly clear with you, Miss Brennan.' He leaned forward and looked at her coolly. 'You haven't been brought here for a candid exchange of views. I appreciate you are probably tense and nervous, which is doubtless why you're cavalier about overstepping the mark, but I suggest it's time to get down from your moral high ground and take a long, hard look at the choices you have made that have landed you in my office.'

Katy flushed. 'I made a mistake with Duncan,' she muttered. 'We all make mistakes.'

'You slept with a married man,' Lucas corrected her bluntly, startling her with the revelation that he'd discovered what he clearly thought was the whole, shameful truth. 'So, while you're waxing lyrical about my tragic, money-orientated life, you might want to consider that, whatever the extent of my greed and arrogance, I would no more sleep with a married woman than I would jump into the ocean with anchors secured to my feet.'

'I…'

Lucas held up one hand. 'No one speaks to me the way you do.' He felt a twinge of discomfort because that one sentence seemed to prove the arrogance of which he had been accused. Since when had he become so *pompous*? He scowled. 'I've done the maths, Miss Brennan and, however much you look at me with those big, green eyes, I should tell you that taking the word of an adulterer is something of a tall order.'

Buffeted by Lucas's freezing contempt and outrageous accusations, Katy rose on shaky legs to direct the full force of her anger at him.

'How *dare you*?' But even in the midst of her anger she was swamped by the oddest sensation of vulnerability as his dark eyes swept coolly over her, electrifying every inch of her heated body.

'With remarkable ease.' Lucas didn't bat an eyelid. 'I'm staring the facts in the face and the facts are telling me a very clear story. You want me to believe that you have nothing to do with the man. Unfortunately, your lack of principles in having anything to do with him in the first place tells a tale of its own.'

The colour had drained away from her face. She hated this man. She didn't think it would be possible to hate anyone more.

'I don't have to stay here and listen to this.' But uneasily she was aware that, without her laying bare her sex life, understandably he would have jumped to the wrong conclusions. Without her confession that she had never slept with Duncan, he would have assumed the obvious. Girls her age had flings and slept with men. Maybe he would be persuaded into believing her if she told him the truth, which was that she had ended their brief relationship as soon as she had found out about his wife and kids. But even if he believed that he certainly wouldn't believe that she hadn't *slept* with the man.

Which would lead to a whole other conversation and it was one she had no intention of having. How would a man like Lucas Cipriani believe that the hussy who slept with married guys was in fact a virgin?

Even Katy didn't like thinking about that. She had never had the urge to rush into sex. Her parents hadn't stamped their values on her but the drip, drip, drip of their gentle advice, and the example she had seen on the doorstep of the vicarage of broken-hearted, often pregnant young girls abandoned by men they had fallen for, had made her realise that when it came to love it paid to be careful.

In fairness, had temptation knocked on the door, then perhaps she might have questioned her old-fashioned take on sex but, whilst she had always got along just fine with the opposite sex, no one had ever grabbed her attention until Duncan had come along with his charm, his overblown flattery and his *persistence*. She had been unsure of where her future lay, and in that brief window of uncertainty and apprehension he had burrowed in and stolen her heart. She had been ripe for the picking and his betrayal had been devastating.

Her virginity was a millstone now, a reminder of the biggest mistake she had ever made. Whilst she hoped that one day she would find the guy for her, she was resigned to the possibility that she might never do so, because somehow she was just out of sync with men and what they wanted.

They wanted sex, first and foremost. To get to the prince, you seemed to have to sleep with hundreds of frogs, and there was no way she would do that. The thought that she might have slept with *one* frog was bad enough.

So what would Lucas Cipriani make of her story?

She pictured the sneer on his face and shuddered.

Disturbed at the direction of her thoughts, she tilted her chin and looked at him with equal cool. 'I expect, after all this, I'm being given the sack and that Personnel will be in touch—so there can't be any reason for me to still be here. And you can't stop me leaving. You'll just have to trust me that I won't be saying anything to anyone about your deal.'

CHAPTER TWO

She didn't get far.

'You leave this office, Miss Brennan, and regrettably I will have to commence legal proceedings against you on the assumption that you have used insider information to adversely influence the outcome of my company's business dealings.'

Katy stopped and slowly turned to look at him.

His dark eyes were flat, hard and expressionless and he was looking right back at her with just the mildest of interest. His absolute calm was what informed her that he wasn't cracking some kind of sick joke at her expense.

Katy knew a lot about the workings of computers. She could create programs that no one else could and was downright gifted when it came to sorting out the nuts and bolts of intricate problems when those programs began to get a little temperamental. It was why she had been carefully headhunted by Lucas's company and why they'd so willingly accommodated her request for a part-time job only.

In the field of advanced technology, she was reasonably well-known.

She didn't, however, know a thing about law. What

was he going on about? She didn't really understand what he was saying but she understood enough to know that it was a threat.

Lucas watched the colour flood her face. Her skin was satiny smooth and flawless. She had the burnished copper-coloured hair of a redhead, yet her creamy complexion was free of any corresponding freckles. The net result was an unusual, absurdly striking prettiness that was all the more dramatic because she seemed so unaware of it.

But then, his cynical brain told him, she was hardly a shrinking violet with no clue of her pulling power, because she *had* had an affair with a married guy with kids.

He wondered whether she thought that she could turn those wide, emerald-green eyes on him and get away scot-free.

If she did, then she had no idea with whom she was dealing. He'd had a lifetime's worth of training when it came to spotting women who felt that their looks were a passport to getting whatever they wanted. He'd spent his formative years watching them do their numbers on his father. This woman might not be an airhead like them, but she was still driven by the sort of emotionalism he steered well clear of.

'Of course—' he shrugged '—my deal would be blown sky-high out of the water, but have you any idea how much damage you would do to yourself in the process? Litigation is something that takes its time. Naturally, your services would be no longer required at my company and your pay would cease immediately. And then there would be the small question of your legal costs. Considerable.'

Her expression was easy to read and Lucas found that he was enjoying the show.

'That's—that's ridiculous,' Katy stuttered. 'You'd find out that I haven't been in touch with…with Duncan for years. In fact, since we broke up. Plus, you'd *also* find out that I haven't breathed a word about the Chinese deal to…well, to anybody.'

'I only have your word for it. Like I said, discovering whether you're telling the truth or not would take time, and all the while you would naturally be without a penny to your name, defending your reputation against the juggernaut of my company's legal department.'

'I have another job.'

'And we've already established that teaching won't pay the rent. And who knows how willing a school would be to employ someone with a potential criminal record?'

Katy flushed. Bit by bit, he was trapping her in a corner and, with a feeling of surrendering to the inexorable advance of a steamroller, she finally said, 'What do you want me to do?'

Lucas stood up and strolled towards the wall of glass that separated him from the city below, before turning to look at her thoughtfully.

'I told you that this was not a straightforward situation, Miss Brennan. I meant it. It isn't a simple case of throwing you out of my company when you can hurt me with privileged information.' He paced the enormous office, obliging her to follow his progress, and all the time she found herself thinking, *he's almost too beautiful to bear looking at.* He was very tall and very lean, and somehow the finely cut, expensive suit did little to conceal something raw and elemental in his physique.

She had to keep dragging her brain back to what he was telling her. She had to keep frowning so that she could give the appearance of not looking like a complete nitwit. She didn't like the man, but did he have this effect on *all* the women he met?

She wondered what sort of women he met anyway, and then chastised herself for losing the thread when her future was at stake.

'The deal is near completion and a fortnight at most should see a satisfactory conclusion. Now, let's just say that I believe you when you tell me that you haven't been gossiping with your boyfriend...'

'I told you that Duncan and I haven't spoken for years! And, for your information, we broke up because *I found out that he was married*. I'm not the sort of person who would ever dream of going out with a married guy—!'

Lucas stopped her in mid-speech. 'Not interested. All I'm interested in is how this situation is dealt with satisfactorily for me. As far as I am concerned, you could spend all your free time hopping in and out of beds with married men.'

Katy opened her mouth and then thought better of defending herself, because it wasn't going to get her anywhere. He seemed ready to hand down her sentence.

'It is imperative that any sensitive information you may have acquired is not shared, and the only way that that can be achieved is if you are incommunicado to the outside world. Ergo that is how it is going to be for the next fortnight, until my deal is concluded.'

'Sorry, Mr Cipriani, but I'm not following you.'

'Which bit, exactly, Miss Brennan, are you not following?'

'The *fortnight* bit. What are you talking about?'

'It's crystal clear, Miss Brennan. You're not going to be talking to anyone, and I mean *anyone,* for the next two weeks until I have all the signatures right where I want them, at which point you may or may not return to your desk in Shoreditch and we can both forget that this unfortunate business ever happened. Can I get any clearer than that? And by "incommunicado", I mean no mobile phone and no computer. To be blunt, you will be under watch until you can no longer be a danger to me.'

'But you can't be serious!'

'Do I look as though I'm doing a stand-up routine?'

No, he didn't. In fact, without her even realising it, he had been pacing the office in ever decreasing circles and he was now towering right in front of her; the last thing he resembled was a man doing a stand-up routine.

Indeed, he looked about as humorous as an executioner; she quailed inside.

Mentally, she added 'bully' to the growing list of things she loathed about him.

'Under watch? What does that even mean? You can't just…just *kidnap* me for weeks on end because you have a deal to complete! That's a crime!'

'Incendiary words, Miss Brennan.' He leaned over and placed both hands on either side of her chair, caging her in so that she automatically cringed back. The power of his personality was so suffocating that she had to make an effort to remember how to breathe. 'I won't be kidnapping you. Far from it. You can walk out of here, but you know the consequences of that if you do. The simple process of consulting a lawyer would start racking up bills you could ill afford, I'm sure. Not to mention the whiff of unemployability that would be attached to you at the end of the long-winded and costly business. I am an extremely powerful man, for my sins. Please do us both a favour by not crossing me.'

'Arrogant.' Katy's green eyes narrowed in a display of bravado she was inwardly far from feeling. 'That's what you are, Mr Cipriani! You're an arrogant, domineering bully!' She collided with eyes that burned with the heat of molten lava, and for a terrifying moment her anger was eclipsed by a dragging sensation that made her breathing sluggish and laborious.

Lucas's eyes drifted to her full lips and for a second he was overwhelmed by a powerful, crazy urge to crush them under his mouth. He drew back, straightened and resumed his seat behind his desk.

'I'm guessing that you're beginning to see sense,' he commented drily.

'It's not ethical,' Katy muttered under her breath. She eyed him with mutinous hostility.

'It's perfectly ethical, if a little unusual, but then again I've never been in the position of harbouring suspicions about the loyalties of any of my employees before. I pay them way above market price and that usually works. This is a first for me, Miss Brennan.'

'I can't just be *kept under watch* for *two weeks*. I'm not a specimen in a jam jar! Plus, I have responsibilities at the school!'

'And a simple phone call should sort that out. If

you want, I can handle the call myself. You just need to inform them that personal circumstances will prevent you from attending for the next fortnight. Same goes for any relatives, boyfriends and random pets that might need sorting out.'

'I can't believe this is happening. How is it going to work?'

'It's simple.' He leaned forward, the very essence of practicality. 'You will be accommodated without benefit of your phone or personal computer for a fortnight. You can consider it a pleasant holiday without the nuisance of having your time interrupted by gadgets.'

'A *pleasant holiday*?' Her breathing was ragged and her imagination, released to run wild, was coming up with all sorts of giddying scenarios.

Lucas had the grace to flush before shrugging. 'I assure you that your accommodation will be of the highest quality. All you need bring with you are your clothes. You will be permitted to return to your house or flat, or wherever it is you live, so that you can pack what you need.'

'Where on earth will I be going? This is mad.'

'I've put the alternative on the table.' Lucas shrugged elegantly.

'But where will I be *put*?'

'To be decided. There are a number of options. Suffice to say that you won't need to bring winter gear.' In truth, he hadn't given this a great deal of thought. His plan had been to delegate to someone else the responsibility of babysitting the headache that had arisen.

Now, however, babysitting her himself was looking good.

Why send a boy to do a man's job? She was lippy, argumentative, stubborn, in short as unpredictable as a keg of dynamite, and he couldn't trust any of his guys to know how to handle her.

She was also dangerously pretty and had no qualms when it came to having fun with a married guy. She said otherwise, but the jury was out on that one.

Dangerously pretty, rebellious and lacking in a moral compass was a recipe for disaster. Lucas looked at her with veiled, brooding speculation. He frankly couldn't think of anyone who would be able to handle this. He had planned to disappear for a week or so to consolidate the finer details of the deal, without fear of constant interruption, and this had become even more pressing since the breach in security. He could easily kill two birds with one stone, rather than delegating the job and then wasting his time wondering whether the task would go belly up.

'So, to cut to the chase, Miss Brennan...' He buzzed and was connected through to his PA. In a fog of sick confusion, and with the distinct feeling of being chucked into a tumble drier with the cycle turned to maximum spin, Katy was aware of him instructing the woman who had escorted her to his office to join them in fifteen minutes.

'Yes?' she said weakly.

'Vicky, my secretary, is going to accompany you back to...wherever you live...and she will supervise your immediate packing of clothes to take with you. Likewise, she will oversee whatever phone calls you feel you have to make to your friends. Needless to say, these will have to be cleared with her.'

'This is ridiculous. I feel as though I'm starring in a low-grade spy movie.'

'Don't be dramatic, Miss Brennan. I'm taking some simple precautions to safeguard my business interests. Carrying on; once you have your bags packed and you've made a couple of calls, you will be chauffeured back here.'

'Can I ask you something?'

'Feel free.'

'Are you always this...*cold*?'

'Are you always this outspoken?' Eyes as black as night clashed with emerald-green. Katy felt something shiver inside her and suddenly, inexplicably, she was aware of her body in a way she had never been in her life before. It felt heavy yet acutely sensitive, tingly and hot, aching as though her limbs had turned to lead.

Her mouth went dry and for a few seconds her mind actually went completely blank. 'I think that, if I have something to say, then why shouldn't I? As long as I'm not being offensive to anyone, we're all entitled to our opinions.' She paused and tilted her chin at a challenging angle. 'To answer your question.'

Lucas grunted. Not even the high-powered women who entered and exited his life made a habit of disagreeing with him, and they certainly never criticised. No one did.

'And to answer yours,' he said coolly, 'I'm cold when the occasion demands. You're not here on a social visit. You're here because a situation has arisen that requires to be dealt with and you're the root cause of the situation. Trust me, Miss Brennan, I'm the opposite of cold, given the right circumstances.'

And then he smiled, a long, slow, lazy smile and her senses shot into frantic overdrive. She licked her lips and her body stiffened as she leant forward in the chair, clutching the sides like a drowning person clutches a lifebelt.

That smile.

It seemed to insinuate into parts of her that she hadn't known existed, and it took a lot of effort actually to remember that the man was frankly insulting her and that sexy smile was not directed at her. Whoever he was thinking of—his current girlfriend, no doubt—had instigated that smile.

Were he to direct a smile at her, it would probably turn her to stone.

'So you stuff me away somewhere...' She finally found her voice and thankfully sounded as composed as he did. 'On a two week *holiday*, probably with those bodyguards of yours who brought me from the office, where I won't be allowed to do anything at all because I'll be minus my mobile phone and minus my computer. And, when you're done with your deal, you might just pop back and collect me, provided I've survived the experience.'

Lucas clicked his tongue impatiently. 'There's no need to be so dramatic.' He raked his fingers through his hair and debated whether he should have taken a slightly different approach.

Nope. He had taken the only possible approach. It just so happened that he was dealing with someone whose feet were not planted on the ground the way his were.

'The bodyguards won't be there.'

'No, I suppose it would be a little *chancy* to stuff

me away with men I don't know. Not that it'll make a scrap of difference whether your henchmen are male or female. I'll still be locked away like a prisoner in a cell with the key thrown away.'

Lucas inhaled deeply and slowly, and hung on to a temper that was never, ever lost. 'No henchmen,' he intoned through gritted teeth. 'You're going to be with me. I wouldn't trust anyone else to keep an eye on you.'

Not without being mauled to death in the process.

'With *you*?' Shot through with an electrifying awareness of him, her heart sped up, sending the blood pulsing hotly through her veins and making it difficult to catch her breath. *Trapped somewhere with him?* And yet the thought, which should have filled her with unremitting horror, kick-started a dark, in-surgent curiosity that frankly terrified her.

'I have no intention of having any interaction with you at all. You will simply be my responsibility for a fortnight and I will make sure that no contact is made with any outside parties until the deal is signed, sealed and delivered. And please don't tell me the prospect of being without a mobile phone or computer for a handful of days amounts to nothing short of torture, an experience which you may or may not survive! It *is* possible to live without gadgets for a fortnight.'

'Could *you*?' But her rebellious mind was some-where else, somewhere she felt it shouldn't be.

'This isn't about me. Bring whatever books you want, or embroidery, or whatever you might enjoy doing, and think about it positively as an unexpected time out for which you will continue to be paid. If you're finding it difficult to kick back and enjoy the experience, then you can always consider the alternative: litigation, legal bills and no job.'

Katy clenched her fists and wanted to say something back in retaliation, even though she was dimly aware of the fact that this was the last person on the planet she wanted to have a scrap with, and not just because he was a man who would have no trouble in making good on his threats. However, the door was opening and through the haze of her anger she heard herself being discussed in a low voice, as if she wasn't in the room at all.

'Right.'

She blinked and Lucas was staring down at her, hands shoved in his trouser pockets. Awkwardly she stood up and instinctively smiled politely at his secretary, who smiled back.

He'd rattled off a chain of events, but she'd only been half listening, and now she didn't honestly know what would happen next.

'I'll have to phone my mum and dad,' she said a little numbly and Lucas inclined his head to one side with a frown.

'Of course.'

'I talk with them every evening.'

His frown deepened, because that seemed a little excessive for someone in her twenties. It didn't tally with the image of a raunchy young woman indulging in a steamy affair with a married man, not that the details of that were his business, unless the steamy affair was ongoing.

'And I don't have any pets.' She gathered her backpack from the ground and headed towards the door in the same daze that had begun settling over her the second his secretary had walked into the room.

'Miss Brennan...'

'Huh?' She blinked and looked up at him.

She was only five-three and wearing flats, so she had to crane her neck up. Her hair tumbled down her back in a riot of colour. Lucas was a big man and he felt as though he could fit her into his pocket. She was delicate, her features fine, her body slender under the oversized white shirt. Was that why he suddenly felt himself soften after the gruelling experience he had put her through? He had never in his life done anything that disturbed his conscience, had always acted fairly and decently towards other people. Yes, undeniably he could be ruthless, but never unjustly so. He felt a little guilty now.

'Don't get worked up about this.' His voice was clipped because this was as close as he was going to get to putting her mind at ease. By nature, he was distrustful, and certainly the situation in which he had encountered her showed all the hallmarks of being dangerous, as she only had to advertise what she knew to her ex. Yet something about her fuelled an unexpected response in him.

Her eyes, he noted as he stared down into them, were a beguiling mix of green and turquoise. 'This isn't a trial by torture. It's just the only way I can deal with a potential problem. You won't spend the fortnight suffering, nor is there any need to fear that I'm going to be following you around every waking moment like a bad conscience. Indeed, you will hardly notice my presence. I will be working all day and you'll be free to do as you like. Without the tools for communicating with the outside world, you can't get up to any mischief.'

'But I don't even know where I'm going!' Katy cried, latching on to that window of empathy before it vanished out of sight.

Lucas raised his eyebrows, and there was that smile again, although the empathy was still there and it was tinged with a certain amount of cool amusement. 'Consider it a surprise,' he murmured. 'A bit like winning the lottery which, incidentally, pretty much sums it up when you think about the alternative.' He nodded to his secretary and glanced at his watch. 'Two hours, Vicky. Think that will do it?'

'I think so.'

'In that case, I will see you both shortly. And, Miss Brennan…don't even think about doing a runner.'

Over the next hour and a half Katy experienced what it felt like to be kidnapped. Oh, he could call it what he liked, but she was going to be held prisoner. She was relieved of her mobile phone by Lucas's secretary, who was brisk but warm, and seemed to see nothing amiss in following her boss's high-handed instructions. It would be delivered to Lucas and held in safekeeping for her.

She packed a bunch of clothes, not knowing where she was going. Outside, it was still, but spring was making way for summer, so the clothes she crammed into her duffel bag were light, with one cardigan in case she ended up somewhere cold.

Although how would she know what the weather was up to when she would probably be locked in a room somewhere with views of the outside world through bars?

And yet, for all her frustration and downright *anger,* she could sort of see why he had reacted the way he had. Obviously the only thing that mattered to Lucas Cipriani was making money and closing deals. If this was to be the biggest deal of his career—and dipping his corporate toes into the Far East would be—then he would be more than happy to do what it took to safeguard his interest.

She was a dispensable little fish in the very big pond in which he was the marauding king of the water.

And the fact that she knew someone at the company he was about to take over, someone who was so far ignorant of what was going on, meant she had the power to pass on highly sensitive and potentially explosive information.

Lucas Cipriani, being the sort of man he was, would never believe that she had no ongoing situation with Duncan Powell because he was suspicious, distrustful, power hungry, arrogant, and would happily feed her to the sharks if it suited him, because he was also ice-cold and utterly emotionless.

'Where am I being taken?' she asked Vicky as they stepped back into the chauffeur-driven car that had delivered her to her flat. 'Or am I going to find myself blindfolded before we get there?'

'To a field on the outskirts of London.' She smiled. 'Mr Cipriani has his own private mode of transport there. And, no, you won't be blindfolded for any of the journey.'

Katy subsided into silence and stared at the scenery

passing by as the silent car left London and expertly took a route with which she was unfamiliar. She seldom left the capital unless it was to take the train up to Yorkshire to see her parents and her friends who still lived in the area. She didn't own a car, so escaping London was rarely an option, although, on a couple of occasions, she *had* gone with Tim and some of the others to Brighton for a holiday, five of them crammed like sardines into his second-hand car.

She hadn't thought about the dynamics of being trapped in a room with just Lucas acting as gaoler outside, but now she did, and she felt that frightening, forbidding tingle again.

Would other people be around? Or would there just be the two of them?

She hated him. She loathed his arrogance and the way he had of assuming that the world should fall in line with whatever he wanted. He was the boss who never made an effort to interact with those employees he felt were beneath him. He paid well not because he was a considerate and fair-minded guy who believed in rewarding hard work, but because he knew that money bought loyalty, and a loyal employee was more likely to do exactly what he demanded without asking questions. Pay an employee enough, and they lost the right to vote.

She hoped that he'd been telling the truth when he'd said that there would be no interaction between them because she couldn't think that they would have anything to talk about.

Then Katy thought about seeing him away from the confines of office walls. Something inside trembled and she had that whooshing feeling again, as if she had been sitting quietly on a chair, only to find that the chair was attached to a rollercoaster and the switch had suddenly been turned on. Her tummy flipped over; she didn't get it, because she really and truly didn't like the guy.

She surfaced from her thoughts to find that they had left the main roads behind and were pulling into a huge parking lot where a long, covered building opened onto an air field.

'I give you Lucas's transport...' Vicky murmured. 'If you look to the right, you'll see his private jet. It's the black one. But today you'll be taking the helicopter.'

Jet? Helicopter?

Katy did a double-take. Her eyes swivelled from private jet to helicopter and, sure enough, there he was, leaning indolently against a black and silver helicopter, dark shades shielding his eyes from the early-afternoon glare.

Her mouth ran dry. He was watching her from behind those shades. Her breathing picked up and her heart began to beat fast as she wondered what the heck she had got herself into, and all because she had stumbled across information she didn't even care about.

She didn't have time to dwell on the quicksand gathering at her feet, however, because with the sort of efficiency that spoke of experience the driver was pulling the car to a stop and she was being offloaded, the driver hurrying towards the helicopter with her bag just as the rotary blades of the aircraft began to *whop, whop, whop* in preparation for taking off, sending a whirlwind of flying dust beneath it.

Lucas had vanished into the helicopter.

Katy wished that she could vanish to the other side of the world.

She was harried, panic-stricken and grubby, because she hadn't had a chance to shower, and her jeans and shirt were sticking to her like glue. When she'd spoken to her mother on the phone, under the eagle eye of Vicky, she had waffled on with some lame excuse about being whipped off to a country house to do an important job, where the reception might be a bit dodgy, so they weren't to worry if contact was sporadic. She had made it sound like an exciting adventure because her parents were prone to worrying about her.

She hadn't thought that she really *would* end up being whipped off to anywhere.

She had envisaged a laborious drive to a poky holding pen in the middle of nowhere, with Internet access cruelly denied her. She hadn't believed him when he had told her to the contrary, and she certainly had not been able to get her head around any concept of an unplanned holiday unless you could call *incarceration* a holiday.

She was floored by what seemed to be a far bigger than average helicopter, but she was still scowling as she battled against the downdraft from the blades to climb aboard.

Lucas had to shout to be heard. As the small craft spun up, up and away, he called out, 'Small bag, Miss Brennan. Where have you stashed the books, the sketch pads and the tin of paints?'

Katy gritted her pearly teeth together but didn't say anything, and he laughed, eyebrows raised.

'Or did you decide to go down the route of being

a good little martyr while being held in captivity against your will? No books…no sketch pads…no tin of paints…and just the slightest temptation to stage a hunger strike to prove a point?'

Clenched fists joined gritted teeth and she glared at him, but he had already looked away and was flicking through the papers on his lap. He only glanced up when, leaning forward and voice raised to be heard above the din, she said, 'Where are you taking me?'

Aggravatingly seeming to read her mind, privy to every dark leap of imagination that had whirled through her head in a series of colourful images, Lucas replied, 'I'm sure that you've already conjured up dire destinations. So, instead of telling you, I'll leave you to carry on with your fictitious scenarios because I suspect that where you subsequently end up can only be better than what you've wasted your time imagining. But to set your mind at rest…'

He patted the pocket of the linen jacket which was dumped on the seat next to him. 'Your mobile phone is safe and sound right there. As soon as we land, you can tell me your password so that I can check every so often: make sure there are no urgent messages from the parents you're in the habit of calling on a daily basis…'

'Or from a married ex-boyfriend?' She couldn't resist prodding the sleeping tiger and he gave her a long, cool look from under the dark fringe of his lashes.

'Or from a married ex-boyfriend,' he drawled. 'Always pays to be careful, in my opinion. Now why don't you let me work and why don't you…enjoy the ride?'

CHAPTER THREE

THE RIDE PROBABLY TOOK HOURS, and felt even longer, with Katy doing her best to pretend that Lucas wasn't sitting within touching distance. When the helicopter began descending, swinging in a loop as it got lower, all she could see was the broad expanse of blue ocean.

Panicked and bewildered, she gazed at Lucas, who hadn't looked up from his papers and, when eventually he did, he certainly didn't glance in her direction.

After a brief hovering, the helicopter delicately landed and then she could see what she had earlier missed.

This wasn't a shabby holding pen.

Lucas was unclicking himself from his seat belt and then he patiently waited for her to do the same. This was all in a day's work for him. He turned to talk to the pilot, a low, clipped, polite exchange of words, then he stood back to allow her through the door and onto the super-yacht on which the helicopter had landed.

It was much, much warmer here and the dying rays of the sun revealed that the yacht was anchored at some distance from land. No intrusive boats huddled anywhere near it. She was standing on a yacht that was almost big enough to be classified as a small liner—sleek, sharp and so impressive that every single left wing thought about money not mattering was temporarily wiped away under a tidal wave of shameless awe.

The dark bank of land rose in the distance, revealing just some pinpricks of light peeping out between the trees and dense foliage that climbed up the side of the island's incline.

She found herself following Lucas as behind them the helicopter swung away and the deafening roar of the rotary blades faded into an ever-diminishing wasp-like whine. And then she couldn't hear it at all because they had left the helipad on the upper deck of the yacht and were moving inside.

'How does it feel to be a prisoner held against your will in a shabby cell?' Lucas drawled, not looking at her at all but heading straight through a vast expanse of polished wood and expensive cream leather furniture. A short, plump lady was hurrying to meet them, her face wreathed in smiles, and they spoke in rapid Italian.

Katy was dimly aware of being introduced to the woman, who was Signora Maria, the resident chef when on board.

Frankly, all she could take in was the breath-taking, obscene splendour of her surroundings. She was on board a billionaire's toy and, in a way, it made her feel more nervous and jumpy than if she had been dumped in that holding pen she had created in her fevered, over-imaginative head.

She'd known the guy was rich but when you were

as rich as this, rich enough to own a yacht of this calibre, then you could do whatever you wanted.

When he'd threatened her with legal proceedings, it hadn't been an empty threat.

Katy decided that she wasn't going to let herself be cowed by this display. She wasn't guilty of anything and she wasn't going to be treated like a criminal because Lucas Cipriani was suspicious by nature.

She had always been encouraged by her parents to speak her mind and she wasn't going to be turned into a rag doll because she was overwhelmed by her surroundings.

'Maria will show you to your suite.' He turned to her, his dark eyes roving up and down her body without expression. 'In it you will find everything you need, including an *en suite* bathroom. You'll be pleased to hear that there is no lock on the outside of your room, so you're free to come and go at will.'

'There's no need to be sarcastic,' Katy told him, mouth set in a sullen line. Her eyes flicked to him and skittered away just as fast before they could dwell for too long on the dark, dramatic beauty of his lean face because, once there, it was stupidly hard to tear her gaze away.

'Correction—there's *every* need to be sarcastic after you've bandied around terms such as *kidnapped*. I told you that you should look on the bright side and see this as a fully paid two-week vacation.' He dismissed Maria with a brief nod, because this looked as though it was shaping up to be another one of *those* conversations, then he shoved his hands in his pockets and stared down at her. She looked irritatingly unrepentant. 'In the absence of your books, you'll find that there is a private home cinema space with a comprehensive selection of movies. There are also two swimming pools—one indoor, one on the upper deck. And of course a library, should you decide that reading is a worthwhile option in the absence of your computer.'

'You're not very nice, are you?'

'Nice people finish last so, yes, that's an accolade I've been more than happy to pass up, which is something you'd do well to remember.'

Katy's eyes narrowed at the bitterness in his voice. Was he speaking from experience? What experience? She didn't want to be curious about him, but she suddenly was. Just for a moment, she realised that underneath the ruthless, cool veneer there would be all sorts of reasons for him being the man he was.

'Nice people don't always finish last,' she murmured sincerely.

'Oh, but they do.' Lucas's voice was cool and he was staring at her, his head at an angle, as if examining something weird he wasn't quite sure about. 'They get wrapped up in pointless sentimentality and emotion and open themselves up to getting exploited, so please don't think I'll be falling victim to that trait while we're out here.'

'Get exploited?' Katy found that she was holding her breath as she waited for his answer.

'Is that the sound of a woman trying to find out what makes me tick?' Lucas raised his eyebrows with wry amusement and began walking. 'Many have tried and failed in that venture, so I shouldn't bother if I were you.'

'It's very arrogant of you to assume that I want

to find out about you,' Katy huffed. 'But, as you've reminded me, we're going to be stuck here together for the next two weeks. I was just trying to have a conversation.'

'Like I said, I don't intend to be around much. When we do converse, we can keep it light.'

'I'm sorry.' She sighed, reaching to loop her long hair over one shoulder. 'Believe it or not, I can almost understand why you dragged me out here.'

'Well, at least *drag* is an improvement on *kidnap,*' Lucas conceded.

'I'm hot, tired and sticky, and sitting quietly at my desk working on my computer feels like a lifetime ago. I'm not in the best of moods.'

'I can't picture you sitting quietly anywhere. Maybe I've been remiss in not getting out and seeing what my employees are doing. What do you think? Should I have left my ivory tower and had a look at which of my employees were sitting and meekly doing their jobs and which ones were pushing the envelope?'

Katy reddened. His voice was suddenly lazy and teasing and her pulses quickened in response. How could he be so ruthless and arrogant one minute and then, in a heartbeat, make the blood rush to her head because of the way he was able to laugh at himself unexpectedly?

She didn't know whether it was because she had been yanked out of her comfort zone, but he was turning her off and on like a tap, and it unsettled her.

After Duncan, she had got her act together; she had looked for the silver lining and realised that he had pointed her in the right direction of what to look for in a man: someone down-to-earth, good-natured, genuine. Someone *normal*. When she found that man, everything else would fall into place, and she was horrified that a guy like Lucas Cipriani could have the sort of effect on her that he did. It didn't make sense and she didn't like it.

'I think my opinion doesn't count one way or another,' she said lightly. 'I can't speak for other people, but no one in my office actually expects you to swoop down and pay a visit.'

'You certainly know how to hit below the belt,' Lucas imparted drily. 'This your normal style when you're with a man?'

'You're not a man.'

Lucas laughed, a rich, throaty laugh that set her senses alight and had her pulses racing. 'Oh, no,' he murmured seriously. 'And here I was thinking that I was…'

'You know what I mean.' Rattled, Katy's gaze slid sideways and skittered away in confusion.

'Do I? Explain.' This wasn't the light conversation he had had in mind, but that wasn't to say that he wasn't enjoying himself, because he was. 'If I'm not a man, then what am I?'

'You're…you're my *captor*.'

Lucas grinned. 'That's a non-answer if ever there was one, but I'll let it go. Besides, I thought we'd got past the kidnap analogy.'

Katy didn't answer. He was being nice to her, teasing her. She knew that he still probably didn't trust her as far as he could throw her, but he was worldly wise and sophisticated, and knew the benefits of smoothing tensions and getting her onside. Constant sniping would bore him. He had been forced into a situation he hadn't banked on, just as she had, but he wasn't throwing temper tantrums. He wasn't interested in having meaningful conversations, because he wasn't interested in her and had no desire to find out anything about her, except what might impact on his business deal; but he would be civil now that he had told her in no uncertain terms what the lay of the land was. He had laughed about being called her captor, but he was, and he called the shots.

Instead of getting hot and bothered around him, she would have to step up to the plate and respond in kind.

They had reached the kitchen and she turned her attention away from him and looked around her. 'This is wonderful.' She ran her fingers over the counter. 'Where is Maria, your...chef?' She remained where she was, watching as he strolled to an over-sized fridge, one of two, and extracted a bottle of wine.

He poured them both a glass and nodded to one of the grey upholstered chairs tucked neatly under the metal kitchen table. Katy sat and sipped the wine very slowly, because she wasn't accustomed to drinking.

'Has her own quarters on the lower deck. I dismissed her rather than let her hang around listening to...a conversation she would have found puzzling. She might not have understood the meaning but she would have got the gist without too much trouble.'

Lucas sat opposite her. 'It is rare for me to be on this yacht with just one other person. It's generally used for client entertaining and occasionally for social gatherings. Under normal circumstances, there would be more than just one member of staff present, but there seemed little need to have an abundance of crew for two people. So, while we're here, Maria will clean and prepare meals.'

'Does she know why I'm here?'

'Why would she?' Lucas sounded genuinely surprised. 'It's none of her business. She's paid handsomely to do a job, no questions asked.'

'But wouldn't she be curious?' Katy couldn't help asking.

Lucas shrugged. 'Do I care?'

'*You* might not care,' she said tartly. 'But maybe *I* do. I don't want her thinking that I'm… I'm…'

'What?'

'I wouldn't want her thinking that I'm one of your women you've brought here to have a bit of fun with.'

Lucas burst out laughing. When he'd sobered up, he stared at her coolly.

'Why does it matter to you what my chef thinks of you? You'll never lay eyes on her again once this two-week stint is over. Besides…' he sipped his wine and looked at her over the rim of his glass '…I often fly Maria over to my place in London and occasionally to New York. She has seen enough of my women over the years to know that you don't fit the mould.'

Katy stared at him, mortified and embarrassed, because somehow she had ended up giving him the impression that…*what*? That she thought he might fancy her? That she thought her precious virtue might be *compromised* by being alone with him on this yacht, when she was only here because of circumstances? The surroundings were luxurious but this wasn't a five-star hotel with the man of her dreams. This was a prison in all but name and he was her gaoler…and since when did gaolers fancy their captives?

'Don't fit the mould?' she heard herself parrot in a jerky voice, and Lucas appeared to give that some consideration before nodding.

'Maria has been with me for a very long time,' he said without a shade of discomfort. 'She's met many of my women over the years. I won't deny that you have a certain appeal, but you're not my type, and she's savvy enough to know that. Whatever she thinks, it won't be that you're here for any reasons other than work. Indeed, I have occasionally used this as a work space with colleagues when I've needed extreme privacy in my transactions, so I wouldn't be a bit surprised if she puts that spin on your presence here.' He tried and failed to think of the woman sitting opposite him in the capacity of *work colleague.*

You have a certain appeal. Katy's brain had clunked to a stop at that throwaway remark and was refusing to budge. Why did it make her feel so flustered; hadn't she, two seconds ago, resolved not to let him get to her? She wanted to be as composed and collected as he was but she was all over the place.

Why was that? Was it the unsettling circumstances that had thrown them together? Lucas was sexy and powerful, but he was still just a man, and male attention, in the wake of Duncan, left her cold. So why did half a sentence from a man who wasn't interested in her make her skin prickle and tingle?

She forced her brain to take a few steps forward and said faintly, 'I didn't realise men had a type.' Which wasn't what she had really wanted to say. What she had *really* wanted to say was '*what's your type?*'

Rich men were always in the tabloids with women dripping from their arms and clinging to them like limpets. Rich men led lives that were always under the microscope, because the public loved reading about the lifestyles of the rich and famous, but she couldn't recall ever having seen Lucas Cipriani in any scandal sheets.

'All men have a *type*,' Lucas informed her. He had a type and he was clever enough to know *why* he had that particular type. As far as he was concerned, knowledge in that particular area was power. He would never fall victim to the type of manipulative women that his father had. He would always be in control of his emotional destiny. He had never had this sort of conversation with a woman in his life before, but then again his association with women ran along two tracks and only two. Either there was a sexual connection or else they were work associates.

Katy was neither. Yes, she worked for him, but she was not his equal in any way, shape or form.

And there was certainly no sexual connection there.

On cue, he gazed away from her face to the small jut of her breasts and the slender fragility of her arms. She really was tiny. A strong wind would knock her off her feet. She was the sort of woman that men instinctively felt the need to protect.

It seemed as good a time as any to remember just the sort of women he went for and, he told himself, keeping in the practical vein, to tell *her*, because, work or no work, aside from his chef there were only the two of them on board his yacht and he didn't want her to start getting any ideas.

She was a nobody suddenly plunged into a world of extreme luxury. He'd had sufficient experience over the years with women whose brains became scrambled in the presence of wealth.

'Here's *my* type,' he murmured, refilling both their glasses and leaning towards her, noting the way she reflexively edged back, amused by it. 'I don't do clingy. I don't do gold-diggers, airheads or any women who think that they can simper and preen their way to my bank balance—but, more than that, I don't care for women who demand more than I am capable of giving them. I lead an extremely pressurised working life. When it comes to my private life, I like women to be soothing and compliant. I enjoy the company of high fliers, career women whose independence matches my own. They know the rules of my game and there are never any unpleasant misunderstandings.'

He thought of the last woman in his life, a ravenhaired beauty who was a leading light in the field of international law. In the end their mutually busy schedules had put paid to anything more than a sixmonth dalliance although, in fairness, he hadn't wanted more. Even the most highly intelligent and ferociously independent woman had a sell-by date in his life.

Katy was trying to imagine these high-flying, saintly paragons who didn't demand and who were also soothing and compliant. 'What would constitute them demanding more than you're capable of giving them?' she asked impulsively and Lucas frowned.

'Come again?'

'You said that you didn't like women who demanded more than you were capable of giving them. Do you mean *love and commitment*?'

'Nicely put,' Lucas drawled. 'Those two things are

off the agenda. An intellectually challenging relationship—with, of course, ample doses of fun—is what
I look for and, fortunately, the women I go out with
are happy with the arrangement.'

'How do you know?'

'How do I know what?'

'That they're happy. Maybe they really want more
but they're too scared to say that because you tell
them that you don't want a committed relationship.'

'Maybe. Who knows? We're getting into another
one of those deep and meaningful conversations
again.' He stood up and stretched, flexing muscles
that rippled under his hand-tailored clothes. 'I've
told you this,' he said, leaning down, hands planted
squarely on the table, 'Because we're here and I
wouldn't want any *wow* moments to go to your head.'

'I beg your pardon?'

'You're here because I need to keep an eye on you
and make sure you don't do anything that could jeop-
ardise a deal I've been working on for the past year
and a half,' he said bluntly, although his voice wasn't
unkind. He was unwillingly fascinated by the way
her face could transmit what she was thinking, like
a shining beacon advertising the lay of the land. 'I
know you're out of your comfort zone but I wouldn't
want you to get any ideas.'

Comprehension came in an angry rush…although,
a little voice whispered treacherously in her head,
hadn't she been looking at him? Had he spotted that
and decided to nip any awkwardness in the bud by
putting down 'no trespass' signs? She wasn't his type
and he was gently but firmly telling her not to start
thinking that she might be. 'You're right.' Katy sat

back and folded her arms. 'I *am* out of my comfort zone and I *am* impressed. Who wouldn't be? But it takes more than a big boat with lots of fancy gadgets to suddenly turn its owner into someone I could *ever* be attracted to.'

'Is that a fact?'

'Yes, it is. I know my place and I'm perfectly happy there. You asked me why do I continue to work in a school? Because I enjoy giving back. I only work for your company, Mr Cipriani, because the pay enables me to afford my rent. If I could somehow be paid more as a teacher, then I would ditch your job in a heartbeat.' Katy thought that, at the rate she was going, she wouldn't have to ditch his job because *it* would be ditching *her*. 'You don't have to warn me off you and you don't have to be afraid that I'm going to start suddenly wanting to have a big boat like this of my own...'

'For goodness' sake, it's a *yacht*, not a *boat*.' And the guy who had overseen its unique construction and charged mightily for the privilege would be incandescent at her condescending referral to it as a boat. Although, Lucas thought, his lips twitching as he fought off a grin, it would certainly be worth seeing. The man, if memory served him right, had embodied all the worst traits of someone happy to suck up to the rich while stamping down hard on the poor.

Katy shrugged. 'You know what I mean. At any rate, Mr Cipriani, you don't want to be stuck here with me and I don't want to be stuck here with you either.'

'Lucas.'

'Sorry?'

'I think it's appropriate that we move onto first names. The name is Lucas.'

Flustered, Katy stared at him. 'I wouldn't feel right calling you by your first name,' she muttered, bright red. 'You're my boss.'

'I'll break the ice. Are you hungry, Katy? Maria will have prepared food and she will be unreasonably insulted if we don't eat what she has cooked. I'll call her up to serve us, after which she'll show you to your quarters.'

'Call her up?'

'The food won't magically appear on our plates.'

'I don't feel comfortable being waited on as though I'm royalty,' Katy told him honestly. 'If you direct me, I'm sure I can do whatever needs doing.'

'You're not the hired help, Katy.'

Katy shivered at the use of her name. It felt...*intimate.* She resolved to avoid calling him by his name unless absolutely necessary: perhaps if she fell overboard and was in the process of drowning. Even then she knew she would be tempted to stick to Mr Cipriani.

'That's not the point.' She stood up and looked at him, waiting to be directed, then she realised that he genuinely had no idea in which direction he should point her. She clicked her tongue and began rustling through the drawers, being nosy in the fridge before finding casserole dishes in the oven.

She could feel his dark, watchful eyes following her every movement, but she was relieved that he hadn't decided to fetch Maria, because this was taking away some of her jitters. Instead of sitting in front of him, perspiring with nerves and with nowhere to rest her eyes except on *him,* which was the least restful place they could ever land, busying herself like this at least occupied her, and it gave her time to get her thoughts together and forgive herself for behaving out of character.

It was understandable. Twenty-four hours ago, she'd been doing her job and going through all the usual daily routines. Suddenly she'd been thrown blindfolded into the deep end of a swimming pool and it was only natural for her to flounder before she found her footing.

She could learn something from this because, after Duncan, being kind to herself had come hard. She had blamed herself for her misjudgements. How could she have gone so wrong when she had spent a lifetime being so careful and knowing just what she wanted? She had spent months beating herself up for her mistake in not spotting the kind of man he had been. She had been raised by two loving parents who had instilled the right values in her, so how had she been sucked into a relationship with a man who had no values at all?

So here she was, acting out of character and going all hot and cold in the company of a man she had just met five seconds ago. It didn't mean anything and she wasn't going to beat herself up over it. There was nothing wrong with her. It was all a very natural reaction to unforeseen circumstances.

Watching her, Lucas thought that this was just the sort of domestic scene he had spent a lifetime avoiding. He also thought that, despite what he had said about his high-flying career women wanting no more than he was willing to give them, many of them had tentatively broached the subject of a relationship that would be more than simply a series of fun one-night stands. He had always shot those makings of uncomfortable conversations down in flames. But looking at the way Katy was pottering in this kitchen, making herself at home, he fancied that many an ex would have been thrilled to do the same.

'I like cooking,' she told him, bringing the food to the table and guilt-tripping him into giving her a hand because, as he had pointed out with spot-on accuracy, she *wasn't* the hired help. 'It's not just because it feels wrong to summon Maria here to do what I could easily do, but I honestly enjoy playing around with food. This smells wonderful. Is she a qualified chef?'

'She's an experienced one,' Lucas murmured.

'Tell me where we're anchored,' Katy encouraged. 'I noticed an island. How big is it? Do you have a house there?'

'The island is big enough for essentials and, although there is some tourism, it's very exclusive, which is the beauty of the place. And, yes, I have a villa there. In fact, I had planned on spending a little time there on my own, working flat-out on finalising my deal without interruptions, but plans changed.'

He didn't dwell on that. He talked, instead, about the island and then, as soon as he was finished eating, he stood up and took his plate to the sink. Katy followed his lead, noticing that his little foray into domesticity didn't last long, because he remained by the sink, leaning against it with his arms folded. She couldn't help but be amused. Just like the perplexed frown when he had first entered the kitchen, his obvious lack of interest in anything domestic was something that came across as ridiculously macho yet curiously endearing. If a man like Lucas Cipriani could ever be *endearing,* she thought drily.

'You can leave that,' was his contribution. 'Maria will take care of it in the morning.'

Katy paused and looked up at him with a half-smile. Looking down at her, he had an insane urge to…to *what?*

She had a mouth that was lush, soft and ripe for kissing. Full, pink lips that settled into a natural, sexy pout. He wondered whether they were the same colour as her nipples, and he inhaled sharply because bringing her here was one thing, but getting ideas into his head about what she might feel like was another.

'I'll show you to your cabin,' he said abruptly, heading off without waiting while she hurriedly stacked the plates into the sink before tripping along behind him.

Let this be a lesson in not overstepping the mark, she thought firmly. They'd had some light conversation, as per his ground rules, but it would help to remember that they weren't pals and his tolerance levels when it came to polite chit chat would only go so far. Right now, he'd used up his day's quota, judging from the sprint in his step as he headed away from the kitchen.

'Have you brought swimsuits?' he threw over his shoulder.

'No.' She didn't even know what had happened to her bag.

Maria, as it turned out, had taken it and delivered it to the cabin she had been assigned. Lucas pushed open the door and Katy stood for a few seconds, looking at the luxurious bedroom suite, complete with a proper king-sized bed and a view of the blue ocean, visible through trendy oversized port holes. Lucas showed her a door that opened out onto a balcony and she followed him and stood outside in a setting that was impossibly romantic. Balmy air blew gently through her hair and, looking down, she saw dark waves slapping lazily against the side of the yacht. She was so conscious of him leaning against the railing next to her that she could scarcely breathe.

'In that case, there's an ample supply of laundered swimsuits and other items of clothing in the walk-in wardrobe in the cabin alongside yours. Feel free to help yourself.'

'Why would that be?'

'People forget things. Maria digs her heels in at throwing them out. I've stopped trying to convince her.' He raked his fingers through his hair and watched as she half-opened her mouth, and that intensely physical charge rushed through him again.

'Okay.'

'You have the freedom of my yacht. I'll work while I'm here and the time will fly past, just as long as we don't get in one another's way...'

CHAPTER FOUR

LUCAS LOOKED AT the document he had been editing for half an hour, only to realise that he had hardly moved past the first two lines.

At this point in time, and after three days of enforced isolation on his yacht, he should have been powering through the intense backlog of work he had brought with him. Instead, he had been wasting time thinking about the woman sharing his space on his yacht.

Frustrated, he stood up, strolled towards the window and stared out, frowning, at a panoramic view of open sea. Every shade of blue and turquoise combined, in the distance, into a dark-blue line where the sea met the skyline. At a little after three, it was still very hot and very still, with almost no breeze at all rippling the glassy surface of the water.

He'd looked at this very skyline a hundred times in the past, stared through this very window of his office on the lower deck, and had never been tempted to leave it for the paradise beckoning outside. He'd never been good at relaxing, and indeed had often found himself succumbing to it more through necessity than anything else. Sitting around in the sun doing nothing was a waste of valuable time, as far as he was concerned; and on the few occasions he had been on weekend breaks with a woman he had found himself enduring the time spent playing tourist with a certain amount of barely concealed impatience.

He was a workaholic and the joys of doing nothing held zero appeal for him.

Yet, he was finding it difficult to concentrate. If he had noticed Katy's delicate, ridiculous prettiness on day one, and thought he could studiously file it away as something he wasn't going to allow to distract him, then he'd made a big mistake because the effect she was having on him was increasing with every second spent in her company.

He'd done his best to limit the time they were together. He'd reminded himself that, were it not for an unfortunate series of events, the woman wouldn't even be on his yacht now, but for all his well-constructed, logical reasons for avoiding her his body remained stubbornly recalcitrant.

Perversely, the more uptight he felt in her company, the more relaxed she seemed to be in his.

Since when had the natural order of things been rearranged? For the first time in his life, he wasn't calling the shots, and *that* was what was responsible for his lack of focus.

Being stuck on the yacht with Katy had made him realise that the sassy, independent career women he dated had not been as challenging as he had always liked to think they were. They'd all been as subservient and eager to please as any vacuous airhead keen to burn a hole in his bank account. In contrast, Katy didn't seem to have a single filter when it came to telling him what she thought about…anything and everything.

So far, he had been regaled with her opinions on money, including his own. She had scoffed at the foolishness of racing towards power and status, without bothering to hide the fact that he was top of her list as a shining example of someone leading the race. She had quizzed him on what he did in his spare time, and demanded to know whether he ever did anything that was actually *ordinary*. She seemed to think that his lack of knowledge of the layout of his own private yacht's kitchen was a shocking crime against humanity, and had then opined that there was such a thing as more money than sense.

In short, she had managed to be as offensive as any human being was capable of being and, to his astonishment, he had done nothing to redress the balance by exerting the sort of authority that would have stalled her mid-sentence.

He had the power in his hands to ruin her career but the thought had not crossed his mind.

She might have been in his company for all the wrong reasons, but he was no longer suspicious of her motives, especially when she had no ability to contact anyone at all, and her openness was strangely engaging.

It was also an uncomfortable reminder as to how far he normally went when it came to getting exactly what he wanted, and that he had surrounded himself with people who had forgotten how to contradict him.

Without giving himself a chance to back out, he headed to his quarters and did the unthinkable: he swapped his khakis for a pair of swimming trunks that hadn't seen the light of day in months, if not years, and a tee-shirt.

Barefoot, grabbing a towel on the way, he headed up to the pool area where he knew Katy was going to be.

She had been oddly reticent about using the swimming pool and, chin tilted at the mutinous angle he was fast becoming accustomed to, she had finally confessed that she didn't like using stuff that didn't belong to her.

'Would you rather the swimsuits all sit unused in cupboards until it's time for the lot to be thrown away?'

'Would you throw away perfectly good clothes?'

'I would if it was cluttering up my space. You wouldn't have to borrow them if you'd thought ahead and brought a few of your own.'

'I had no idea I would be anywhere near a pool,' she had been quick to point out, and he had dealt her a slashing grin, enjoying the way the colour had rushed into her cheeks.

'And now you are. Roll with the punches, would be my advice.'

His cabin was air-conditioned, and as he headed up towards the pool on the upper deck he was assailed by heat. It occurred to him that she might not be there, that she might have gone against her original plan of reading in the afternoon and working on ideas for an app to help the kids in her class with their homework, something he had discovered after some probing. If she wasn't there, he'd be bloody disappointed, and that nearly stopped him in his tracks because disappointment wasn't something he associated with the opposite sex.

He enjoyed the company of women. He wasn't promiscuous but the truth was that no woman had ever had the power to hold his attention for any sustained length of time, so he had always been the first to do the dispatching. By which point, he was always guiltily relieved to put the relationship behind him. In that scenario, disappointment wasn't something that had ever featured.

Katy, with her quirky ways and forthright manner, was yanking him along by some sort of invisible chain and he was uneasily aware that it was something he should really put a stop to.

Indeed, he paused, considering that option. It would take him less than a minute to make it back down to his office where he could resume work.

Except...would he be able to? Or would he sit at his desk allowing his mind idly to drift off to the taboo subject of his sexy captive?

Lucas had no idea what he hoped to gain by hitting the upper deck and joining her by the pool. So what if she was attractive? The world was full of attractive women and he knew, without a shred of vanity, that he could have pretty much any of them he wanted.

Playing with his reluctant prisoner wasn't on the cards. He'd warned her off getting any ideas into her head so there was no way he was going to try to get her into his bed now.

Just thinking about that, even as he was fast shoving it out of his head, conjured up a series of images that sent his pulses racing and fired up his libido as though reacting to a gun at the starting post.

He reached out one hand and supported himself heavily against the wall, allowing his breathing to settle. His common sense was fighting a losing battle with temptation, telling him to hot foot it back to the office and slam the metaphorical door on the siren lure of a woman who most definitely wasn't his sort.

He continued on, passing Maria in the kitchen preparing supper, and giving a brief nod before heading up. Then the sun was beating down on him as he took a few seconds to appreciate the sight of the woman reclining on a deck chair, eyes closed, arms hanging loosely over the sides of the chair, one leg bent at the knee, the other outstretched.

She had tied her long, vibrant hair into some kind of rough bun and a book lay open on the ground next to her.

Lucas walked softly towards her. He hadn't seen her like this, only just about decently clothed, and his breathing became sluggish as he took in the slender daintiness of her body: flat stomach, long, smooth legs, small breasts.

He cleared his throat and wondered whether he would be able to get his vocal cords to operate. 'Good job I decided to come up here...' He was inordinately thankful for the dark sunglasses that shielded his expression. 'You're going pink. Where's your sunblock? With your skin colouring, too much sun and you'll end up resembling a lobster—and your two-week prison sentence might well end up being longer than you'd bargained for. Sun burn can be a serious condition.'

'What are you *doing* here?' Katy jack-knifed into a sitting position and drew her knees up to her chest, hugging herself and glowering from a position of disadvantage as he towered over her, all six-foot-something of bronzed, rippling muscle.

Her eyes darted down to his legs and darted away again just as fast. Something about the dark, silky hair shadowing his calves and thighs brought her out in a sweat.

She licked her lips and steadied her racing pulse. She'd kept up a barrage of easy chatter for the past few days, had striven to project the careless, outspoken insouciance that she hoped would indicate to him that she wasn't affected by him, *not at all,* and she wasn't going to ruin the impression now.

He'd warned her not to go getting any ideas and that had been the trigger for her to stop gaping and allowing him to get under her skin. She was sure that the only reason he had issued that warning was because he had noticed her reaction to him and, from that moment onwards, she had striven to subdue any wayward reactions under a never-ending stream of small talk.

To start with, she'd aimed to keep the small talk *very* small, anything to break the silence as they had shared meals. In the evenings, before he left to return to the bowels of the yacht, they'd found themselves continuing to talk over coffee and wine.

Her aim had been harder to stick to than she'd thought because something about him fired her up. Whilst she managed to contain her body's natural impulse to be disobedient—by making sure she was physically as far away from him as possible without being too obvious—she'd been seduced into provoking him, enjoying the way he looked at her when she said something incendiary, head to one side, his dark eyes veiled and assessing.

It was a subtle form of intellectual arousal that

kept her on a permanent high and it was as addictive as a drug.

In Lucas's presence, Duncan no longer existed.

In fact, thanks to Lucas's all-consuming and wholly irrational ability to rivet her attention, Katy had reluctantly become aware of just how affected she had been by Duncan's betrayal. Even when she had thought she'd moved on, he had still been there in the background, a troubling spectre that had moulded her relationships with the opposite sex.

'I own the yacht,' Lucas reminded her lazily. He began stripping off the tee-shirt and tossed it onto a deckchair, which he pulled over with his foot so that it was right next to her. 'Do you think I should have asked your permission before I decided to come up here and use the pool?'

'No, of course not,' Katy replied, flustered. 'I just thought that you had your afternoon routine and you worked until seven in the evening...'

'Routines are made to be broken.' He settled down onto the deck chair and turned so that he was looking at her, still from behind the dark shades that gave him a distinct advantage. 'Haven't you been lecturing me daily on my evil workaholic ways?'

'I never said that they were *evil*.'

'But you were so persuasive in convincing me that I was destined for an early grave that I decided to follow your advice and take some time out.' He grinned and tilted his shades up to look at her. 'You're not reacting with the sort of smug satisfaction I might have expected.'

'I didn't think that you would actually listen to

what I said,' Katy muttered, her whole body as rigid as a plank of wood.

She wanted to look away but her greedy eyes kept skittering back to him. He was just so unbelievably perfect. More perfect than anything she had conjured up in her fevered imaginings. His chest was broad and muscular, with just the right dusting of dark hair that made her draw her breath in sharply, and the line of dark hair running down from his belly button electrified her senses like a live wire. How was it possible for a man to be so sexy? So sinfully, darkly and *dangerously* sexy?

Every inch of him eclipsed her painful memories of Duncan and she was shocked that those memories had lingered for as long as they had.

Watching him, her imagination took flight. She thought of those long, clever fingers stroking her, touching her breasts, lingering to circle her nipples. She felt faint. Her nipples were tight and pinched, and between her legs liquid heat was pooling and dampening her bikini bottoms.

She realised that she had been fantasising about this man since they had stepped foot on the yacht, but those fantasies had been vague and hazy compared to the force of the graphic images filling her head as she looked away with a tight, determined expression.

It was his body, she thought. Seeing him like that, in nothing but a pair of black trunks, was like fodder for her already fevered imagination.

Under normal circumstances, she might have looked at him and appreciated him for the drop-dead, gorgeous guy that he was, but actually she wouldn't have turned that very natural appreciation into a full-on mental sexual striptease that had him parading naked in her head.

But these weren't normal circumstances and *that* was why her pragmatic, easy-going and level-headed approach to the opposite sex had suddenly deserted her.

'Tell me about the deal.' She launched weakly into the first topic of conversation that came into her head, and Lucas flung himself back into the deck chair and stared up at a faultlessly blue, cloudless sky.

He was usually more than happy to discuss work-related issues, except right now and right here that was the last thing he wanted to do. 'Persuade me that you give a damn about it.' He slanted a sideways look at her and then kept looking as delicate colour tinged her cheeks.

'Of course I do.' Katy cleared her throat. 'I'm here *because* of it, aren't I?'

'Are you enjoying yourself?' He folded his arms behind his head and stared at her. 'You're only here because of the deal but, now that you *are* here, are you having a good time?'

Katy opened her mouth to ask him what kind of question that was, because how on earth could she be having a good time when life as she knew it had been turned upside down? Except she blinked and thought that she *was* having a good time. 'I've never been anywhere like this before,' she told him. 'When I was a kid, holidays were a week in a freezing-cold British seaside town. Don't get me wrong, I adored my holidays, but this is…out of this world.'

She looked around her and breathed in the warm breeze, rich with the salty smell of the sea. 'It's a different kind of life having a father who's the local parish priest,' she confided honestly. 'On the one hand, it was brilliant, because I never lacked love and support from both my parents, especially as I was an only child. They wanted more but couldn't have them. My mum once told me that she had to restrain herself from lavishing gifts on me, but of course there was always a limit to what they could afford. And besides, as I've told you, they always made sure to tell me that money wasn't the be-all and end-all.' She looked at Lucas and smiled, somewhat surprised that she was telling him all this, not that any of it was a secret.

Never one to encourage confidences from women, Lucas was oddly touched by her confession because she was usually so outspoken in a tomboyish, challenging way.

'Hence your entrenched disregard for money,' he suggested drily. 'Tell me about the down sides of life in a vicarage. I'll be honest with you, you're the first daughter of a man of the cloth I've ever met.'

The image of the happy family stuck in his mind and, in a rare bout of introspection, he thought back to his own troubled youth after his mother had died. His father had had the love, but he had just not quite known how to deliver it and, caught up in his own grief and his never-ending quest to find a substitute for the loss of his wife, he had left a young Lucas to find his own way. The independence Lucas was now so proud of, the mastery over his own emotions and his talent for self-control, suddenly seemed a little tarnished at the edges, too hard-won to be of any real value.

He dismissed the worrying train of thought and

encouraged her to keep talking. She had a very melodic voice and he enjoyed the sound of it as much as he enjoyed the animation that lit up her ravishingly pretty, heart-shaped face.

'Down sides... Well, now, let me have a think...!' She smiled and lay down on the deck chair so that they were now both side by side, faces upturned to the brilliant blue sky above. She glanced across at him, expecting to see amusement and polite interest, just a couple of people chatting about nothing in particular. Certainly nothing that would hold the interest of a man like Lucas Cipriani. But his dark, fathomless eyes were strangely serious as he caught her gaze and held it for a few seconds, and she shivered, mouth going dry, ensnared by the gravity of his expression.

'So?' Lucas murmured, closing his eyes and enjoying the warmth and the rarity of not doing anything.

'So...you end up always knowing that you have to set a good example because your parents are pillars of the community. I could never afford to be a rebel.'

Even when she had gone to university her background had followed her. She'd been able to have a good time, and stay out late and drink with the best of them, but she had never slept around or even come close to it. Maybe if she hadn't had so many morals drilled into her from an early age she would have just got sex out of the way and then would have been relaxed when it came to finding relationships. Maybe she would have accepted that not all relationships were serious, that some were destined to fall by the wayside, but that didn't mean they weren't worthwhile.

It was a new way of thinking for Katy and she gave

it some thought because she had always assumed, post-Duncan, that she would hang on to her virginity, would have learned her lesson, would be better equipped to make the right judgement calls.

Thinking that she could deviate from that path gave her a little frisson of excitement.

'Not that I was ever tempted,' she hurriedly expanded. 'I had too much experience of seeing where drugs and drink and casual sex could lead a person. My dad is very active in the community and does a lot outside the village for down-and-outs. A lot of them ended up where they did because of poor choices along the way.'

'I feel like I'm talking to someone from another planet.'

'Why?'

'Because your life is so vastly different from anything I've come across.'

Katy laughed. Lying side by side made it easier to talk to him. If they'd been sitting opposite one another at the table in the kitchen, with the yacht rocking softly as they ate, she wasn't sure she would have been able to open up like this. She could spar with him and provoke him until she could see him gritting his teeth in frustration—in fact, she got a kick out of that—but this was different.

She couldn't even remember having a conversation like this with Duncan, who had split his time talking about himself and flirting relentlessly with her.

'What do you come across?' she asked lightly, dropping her hands to either side of the deck chair and tracing little circles on the wooden decking.

'Tough career women who don't make a habit of

getting too close to down-and-outs,' Lucas told her wryly. 'Unless, in the case of at least a couple of them who were top barristers, a crime had been committed and they happened to be confronted with one of those down-and-outs in a court of law.'

'I remember you telling me,' Katy murmured, 'About those tough career women who never wanted more than you were prepared to give them and were always soothing and agreeable.'

Lucas laughed. That had been when he'd been warning her off him, just in case she got ideas into her head. On cue, he inclined his head slightly and looked at her. She was staring up at the sky, eyes closed. Her long, dark lashes cast shadows on her cheeks and her mouth, in repose, was a full, pink pout. The sun had turned her a pale biscuit-gold colour and brought out shades of strawberry blonde amidst the deep russets and copper of her hair. Eyes drifting down, he followed the line of her shoulders and the swell of her breasts under the bikini, which he had not really been able to appreciate when she had been hugging her knees to herself, making sure that as little of her body was on show as humanly possible.

The bikini was black and modest by any modern standard but nothing could conceal the tempting swell of her pert, small breasts, the barely there cleavage, the jut of her hip bones and the silky smoothness of her thighs.

Lucas didn't bother to give in to consternation at the hot, pulsing swell of his arousal which, had she only opened her big green eyes and cast a sideways glance at him, she'd have noticed was distorting his swimming trunks.

He'd acknowledged her appeal from day one, from the very second she had walked into his office. No red-blooded male could have failed to. He'd also noted her belligerence and lack of filter when it came to speaking her mind, which was why he had decided to take on babysitting duties personally until his deal was safely in the bag. When you took into account that she had shimmered into his line of vision as a woman not averse to sleeping with married men, one who could not be trusted, it had seemed the obvious course of action.

But he knew, deep down, that even though he had dismissed any notion of going anywhere near Katy the prospect of being holed up with her for a fortnight had not exactly filled him with distaste.

He wondered whether he had even played with the forbidden thought of doing what his body wanted against the wishes of his brain. Or maybe he had been invigorated just by the novelty of having that mental tussle at all. In his well-ordered life, getting what he wanted had never posed a challenge, and internal debates about what he should or shouldn't do rarely featured, especially when it came to women.

He thought that if she had lived down to expectations and proved herself to be the sort of girl who had no morals, and really *might* have tried her luck with him, he would have had no trouble in eating, breathing and sleeping work. However, she hadn't, and the more his curiosity about her had been piqued the more he had been drawn to her like a wanderer hearing the call of a siren.

Which was so not him *at all* that he almost didn't know how to deal with it.

Except, his body was dealing with it in the time-honoured way, he thought, and then hard on the heels of that thought he wondered what she would do if she looked and saw the kind of response she'd awakened in him.

Katy wasn't sure whether it was the sudden silence, or just something thick and electric in the air, but she opened her eyes and turned her head, her mouth already opening to say something bland and chirpy to dispel the sudden tension.

His eyes caught hers and she stopped breathing. She had a drowning sensation as she was swallowed up in the deep, dark, quiet depths of his eyes. Those eyes were telegraphing a message to her, or they seemed to be. Was she imagining it? She had no experience of a man like him. That cool, brooding, speculative expression seemed to be inviting a response, but was it? Flustered and confused, her eyes dipped...

And then there was no doubt exactly what message was being telegraphed.

For a few seconds, Katy froze while her mind went into free fall. He was *turned on*. Did he think that he could try it on and she would fall in line because she was easy? Who knew, he probably still believed that she was the sort who had affairs with married men, even though he surely should know better, because she had shared stuff with him, told him about her childhood and her parents and the morals they had instilled in her. Maybe he hadn't believed her. Maybe he had taken it all with a pinch of salt because he was suspicious and mistrustful.

She *wasn't* easy. And yet, unleashed desire flooded through her in an unwanted torrent, crashing through common sense and good intentions. *She wanted this man, this unsuitable man, and she wanted him with a craving that was as powerful as a depth charge.*

The shocking intensity of a physical response she had never, *ever* felt towards any man, including Duncan, scared the living daylights out of her. Mumbling something under her breath, she leapt to her feet, the glittering blue of the infinity pool beckoning like an oasis of safety away from the onslaught of confusion overwhelming her.

Heart hammering in her chest, she scrambled forward, missed the step that gave down to the smooth wood around the pool and found herself flying forward.

She landed with a painful thump, her knees stinging where she had grazed them after her airborne flight.

Clutching her leg, she watched in fascinated slow motion as Lucas strode towards her, every lean muscle of his body intent.

'What were you thinking?' he asked urgently, scooping her up and ignoring her protests that he put her down because she was *absolutely fine*. 'You took off like a bat out of hell. Something I said?'

He was striding away from the pool area, carrying her as easily as he would carry a couple of cushions. Katy clutched his broad shoulders, horribly aware that in this semi-folded position there were bits of her on view that made her want to die an early death from embarrassment.

One glance down and he would practically be able to see the shadow of one of her nipples.

'Where are you taking me?' she croaked. 'This is ridiculous. I tripped and fell!'

'You could have broken something.'

'I haven't broken *anything*!' Katy practically sobbed.

'How do you know?'

'Because if I had I wouldn't be able to walk!'

'You're not walking. I'm carrying you. How much do you weigh, by the way? You're as light as a feather. If I didn't see how much food you're capable of putting away, I'd be worried.'

'I've always been thin,' Katy said faintly, barely noticing where they were going because she was concentrating very hard on making sure no more of her bikini-clad body went on show. She felt she might be on the verge of passing out. 'Please just take me to my cabin. That would be fine. I can clean my knee up and I'll be as right as rain.'

'Nonsense. How could I live with myself if I didn't do the gentlemanly thing and make sure you're all right? I wasn't brought up to ignore damsels in distress.'

'I'm not one of those!'

'Here we are,' Lucas intoned with satisfaction. He kicked open the door and, when Katy tore her focus away from her excruciating attempts to keep her body safely tucked away in the swimsuit, she realised where he had taken her.

Away from the safety of the pool and straight into the hellfire of his private quarters.

CHAPTER FIVE

LUCAS'S CABIN WAS different from hers insofar as it was twice the size and unnervingly masculine: dark-grey silky throw on the bed, dark-grey pillows, built-in furniture in rich walnut that matched the wooden flooring. He laid her on the bed and she immediately wriggled into a sitting position, wishing that she had something to tug down to cover herself, but instead having to make do with arranging herself into the most modest position possible, back upright, legs rammed close together and hands primly folded on her lap.

Sick with tension, she watched him disappear into an adjoining bathroom, that made hers look like a shower cubicle, to return a minute later with a first-aid kit.

'This really isn't necessary…er… Lucas.'

'You managed the first name. Congratulations. I wondered whether you would.'

'I have a few grazes, that's all.'

He was kneeling in front of her and he began to feel her ankle with surprisingly gently fingers. 'Tell me if anything hurts.'

'Nothing,' Katy stated firmly. She gave a trial tug

of her leg so that Lucas could get the hint that this was all pretty ridiculous and overblown but he wasn't having it.

Relax, she told herself sternly; *relax and it'll be over and done with in a second and you can bolt back to your cabin.* But how could she even begin to relax when those fingers were doing all sorts of things to her body?

The feathery delicacy of his touch was stirring her up, making her breathing quicken and sending tingling, delicious sensations racing through her body like little lightning sparks. She looked at his down-bent head, the raven-black hair, and had to stop herself from reaching out and touching it just to see what it felt like between her fingers.

Then she thought of the bulge of his arousal and felt faint all over again.

'I'm surprised you have a first-aid kit to hand,' she said breathlessly, tearing her fascinated gaze away from him and focusing hard on trying to normalise the situation with pointless conversation.

'Why?' Lucas glanced up briefly before continuing with his exceedingly slow exploration of her foot.

'Because you don't seem to be the type to do this sort of thing,' Katy said honestly.

'It's essential to have a first-aid kit on board a sailing vessel. In fact, this is just one of many. There's a comprehensive supply of medical equipment in a store room on the middle deck. You would be surprised at the sort of unexpected accidents that can happen when you're out at sea, and there's no ambulance available to make a five-minute dash to collect and take you to the nearest hospital.' He was working his way gently up her calf, which was smooth, slender and sprinkled with golden hair. Her skin was like satin and still warm from the sun.

'And you know how to deal with all those unexpected accidents?' Lucas's long, clever fingers were getting higher and, with each encroaching inch, her body lit up like a Christmas tree just a tiny bit more. Any higher and she would go up in flames.

'You'd be surprised,' Lucas drawled. 'Your knees are in a pretty terrible state, but after I've cleaned them up you should be fine. You'll be pleased to know that nothing's been broken.'

'I told you that,' Katy reminded him. 'Why would I be surprised?'

He was now gently swabbing her raw, torn skin and she winced as he patted the area with some oversized alcohol wipes, making sure to get rid of every last bit of dirt.

'Because,' Lucas said wryly, not looking at her, 'I get the feeling you've pigeonholed me as the sort of money-hungry, ambitious businessman who hasn't got time for anything other than getting richer and richer and richer, probably at the expense of everyone around him. Am I right?'

'I never said that,' Katy told him faintly.

'It's hard not to join the dots when your opening words to me were to accuse me of being capable of kidnapping you.'

'You *were* kidnapping me, in a manner of speaking!'

'Tell me how it feels to be a kidnap victim.' His voice was light and teasing as he continued to tend to her knee, now applying some kind of transparent ointment, before laboriously bandaging it and then turning his attention to foot number two. 'I always wanted to be a doctor,' he surprised her and himself by saying.

'What happened?' For the first time since she had been deposited on his bed, Katy felt herself begin to relax, the nervous tension temporarily driven away by a piercing curiosity. Lucas could be many things, as she had discovered over the past few days. He could be witty, amusing, arrogant and always, always wildly, extravagantly intelligent. But confiding? No.

'My father's various wives happened,' Lucas said drily. 'One after each other. They looked alike and they certainly were all cut from the same cloth. They had their eyes on the main prize and, when their tenure ran out, my father's fortune was vastly diminished. By the time I hit sixteen, I realised that, left to his own devices, he would end up with nothing to live on. It would have killed my father to have seen the empire his grandfather had built dwindle away in a series of lawsuits and maintenance payments to greedy ex-wives.

'I knew my father had planned on my inheriting the business and taking over, and I had always thought that I'd talk to him about that change of plan when the time was right; but, as it turned out, the time never became right because without me the company would have ended up subdivided amongst a string of gold-diggers and that would have been that.'

'So you gave up your hopes and dreams?'

'Don't get too heavy on the pity card.' Lucas laughed, sitting back on his heels to inspect his work, head tilted to one side. He looked at her and her mouth went dry as their eyes tangled. 'I enjoy my life.'

'But it's a far cry from being a doctor.' She had never imagined him having anything to do with the caring profession and something else was added to the swirling mix of complex responses she was stock-piling towards him. She thought that the medical profession had lost something pretty big when he had decided to pursue a career in finance because, knowing the determination and drive he brought to his chosen field of work, he surely would have brought tenfold to the field of medicine.

'So it is,' Lucas concurred. 'Hence the fact that I actually enjoy being hands-on when it comes to dealing with situations like this.'

'And have you had to deal with many of them?' She thought of him touching another woman, one of the skinny, leggy ones to whom those thong swimsuits forgotten on the yacht belonged, carefully stored just in case someone like her might come along and need to borrow one of them.

'No.' He stood up. 'Like I said, my time on this yacht is limited, and no one to date has obliged me by requiring mouth-to-mouth resuscitation whilst out to sea.' He disappeared back into the bathroom with the kit and, instead of taking the opportunity to stand up and prepare herself for a speedy exit, Katy remained on the bed, gently flexing both her legs and getting accustomed to the stiffness where the bandages had been applied expertly over her wounds.

'So I'm your first patient?'

Lucas remained by the door to the bathroom, lounging against the doorframe.

Katy was riveted at the sight. He was still wearing his bathing trunks although, without her even noticing when he had done it, he had slung on his tee-shirt. He was barefoot and he exuded a raw, animal sexiness that took her breath away.

'Cuts and grazes don't honestly count.' Lucas grinned and strolled towards her, holding her spellbound with his easy, graceful strides across the room. He moved to stand by the window which, as did hers, looked out on the blue of an ocean that was as placid as the deepest of lakes. His quarters were air-conditioned, as were hers, but you could almost feel the heat outside because the sun was so bright and the sky was so blue and cloudless.

'I'm sorry if I ruined your down time.'

'You never told me why you leapt off your deck-chair and raced for the pool as though the hounds of hell were after you,' Lucas murmured.

She was in his bedroom and touching her had ignited a fire inside him, the same fire that had been burning steadily ever since they had been on his yacht. He knew why she had leapt off that deck chair. He had enough experience of the opposite sex to register when a woman wanted him, and it tickled him to think that she wasn't doing what every other woman would have done and flirting with him. Was that because she worked for him? Was that holding her back? Maybe she thought that he would sack her if she was too obvious. Or maybe she had paid attention to the speech he had given her at the start when he had told her not to get any crazy ideas about a relationship developing between them.

He almost wished that he hadn't bothered with that

speech because it turned him on to imagine her making a pass at him.

Lucas enjoyed a couple of seconds wondering what it would feel like to have her begin to touch him, blushing and awkward, but then his innate pragmatism kicked in and he knew that she was probably playing hard to get, which was the oldest game in the world when it came to women. She had revealed all sorts of sides to her that he hadn't expected, but the reality was that she *had* had an affair with a married man. She'd denied that she'd known about the wife and kiddies, and maybe she hadn't. Certainly there was an honesty about her that he found quite charming but, even so, he wasn't going to be putting any money on her so-called innocence any time soon.

'It was very hot out there,' Katy muttered awkwardly, heating up as she recalled the pivotal moment when raging, uncontrolled desire had taken her over like a fast-moving virus and she had just *had to escape*. 'I just fancied a dip in the pool and unfortunately I didn't really look where I was going. I should head back to my room now. I think I'll give my legs a rest just while I have these bandages on—and, by the way, thank you very much for sorting it out. There was no need, but thanks anyway.'

'How long do you think we should carry on pretending that there's nothing happening between us?' Which, frankly, was a question Lucas had never had to address to any other women because other women had never needed persuading into his bed. Actually, it was a question he had not envisaged having to ask *her,* considering the circumstances that had brought them together. But he wanted her and there was no point having a mental tussle over the whys and wherefores or asking himself whether it made sense or not.

On this occasion, self-denial probably made sense, but Lucas knew himself and he knew that, given the option of going down the route of what made sense or the less sensible route of scratching an itch, then the less sensible route was going to win the day hands down every time.

He also knew that he wasn't a man who was into breaking down barriers and jumping obstacles in order to get any woman between the sheets—and why would he do that anyway? This wasn't a game of courtship that was going anywhere. It was a case of two adults who fancied one another marooned on a yacht for a couple of weeks..

In receipt of this blunt question, presented to her without the benefit of any pretty packaging, Katy's eyes opened wide and her mouth fell open.

'I beg your pardon?'

'I've seen the way you look at me,' Lucas murmured, moving to sit on the bed right next to her, and depressing the mattress with his weight so that Katy had to shift to adjust her body and stop herself from sliding against him.

She should have bolted. His lazy, dark eyes on her were like lasers burning a hole right through the good, old-fashioned, grounded common sense that had dictated her behaviour all through her life—with the exception of those few disastrous months when she had fallen for Duncan.

The slow burning heat that had been coursing through her, the exciting tingle between her legs and the tender pinching of her sensitive nipples—all responses activated by being in his presence and feeling his cool fingers on her—were fast disappearing under a tidal wave of building anger.

'The way I *look at you*?'

'Don't be embarrassed. Believe me, it isn't usually my style to force anyone's hand, but we're here and there's a sexual chemistry between us. Are you going to dispute that? It's in the air like an invisible electric charge.' He laughed with some incredulity. 'You're not going to believe this, but it's something I can't remember feeling in a very long time, if ever.'

'And you think I should be *flattered*?'

Lucas frowned because this wasn't the reaction he had been expecting. 'Frankly, yes,' he told her with complete honesty.

Katy gaped, even though she knew very well why a woman would be flattered to be the object of attention from Lucas Cipriani. He was drop-dead gorgeous and a billionaire to boot. If he made a pass at a woman, then what woman was going to stalk off in the opposite direction and slam the door in his face? He probably had a queue of them waiting to be picked.

Her lips tightened because what he saw as a flattering, complimentary approach was, to her, downright insulting.

At least the creep Duncan had had the wit to approach her a little less like a bull stampeding through a china shop.

But then, Katy concluded sourly, time wasn't on Lucas's side. They were here for a limited duration, so why waste any precious time trying to seduce her into bed the old-fashioned way?

'That's the most egotistical, arrogant thing I have ever heard *in my entire life*!'

'Because I've been honest?' But Lucas flushed darkly. 'I thought you were all in favour of the honest approach?'

'Who do you think I am?'

'I have no idea where you're going with this.'

'You think that you just have to snap your fingers and someone like me will dump all her principles and come running, don't you?'

'Someone like you?' But she had scored a direct hit, and he was guiltily aware that he *had* indeed compartmentalised her, however much he had seen evidence to the contrary.

'The sort of person,' Katy informed him with scathing distaste, 'Who needs a good, long lecture on making sure her little head doesn't get turned by being on a big, expensive boat—oh, sorry, *super-yacht*—with the great Lucas Cipriani! The sort of person,' she added for good measure, 'Who comes with a dubious reputation as someone who thinks it's okay to hop into bed with a married guy!' It made her even madder to think that she had fallen into the trap of forgetting who he really was, won over by his charm and the random confidences he had thrown her way which she had sucked up with lamentable enthusiasm.

And what made her even madder *still* was the fact that he had managed to read her so correctly! She thought she'd been the model of politeness, but he'd seen right through that and homed in laser-like on the fevered core of her that was attracted to him.

'You're over-analysing.' Lucas raked his fingers

through his hair and sprang to his feet to pace the cabin before standing by the window to look at her.

'I am *not* over-analysing,' Katy told him fiercely. 'I know what you think of me.'

'You don't.' Unaccustomed to apologising for anything he said or did, Lucas now felt…like a cad. He couldn't credit how she had taken his interest in her and transformed it into an insult, yet he had to admit to himself that his approach had hardly been handled with finesse. He'd been clumsy, and in no one's wildest imagination could it have passed for *honesty*.

'I know exactly what you think of me! And you've got a damned cheek to imagine that I would be so easy that I'd just fall into bed with you because you happened to extend the invite.'

'I… I apologise,' Lucas said heavily, and that apology was so unexpected that Katy could only stare at him with her mouth open. He looked at her with a roughened sincerity and she fought against relenting.

Glaring, she stood up. Her good intentions of sweeping out of his cabin with her head held high, now that she had roundly given him a piece of her mind, were undermined by the fact that she was wearing next to nothing and had to hobble a bit because the grazes on her knees were killing her.

'Katy,' he murmured huskily, stopping her in her tracks. He reached out to stay her and the pressure on her arm where his fingers circled her skin was as powerful as a branding iron. She had to try not to flinch. Awareness shot through her, rooting her to the spot. 'I don't, actually, think that you're easy and I certainly don't take it for granted that you're going to fall into bed with me because that's the kind of person you are. And,' he continued with grudging sincerity, 'If there's a part of me that is still wary, it's because it's my nature to be suspicious. The bottom line is that I want you, and I might be wrong but I think it's mutual. So tell me…is it?'

He took half a step closer to her, looked down and suppressed a groan at the delicious sight of her delicate breasts encased in stretchy fabric. 'If I've misread the signals,' he told her, 'Then tell me now and I'll back off. You have my word. Nor will I let it affect whatever lies down the line in terms of your position in my company. Say no, and this is never mentioned again. It will never have happened.'

Katy hesitated. She so badly wanted to tell him that, no, she most certainly was *not* interested in him *that* way, but then she thought of him backing away and leaving her alone and she realised with a jolt how much she enjoyed spending time in his company when they were tossing ideas around and sparring with one another. She also now realised that underneath that sparring had been the very thread of sexual attraction which he had picked up with his highly developed antennae.

'That's not the point,' she dodged feebly.

'What do you mean?'

'I mean…' Katy muttered *sotto voce*, red-faced and uncomfortable, 'It doesn't matter whether we're attracted to one another or not. It would be mad for us to do anything about it. Not that I would,' she continued at speed, face as red as a beetroot. 'After Duncan, I swore to myself that I would never make the mistake of throwing myself into anything with someone unless I really felt that they were perfect for me.'

'I've never heard such nonsense in my entire life,' Lucas said bluntly, and, feathers ruffled, Katy tensed and bristled.

'What's wrong with wanting the best?' she demanded, folding her arms, neither leaving the room nor returning to the bed, instead just standing in the middle as awkward as anything. He, on the other hand, looked totally at ease even though he was as scantily clad as she was. But then, he obviously wasn't the sort who gave a jot if his body was on display.

'Nothing's wrong with wanting the best,' Lucas concurred. 'But tell me, how do you intend to find it? Are you going to present each and every candidate with a questionnaire which they will be obliged to fill out before proceeding? I'm going to take a leap of faith here and assume that you didn't know about Powell's marital status. You went out with the man and presumably you believed that he was the right one for you.'

'I made a mistake,' Katy said defensively.

'And mistakes happen. Even if you're not being deliberately misled by a guy, you could both go out in good faith, thinking that it will go somewhere, only to discover that you hit obstacles along the way that make it impossible for you both to consider a life together.'

'And you're an expert because...?' Katy asked sarcastically.

'People are fond of self-deception,' Lucas delivered with all-knowing cool. 'I should know because I witnessed it first-hand with my father. You want something badly enough and you try and make it work and, if it all makes sense on paper, then you try all the harder to make it work. In a worst case scenario, you might actually walk up the aisle and then into a maternity ward, still kidding yourself that you've got the real deal, only to be forced to concede defeat, then cutting the ties is a thousand times more complicated.'

'You're so cynical…about *everything*.' She harked back to the lack of trust that had made him think that the only solution to saving his deal was to isolate her just in case.

'There's no such thing as the perfect man, Katy. With Powell, you got someone who deliberately set out to deceive you.' He shrugged. 'You might think I'm cynical but I'm also honest. I have never in my life set out to deceive anyone. I've never promised a bed of roses or a walk up the aisle.' He looked at her thoughtfully. 'You had a crap time with some guy who strung you along…'

'Which is why you should have believed me when I told you that I'd rather have walked on a bed of hot coals than have anything to do with him in my life again.'

'That's beside the point. At the time, I looked at the facts and evaluated them accordingly. What I'm trying to tell you is this: the world is full of men who will do whatever it takes to get a woman into bed, and that includes making promises they have no intention of keeping. With me, what you see is what you get. We're here, we're attracted to one another and that's all there is to it.'

'Sex for the sake of sex.' That was something she had never considered and surely *would* never consider. It contravened pretty much everything she had been taught to believe in. Didn't it? It was what Duncan had been after and that had repulsed her. Sex and love were entwined and to disentangle them was to reduce the value of both.

Lucas laughed at the disapproving, tight-lipped expression on her face. 'It could be worse,' he drawled. 'It could be sex for the sake of a happy-ever-after that is never going to be delivered.'

The air sizzled between them. Katy was mesmerised by the dark glitter in his eyes and could feel herself being seduced by opinions that were so far removed from her own. Yet he made them sound so plausible. Instead of giving her the freedom to enjoy a healthy and varied sex life, to take her time finding the right man for her, her experience with Duncan had propelled her ever further into a mind-set that rigidly refused to countenance anything but the guy who ticked all the boxes.

Wasn't Lucas right in many ways? How could you ever be sure of finding Mr Right unless you were prepared to bravely face down the probability that you might have to risk some Mr Wrongs first?

And who was to say that all Mr Wrongs were going to be creeps like Duncan? Some Mr Wrongs might actually be *fun*. Not marriage material, but *fun*.

Like Lucas Cipriani. He had Mr Wrong stamped all over him and yet...wouldn't he be fun?

For the first time in her life, Katy wondered when and how she had become so protective of her emotions and so incapable of enjoying herself in the way all other girls of her age would. Her parents had never laid down any hard and fast rules but she suspected now, looking back down the years, that she had picked things up in overheard conversations about some of the young women in distress they had helped. She had seen how unwanted pregnancies and careless emotional choices could destroy lives and she had consigned those lessons to the back of her mind, little knowing how much they would influence her later decisions.

Lucas could see the range of conflicting emotions shadowing her expression.

The man had really done a number on her, he thought, and along with that thought came another, which was that the first thing he would do, provided the deal went through, was to sling Powell out on his backside.

Whatever experiences she had had before the guy, he had clearly been the one she had set her sights on for a permanent relationship, and throwing herself into something only to find it was built on lies and deceit would have hit her hard.

For all her feisty, strong-willed, argumentative personality, she was a romantic at heart and that probably stemmed from her background. Sure she would have enjoyed herself as a girl, would have had the usual sexual experiences, but she would have kept her heart intact for the man she hoped to spend the rest of her life with, and it was unfortunate that that man happened to have been a married guy with a penchant for playing away.

'You may think that I don't have the sort of high moral code that you look for,' Lucas told her seriously. 'But I have my own code. It's based on honesty. I'm not in search of involvement and I don't pretend to be. You were hurt by Powell but you could never be hurt by me because emotions wouldn't enter the equation.'

Katy looked at him dubiously. She was surprised that she was even bothering to listen but a Pandora's box had been opened and all sorts of doubts and misgivings about that high moral code he had mentioned were flying around like angry, buzzing wasps.

'I'm not the type you would ever go for.' Lucas had never thought he'd see the day he actually uttered those words to a woman. 'And quite honestly, I second that, because I would be no good for you. This isn't a relationship where two people are exploring one another in the hope of taking things to the next level. This is about sex.'

'You're confusing me.'

'I'm taking you out of your comfort zone,' Lucas murmured, yearning to touch her, only just managing to keep his hands under lock and key. 'I'm giving you food for thought. That can't be a bad thing.'

Katy looked at him and collided with eyes the colour of the deepest, darkest night. Her heart did a series of somersaults inside her chest. He was temptation in a form she was finding irresistible. Every word he had said and every argument he had proffered combined to produce a battering ram that rendered her defenceless.

'You're just bored,' she ventured feebly, a last-ditch attempt to stave off the crashing ache to grab hold of what he was offering and hold on tight. 'Stuck here without a playmate.'

'How shallow do you think I am?' Lucas grinned, his expression lightening, his eyes rich with open amusement. 'Do you think I need to satisfy my raging libido every other hour or risk exploding? I'm tired of talking. I don't think I've ever spent this much time trying to persuade a woman into bed with me.'

'Should I be flattered?'

'Most definitely,' Lucas returned, without the slightest hesitation.

Then he reached out, trailed a long finger against her cheek and tucked some strands of coppery hair behind one ear. When he should have stopped and given her time to gather herself, because she was all over the place, he devastated her instead by feathering his touch along her collarbone then dipping it down to her cleavage.

Gaze welded to his darkly handsome face, Katy remained rooted to the spot. Her nipples were pinched buds straining against the bikini top. If she looked down she knew that she would see their roused imprint against the fabric. Her eyelids fluttered and then she breathed in sharply as he stepped closer to her and placed both of his big hands on her rib cage.

He had been backing her towards the bed without her even noticing and suddenly she tumbled back against the mattress and lay there, staring up at him.

She was about to break all her rules for a one-night stand and she wasn't going to waste any more time trying to tell herself not to.

CHAPTER SIX

EXCEPT KATY WASN'T entirely sure how she was going to initiate breaking all those rules. She'd never done so before and she was dealing with a man who had probably cut his teeth breaking rules. He'd made no bones about being experienced. Was he expecting a similar level of experience? Of course he was!

She quailed. Mouth dry, she stared at him in silence as he whipped off his shirt in one fluid movement and then stood there, a bronzed god, staring down at her. She greedily ate him up with her eyes, from his broad shoulders to his six-pack and the dark line of hair that disappeared under the low-slung swimming trunks.

Lucas hooked his fingers under the waistband of the trunks and Katy shot up onto her elbows, fired with a heady mixture of thrilling excitement and crippling apprehension.

What would he do if she were to tell him that she was a virgin? *Run a mile*, was the first thought that sprang to mind. Katy didn't want him to run a mile. She wanted him near her and against her and inside her. It made her feel giddy just thinking about it.

In the spirit of trying to be someone who might actually know what to do in a situation like this, she reached behind her to fumble unsuccessfully with the almost non-existent spaghetti strings that kept the bikini top in position.

Lucas couldn't have been more turned on. He liked that shyness. It wasn't something with which he was familiar. He leant over her, caging her in.

'You smell of the sun,' he murmured. 'And I don't think I've ever wanted any woman as much as I want you right now.'

'I want you too,' Katy replied huskily. She tentatively traced the column of his neck then, emboldened, his firm jawline and then the bunched muscles of his shoulder blades. Her heart was thumping hard and every jerky breath she took threatened to turn into a groan.

He eased her lips apart and flicked his tongue inside her mouth, exploring and tasting her, and setting off a dizzying series of reactions that galvanised every part of her body into furious response. Her small hands tightened on his shoulders and she rubbed her thighs together, frantic to ease the tingling between them.

Lucas nudged her with his bulging erection, gently prising her legs apart and settling himself between them, then moving slowly as he continued to kiss her.

He tugged at her lower lip with his teeth, teasing her until she was holding her breath, closing her eyes and trembling like a leaf.

Katy didn't think that anything in the world could have tasted as good as his mouth on her and she pulled him against her with urgent hands.

She wished she'd rid herself of her bikini because now it was an encumbrance, separating their bodies.

She wriggled under him, reaching behind herself and, knowing what she wanted to do, Lucas obliged, urging her up so that he could tug free the ties. Then he rose up to straddle her and looked down, his dark eyes slumberous with desire.

Katy had never thought about sex without thinking about love and she had never thought about love without painting a tableau of the whole big deal, from marriage to babies in a thirty-second fast-forward film reel in her head.

Big mistake. In all those imaginings, her body had just been something all tied up with the bigger picture and not something needing fulfilment in its own right. The fact she had never been tempted had only consolidated in her head that sex was not at all what everyone shouted about.

Even the momentous decision that desire had propelled her into making, to ditch her hard and fast principles and sleep with him, had been made with no real prior knowledge of just how wonderfully liberating it would feel for her.

Yes, she had imagined it.

In practice, it was all oh, so wildly different. She felt joyously free and absolutely certain that what she was doing was the right thing for her to do.

Burning up, she watched Lucas as he looked at her. He was so big, so dangerously, *sinfully* handsome, and he was gazing at her as though she was something priceless. The open hunger in his eyes drove away all her inhibitions and she closed her eyes on a whimper as he leaned back down to trail his tongue against her collarbone.

Then he pinned her hands to her sides, turning her

into a willing captive so that he could fasten his mouth on one nipple. He suckled, pulling it into his mouth while grazing the stiffened bud with his tongue.

This was sex as Katy had never imagined it. Wild, raw and basic, carrying her away on a tide of passion that was as forceful as a tsunami. This wasn't the physical connection from a kind, considerate and thoughtful guy who had wooed her with flowers and talked about a happy-ever-after future. This was the physical connection from a guy who had promised nothing but sex and would walk away from her the minute their stay on his yacht had come to an end.

His mouth and tongue against her nipple were sending piercing arrows of sensation through her body. She was on fire when he drew back to rid himself of his swimming trunks. The bulge she had felt pressing against her was impressively big, big enough for her to feel a moment of sheer panic, because how on earth could something so big fit inside her and actually feel good?

But that fear wasn't allowed to take root because desire was smothering it. He settled back on the bed and then tugged down the bikini bottoms.

Katy closed her eyes and heard him laugh softly.

'Don't you like what you see?' Lucas teased and she cautiously looked at him. 'Because I very much like what *I* see.'

'Do you?' Katy whispered, very much out of her depth and feverishly making all sorts of comparisons in her head between her boyish figure and the women he probably took to his bed. She wasn't going to dwell on it, but she wasn't an idiot. Lucas Cipriani could have any woman he wanted and, whilst she was confident enough about her looks, that confidence took a very understandable beating when she considered that the man in bed with her was every woman's dream guy. 'Sexy' didn't get more outrageous.

Lucas felt a spurt of pure rage against Powell, a man whose existence he had known nothing about a week ago. Not only had he destroyed Katy's faith in the opposite sex, but he had also pummelled her self-esteem. Any human being with functioning eyesight could have told her that she was a show-stopper.

He bent over to taste her pouting mouth whilst at the same time gently inserting his hand between her thighs.

She wasn't clean-shaven down there and he liked that; he enjoyed the feel of her soft, downy fluff against his fingers. He liked playing with it before inserting one long finger into her.

It was electrifying. He slid his finger lazily in long strokes, finding the core of her and the tight little bud that throbbed as he zeroed in on it. In the grip of sensations she had never known before, Katy whimpered and clutched him, all frantic need and craving. She was desperate to ride the crest of a building wave and her whimpers turned into soft, hitched moans as she began to arch her spine, pushing her slight breasts up, inviting him to tease a nipple with his tongue.

He released her briefly to fetch a condom from his wallet then he was over her, nudging her legs apart with his thigh and settling between them. Nerves firmly back in place, Katy smoothed exploratory hands along his back, tracing the hardness of muscle and sinew.

Her coppery hair was in tangles over her shoulders,

spread like flames across the pillows. Lucas stroked some of the tangles back and kissed her.

'I want you,' Katy muttered into his mouth, and she felt him smile. Desire was a raging force inside her, ripping all control out of her grasp and stripping her of her ability to think straight, or even to think at all.

She felt his impatience and his need matching hers as he pushed into her, a deep, long thrust that made her cry out. He stilled and frowned.

'Don't stop,' she begged him, rising up so that he could sink deeper into her. She was so wet for him and so ready for this.

'You're so tight,' Lucas murmured huskily in a driven undertone. 'I can't describe the sensation, *mia bella.*'

'Don't talk!' Katy gasped, urging him on until he was thrusting hard, and the tight pain gave way to a soaring sense of pleasure as he carried her higher and higher until, at last, she came…and it was the most out-of-body experience she could ever have imagined. Wracked with shudders, she let herself fly until she weakly descended back down to planet Earth. Then, all she wanted to do was wrap her arms around him and hold him tightly against her.

Lucas was amused when she hugged him. He wasn't one for hugs, but there was something extraordinarily disingenuous about her and he found that appealing.

He gently moved off her and then looked down and frowned, his brain only slowly making connections that began to form into a complete picture, one that he could scarcely credit.

There wasn't much blood, just a few drops, enough

for him to work out that none of that shyness and hesitancy had been put on. She'd blushed like a virgin because that was exactly what she was. He looked at her as the colour drained from her face.

'This is your first time, isn't it?'

For Katy, that was the equivalent of a bucket of cold water being poured over her. She hadn't thought that he would find out. She had vaguely assumed that if she didn't say anything then Lucas would never know that she had lost her virginity to him. She hadn't wanted him to know because she had sensed, with every pore of her being, that he wouldn't be thrilled.

For a man who didn't do commitment, and who gave warnings about the perils of involvement, a virgin would represent the last word in unacceptable.

She quailed and clenched her fists because making love to Lucas had been the most wonderful thing in her life, just the most beautiful, *right* thing she had ever done, and now it was going to be spoiled because, quite rightly, he was going to hit the roof.

She wriggled and tried to yank some of the covers up because there was no way she was going to have an argument with him in the nude.

'So what?' She eyed him mutinously under the thick fringe of her lashes and glowered. 'It's really no big deal.'

'No big deal?' Lucas parroted incredulously. 'Why didn't you tell me?'

'Because I know how you would have reacted,' Katy muttered, hugging her knees to her chest and refusing to meet his eyes for fear of the message she would read there.

'You know, do you?'

Katy sneaked a glance at him, and just as fast her eyes skittered away. He was sprawled indolently on the bed, an in-your-face reminder of the intimacy they had just shared. She was covering up for all she was worth but he was carelessly oblivious to his nakedness.

'I wanted to do it.' She stuck her chin up and challenged him to argue with that. 'And I knew that if I told you that I'd never slept with anyone before you'd have run a mile. Wouldn't you?'

Lucas grimaced. 'I probably would have been a little cautious,' he conceded.

'Run a mile.'

'But I would have been flattered,' he admitted with even more honesty. 'I would also have been more gentle and taken my time.' He raked his fingers through his hair and vaulted out of the bed to pace the floor, before snatching a towel which was slung over the back of a chair and loosely settling it around his waist. Then he circled to sit on the bed next to her. 'It *is* a big deal,' he said gently. He took her hands in his and stroked her wrists until her clenched fists relaxed. 'And if I was a little rough for you, then I apologise.'

'Please don't apologise.' She smiled cautiously and stroked his face, and it was such an intimate gesture that she almost yanked her hand back, but he didn't seem to mind; indeed he caught her hand and turned it over so that he could place a very tender kiss on the underside of her wrist.

'You're beautiful, *cara*. I don't understand how it is that you've remained a virgin. Surely there must have been other men before Powell?'

Katy winced at the reminder of the man who had

been responsible for landing them here together on this yacht. It was fair to say that, however hateful her memories of him were, they seemed a lot less hateful now. Maybe one day she might even mentally thank him because she couldn't see how she could ever regret having slept with Lucas.

'That was another of those down sides to having parents who were pillars of the community.' Katy let loose a laugh. 'There were always expectations. And especially in a tiny place, when you're growing up, everyone knows everyone else. Reputations are lost in the snap of a finger. I didn't really think about that, though,' she said thoughtfully. 'I just knew that I wanted the whole love and marriage thing, so my standards were maybe a bit on the high side.'

She sighed and smiled ruefully at Lucas, who was looking at her with such sizzling interest that every pulse in her body raced into overdrive.

'When Duncan came along, I'd just returned from university and I wasn't quite sure what direction my life was going to take. I remember my mother and I talking about the social scene at university, and my mum asking me about the boys, and something must have registered that I needed to take the next step, which was finding someone special.' She gazed at Lucas. 'I slept with you because I really wanted to. You said a lot of stuff…basically about seizing the day…'

'I had no idea I was addressing a girl who had no experience.'

'But, you see, that's not the point.' Katy was keen to impress this on him. 'The point is that you made me think about things differently. I know this isn't going anywhere but at least you were honest about that and you gave me a choice.' Duncan had denied her the truth about himself and, even if this was just a one night stand, which was something she had always promised herself she would never do, was it really worse to lose her virginity to Lucas than to a liar like Duncan?

She gazed up at him earnestly and Lucas lowered his head and very tenderly kissed her on the lips. He could have taken her again, right then, but she would be sore. Next time, he intended to make it up to her, to take his time. It blew his mind to think that she had come to him as a virgin. It was a precious gift and he knew that, even though he couldn't fully understand what had led her to give it to him.

'Yes, *cara,* there will be no "for ever after" with us but believe me when I tell you that, for the time we're together, I will take you to paradise and back. But before that…can I interest you in a shower?' He stood up and looked down at her slender perfection.

'With you?'

'Why not?' Lucas raised his eyebrows. 'You'd be surprised how different an experience it can be when you're in a shower with your lover.'

Katy shivered pleasurably at that word…*lover.* She shook her head and laughed. 'I think I'm going to relax here for a bit, then I'll go back to my cabin.'

Of course there would be no 'for ever after'…and she was tempted to tell him that she understood that well enough without having to be reminded of it.

'Why?' Lucas frowned and then heard himself inviting her to stay with him, which was astonishing, because he had always relished his privacy, even when he was involved with someone. Sex was a great outlet, and his appetite for it was as healthy as the next man's, but when the sex was over his craving for his own space always took precedence over post-coital closeness. He'd never spent the night with a woman.

'Because I need to be on my own for a bit.'

Right then, Lucas felt that by the time they were ready to leave this yacht he would have introduced her to the joys of sharing showers and shown her how rewarding it could be to spend the night in his bed...

Katy had fallen into something of a sleep when she heard the bang on the door to her cabin. For the first time since she had arrived on Lucas's cruiser, she had retired to bed without anything to eat, but then it had been late by the time she had eventually left his cabin.

Having intended to sneak out while he was showering, she had remained where she was and they had spent the next few hours in one another's arms. To his credit, he had not tried to initiate sex again.

'I can show you a lot of other ways we can satisfy one another,' he had murmured, and he had proceeded to do just that.

In the end, *she* had been the one whose body had demanded more than just the touch of his mouth and the feel of his long, skilful fingers. *She* had been the one to guide him into her and to demand that he come inside her.

It had been a marathon session and she had made her way back to her cabin exhaustedly, still determined not to stay the night in his room, because if she slept in her own bed then she would somehow be able to keep control of the situation.

'Katy! Open up!'

Katy jerked up with a start at the sound of Lucas's voice bellowing at her through the locked door. She leapt out of the bed, half-drugged with sleep, and yanked open the door, every fibre in her body responding with panic to the urgency in his voice.

She looked at him in consternation. He was in a pair of jeans and a black, figure-hugging tee-shirt. Not the sort of clothes anyone would consider wearing for a good night's sleep. Her already panicked antennae went into overdrive.

'Lucas! What time is it?'

'You need to get dressed immediately. It's a little after five in the morning.'

'But why?'

'Don't ask questions, Katy. Just do it.' He forged into the room and began opening drawers, yanking out a pair of jeans, quickly followed by the first tee-shirt that came to hand. Even at that hour in the morning, it would be balmy outside. 'Maria is sick.' He looked at his watch. 'Very sick. It has all the makings of acute appendicitis. Any delay and peritonitis will kick in, so you need to dress and you need to dress fast. I can't leave you on this yacht alone.'

Katy dashed into the bathroom and began stripping off the oversized tee-shirt she slept in, replacing it with the jeans and tee-shirt she had grabbed from his outstretched hand.

'Do you think I might get up to no good if you're not around to keep an eye on me?' she asked breathlessly, only half-joking because that deeply intimate step she had taken with him had clearly not been a deeply intimate step for him. He was a man who could detach, as he had made perfectly clear.

'Not now, Katy.'

'How will we get her to the hospital?' She flushed, ashamed that her thoughts had not been one hundred percent on the woman of whom she had grown fond during the short time she had been on the yacht.

'Not by helicopter,' Lucas told her, his every movement invested with speed as he took her arm and began leading her hurriedly out of the bedroom. 'Too long to get my pilot here and nowhere to land near the hospital.'

They were walking quickly to a part of the yacht Katy hadn't known existed, somewhere in the bowels of the massive cruiser.

'Fortunately, I am equipped to deal with any emergency. And to answer your earlier question...' He briefly glanced down at her, rosy, tousled and so utterly adorable that she literally took his breath away. 'I'm not taking you with me because I think you might get up to no good in my absence. I'm taking you with me because if something happened to you and I wasn't around I would never forgive myself.'

Something flared inside her and she felt a lump in her throat, then she quickly told herself not to be an idiot, because that wasn't a declaration of caring; it was a simple statement of fact. If she was left alone on the yacht and she needed help of any sort, she would be unable to swim to shore and unable to contact him. How would he, or anyone in his position, be able to live with that?

Things were happening at the speed of light now. In a move she thought was as impressive as a master magician's sleight of hand, the side of the yacht opened up to reveal a speedboat, an expensive toy within an expensive toy. Maria, clearly in a great deal of pain but smiling bravely, was waiting for them and was soon ensconced, to be taken to the island.

Dawn was breaking as they hit the island, a rosy, blushing dawn that revealed lush trees and flowers and narrow, winding roads disappearing up sloping hills.

A car was waiting for them, a four-wheel drive with an elderly man behind the wheel. They reached the town in under half an hour and then Maria was met in Accident and Emergency and whizzed through in a wheelchair, everything moving as though orchestrated.

Katy had barely had time to draw breath. Only when the older woman had been wheeled into the operating theatre, and they were sitting in the small hospital café with a cup of coffee in front of them, did she begin to pay attention to her surroundings… and then it registered.

'Your name is all over this hospital…'

Lucas shifted uncomfortably and glanced around him. 'So it would seem.'

'But why?'

'My money went towards building most of it.' He shrugged, as though that was the most natural response in the world. 'My father's family owned a villa here and he spent his holidays on the island with my mother and me when I was very young. It's about the only thing my father didn't end up giving away to one of the ex-wives who fleeced him in their divorce proceedings. I expect he had strong sentimental attachments to it. There was a prolonged period when the villa got very little use but, as soon as I was able, I began the process of renovation. I have the money, so when the head of the hospital came to me for help it was only natural for me to offer it.'

It felt odd to be offering her this slither of personal information and for a few seconds he was uncomfortable with what felt like a loss of his prized self-control.

What was it about this woman that made him behave out of character? Not in ways that should be disconcerting, because she neither said nor did anything that raised red flags, but still...

He was intensely private, not given to sharing. However, this was the first time he had been on the island with any woman. He rarely came here but, when he did, he came on his own, relishing the feeling of being swept back to happier times. Was Katy's necessary presence here the reason why he was opening up? And why was he making a big deal of it anyway? he thought with prosaic irony. She couldn't help but have noticed his name on some of the wards, just as she couldn't have failed to notice how eager the staff were to please.

'The old hospital, which was frankly far from perfect, was largely destroyed some time ago in a storm. I made sure that it was rebuilt to the highest specification. The infrastructure here is not complex but it is essential it all works. The locals depend on exporting produce, and naturally on some tourism. The tourists, in particular, are the wealthy sort who expect things to run like clockwork. Including the hospital, should one of them decide to take ill.' He grinned. 'There's nothing more obnoxious than a rich tourist who finds himself inconvenienced.'

'And I'm guessing you don't include yourself in that category?' Katy teased. Their eyes met; butterflies fluttered in her tummy and her heart lurched. They hadn't had a chance to talk about what had happened because she had disappeared off to her own quarters, and here they were now, caught up in unexpected circumstances.

She had no idea whether this was something that would be more than a one-night stand. She hoped it was. She had connected with him and she would feel lost if the connection were abruptly to be cut. It panicked her to think like that but she had to be honest with herself and admit that Lucas was not the man she had originally thought he was. He still remained the last person on earth she could ever contemplate having an emotional relationship with, but he had shown her the power of a sexual relationship and, like a starving person suddenly led to a banquet, she didn't want the experience to end. Just yet.

But nothing had been said and she wasn't going to engineer round to the conversation.

'Do *you* think I'm obnoxious?' Lucas questioned softly and she blushed and squirmed, so very aware of those dark eyes fastened to her face.

'My opinion of you *has* changed,' Katy admitted, thinking back to the ice-cold man who had forced her hand for the sake of a deal. She thought that her opinion also *kept* changing. She didn't want to dwell on that, so instead she changed the subject. 'What about Maria? When will we find out what the outcome is?'

'There's every chance it will be a positive one.'

Lucas glanced at his watch. 'I personally know the surgeon and there's no one better. I've contacted her family, who will be in the waiting area, and as soon as the operation is over I've asked to be called. I don't anticipate any problems at all. However...'

'However?'

'It does mean that there will be a small change of plan.'

'How do you mean?'

'We will no longer be based on the yacht. For a start, without Maria around, there will be no one to attend to the cooking and all the other little things she takes care of, and it's too late to find a replacement who can stay on board. So we'll have to relocate to my villa. I can get someone to come in on a daily basis and, furthermore, I will be on hand in case there are any complications following surgery.'

He paused. 'Maria worked for my father before he...began steadily going off the rails. My mother was very fond of her, so I've made sure to look out for her and her family, and also made sure to carry on employing her in some capacity when my father's various wives decided that they would rather have somewhat smarter people holding the fort in the various properties.'

His mobile phone buzzed and he held up one hand as he spoke in rapid Italian to the consultant, the concerned lines on his face quickly smoothing over in reaction to whatever was being said on the other end.

'All's gone according to plan,' he said. 'But, had she not reached the hospital when she did, then it would have been quite a different story. Now, why don't you wait here while I have a word with some of her family? I won't be long. I'll also arrange for your clothes and possessions to be transported to the villa.' He looked at her, head tilted to one side, then he patted his pocket. 'You can call your parents, if you like,' he said gruffly. 'I've been checking your phone, and I see that they've taken you at your word and not texted, but I expect they'd like to hear from you.'

He handed over the phone and her eyes shone, because more than anything else this demonstrated that he finally trusted her, and she found that that meant a great deal to her.

'What can I say to them?' she asked, riding high on the fact that she was no longer under suspicion. A barrier between them had been crossed and that felt good in the wake of what they had shared.

'Use your discretion,' Lucas told her drily. 'But it might be as well not to mention too many names, not that I think anything can go wrong with the deal at this stage. It's a hair's breadth away from being signed.' He stood up, leaving her with her mobile phone, and it felt like the greatest honour bestowed on her possible. 'I'll see you shortly and then we'll be on our way.'

CHAPTER SEVEN

LYING ON THE wooden deckchair by the side of the infinity pool that graced the lush grounds of his villa and overlooked the distant turquoise of the ocean, Lucas looked at Katy as she scythed through the water with the gracefulness of a fish.

The finalising of the deal had taken slightly longer than Lucas had anticipated, but he wasn't complaining. Indeed, he had encouraged his Chinese counterparts to take their time in sorting out all the essential details on which the takeover pivoted. In the meantime…

Katy swam to the side of the pool and gazed at him with a smile.

Up above, the sun had burnt through the early-morning clouds to leave a perfectly clear, milky, blue sky. Around them, the villa afforded absolute isolation. It was ringed with trees and perched atop a hill commanding views of the sea. Lucas had always valued his privacy and never more so than now, when he didn't want a single second of his time with her interrupted by so much as a passing tradesman. Not that any passing tradesman would be able to make it past the imposing wrought-iron gates that guarded the property.

He had dismissed all help, ensuring that the villa was stocked with sufficient food for their stay.

Just him…and her…

Right now, she was naked. He had half-expected, after that tentative surrender four days ago when she had placed her small hand on his thigh and sent his blood pressure through the roof, that a three-steps-forward, one-step-back game might ensue. He had predicted a tussle with her virtuous conscience, with lust holding the trump card, but in fact she had given herself to him without a trace of doubt or hesitation. He had admired her for that. Whatever inner battles she had fought, she had put them behind her and given generously.

'It's beautiful in here.' She grinned. 'Stop being so lazy and come and swim.'

'I hope that's not the sound of a challenge,' Lucas drawled, standing up, as naked as she was. He couldn't see her without his libido reacting like a lit rocket and now was no exception.

'Is sex *all* you ever think about, Lucas?' But she was laughing as she stepped out of the pool, the water streaming off her slick body.

'Are you complaining?' His eyes darkened and he balled his hands into fists. The urge to take her was so powerful it made him feel faint. He wanted to settle her on a towel on the ground and have her hard and fast, like a teenager in the grip of too much testosterone. Around her he lost his cool.

'Not at the moment,' Katy said breathlessly, walking straight into his arms. They had a lot of sex but, in fact, they also talked as well, and laughed, and en-

joyed a level of compatibility she would never have
thought possible when she had first met him.

He was still the most arrogant man she had ever
met but there was so much more to him as well. She
had no idea what was going to happen when they returned to London and she didn't think about it. Maybe
they would carry on seeing one another...although
how that would work out when she was his employee
she couldn't quite fathom. The gossip would be out
of control and he would loathe that.

For the first time in her life, Katy was living in
the moment, and she wasn't going to let fear of what
might or might not lie round the corner destroy her
happiness.

Lucas cupped her pert bottom, which was wet from
swimming, and kneaded it between his hands, driving her closer to him so that his rock-hard erection
pushed against her belly.

She held him, played with him, felt the way
his breathing changed and his body stiffened. She
couldn't stop loving the way he reacted to her. It
made her feel powerful and sexy and very, very fem-
inine.

'I'm too big for deck-chair sex,' Lucas murmured.

'Who said anything about sex?' Katy breathed.
'We could just...you know...'

'I think I'm getting the picture.' He emitted a low,
husky laugh and settled her on the cushioned deck
chair, arranging her as carefully as an artist arranging a model he was about to paint, lying her in just
the right place with her legs parted, hanging over either side of the chair, leaving her open for his atten-
tive ministrations.

Then, sitting at the foot of the chair on his over-sized beach towel, he tugged her gently down towards his mouth and began tasting her. He slid his tongue into her, found the bud of her clitoris and licked it delicately, feathering little explosions of sensation through her, and he continued licking and teasing, knowing at which point she would begin to buck against his mouth as those little explosions became more and more impossible to control.

When he glanced up, he could see her small breasts, pointed and crowned with the dusky pink of her nipples, which were pinched from the water cooling on them. Her lips were parted, her nostrils flared as she breathed laboriously and her eyes were closed.

A thought flashed through his head. His condoms were nowhere to hand. What would happen if he were to sweep her up right now, hoist her onto him and let her ride them both to one of the body-shattering orgasms that they seemed strangely adept at giving one another? What if he were to feel himself in her without the barrier of a condom? Would it be such a bad thing? It wasn't as if pregnancy would be a certainty.

Shock at even thinking such a thing stilled him for a second. He'd never had thoughts like that in his life before and it implied a lack of self-control he found disturbing.

He killed the wayward thought that had sprung from nowhere and drove a finger into her, rousing her deep inside, and feeling her begin to spasm as she began to soar towards a climax.

She came against his mouth, arching up with an

abandoned cry of intense satisfaction, and then and only then did he allow her to touch him, with her mouth and with her hands.

The errant desire to take her without protection had been ruthlessly banished from his head but it left a lingering taste of unease in his mouth as they both subsided and flopped back into the pool to cool off.

Katy swam to Lucas but he stiffened and turned away, striking out into the water and rapidly swimming four lengths, barely surfacing for air as she watched from the side. He'd rejected her just then. Or maybe she'd been imagining it. Had she? He certainly hadn't done the usual and held her against him, coming down from a high with his body still pressed up against hers.

Sensitive to the fact that this was not a normal situation, that it was the equivalent of a one-night stand stretched out for slightly longer than the one night, Katy got out of the pool and walked over to her towel, anchoring it firmly around her so that she was covered up. Then she watched him as he continued swimming, his strong, brown body slicing through the water with speed and efficiency.

He didn't spare her a glance and after five minutes she retired to the villa and to the *en suite* bathroom which had been designated for her but rarely used, now she and Lucas were lovers.

The villa was magnificent, interestingly laid out with lots of nooks and crannies in which to relax, and huge, open windows through which breezes could circulate freely through the house. It lacked the slick sophistication of his yacht and was rather colonial in style with a stunning mixture of wood, billowing muslin at the windows, shutters and over-head fans. Katy loved it. She settled with her book into a rocking chair on the wide veranda that fronted the villa.

She kept waiting for Lucas to show up but eventually she gave up and nodded off. It was a little after four but still baking hot and, as always, cloudless.

Allowing her mind to drift, yanking it back every time it tried to break the leash and worry away at Lucas's reaction earlier on, she was scarcely aware of time going by, and it was only when she noticed the tell-tale signs of the sun beginning to dip that she realised that several hours must have passed.

In a panic, she scrambled to her feet and turned round, to find the object of her feverish imaginings standing framed in the doorway…and he wasn't smiling. Indeed, the humorous, sexy guy she had spent the past week with was noticeably absent.

'Lucas!' She plastered a smile on her face. 'How long have you been standing there? I was reading… er… I must have nodded off…'

Lucas saw the hurt beneath the bright smile and he knew that he had put it there. He had turned his back on her and swam off, and he had carried on swimming because he had needed to clear his head. When he'd finally stopped, she was gone and he had fought against the desire to seek her out because he was not going to allow a simple sexual liaison to get out of control. When they returned to London, this would finish and his life would return to normal, which was exactly as it should be. So he'd kept his distance and that would have upset her. He clenched his jaw and focused on what really mattered now, which was a turn of events that neither of them could have predicted.

'You've been talking to your parents. What, exactly, have you told them?'

'Lucas, I have no idea what you're talking about.'

'Just try and think.' He moved to stand in front of her, the beautiful lines of his handsome face taut and forbidding. 'Did you tell either of them where you were? What you were doing here? Who you were with?'

'I...you're making me nervous, Lucas. Let me think...no; *no*. I just told Mum that I was in Italy and that it was lovely and warm and that I was fine and having a good time...'

'I have just spent the past hour on the phone with the Chinese company. It seems that they were told by Powell that I was the wrong kind of person to be doing business with—that I was the sort of guy who seduces innocent girls and shouldn't be trusted as far as I can be thrown. It would seem that news travelled and connections were made. Someone, somewhere, figured out that we're here together and social media has taken the information right into Powell's hands and given the man ammunition to blow my deal sky-high at the last minute.'

The colour drained from Katy's face. When he said that 'connections were made', it was easy to see how. They had been into the little town several times over the past few days, checking on Maria and doing all sorts of touristy things. He could have been recognised and, whilst *she* wouldn't have been, someone could have sneakily taken a picture of them together and tagged them in something they posted online. The mind boggled.

'This is *not* my fault, Lucas. You know how pervasive social media is.' But it *was* her fault. She was the one with the connection to Duncan and, if gossip had been spread, then who knew what her mum might have mentioned to anyone in the village? Someone might be friends with Duncan on Facebook or whatever. Guilt pinked her cheeks, but before she could go on the defensive he held up one imperious hand to close down her protest.

'I'm not going to waste time going back and forth with this.' He frowned down at her and sighed. 'I'm not playing blame games here, Katy, and you're right: there's no privacy left anywhere. If anyone is to blame, then it's me, because I should have been more circumspect in my movements here. The place is small, I'm a well-known face, it's close to the busiest time of year for tourists and they have smart phones. But the fact remains that I have now been left with a considerable problem.

'No, perhaps I should amend that: when I say that *I* have a considerable problem, it might be fairer to say that we *both* have a considerable problem. Your ex approached Ken Huang and told him a story, and there's an underlying threat to go to the press and take public this sordid tale of a young, innocent girl being taken advantage of by an unscrupulous billionaire womaniser.'

Katy paled. 'Duncan wouldn't...'

But he would.

'He's played up your innocence to the hilt.'

'He knew...' Katy swallowed painfully. 'He knew

that I was inexperienced. I never thought that he would use the information against me. I trusted him when I confided in him.'

In the midst of an unfolding nightmare, Lucas discovered that the deal which should have been uppermost in his mind was overshadowed by a gut-wrenching sympathy for her vulnerability, which Powell had thoroughly taken advantage of.

Lucas dragged over a chair to join hers and sat heavily, closing his eyes for a few seconds while he sifted through the possibilities for damage limitation. Then he looked at her.

'The man has an axe to grind,' Lucas stated flatly. 'Tell me why.'

'Does it matter?'

'In this instance, everything matters. If I need to use leverage, then I need to know where to apply it. I don't play dirty but I'm willing to make an exception in this case.'

'It ended really badly between me and Duncan.' She shot him a guilty, sidelong look before lowering her eyes. 'As you may have gathered. It wouldn't have been so bad if I'd found out about his wife and children *after* I'd slept with him, but I think he was doubly enraged that, not only did I find out that he was married, but he hadn't even succeeded in getting me into bed *before* I'd had a chance to find out.'

'Some men are bastards,' Lucas told her in a matter-of-fact voice. 'It has to be said that some women leave a lot to be desired as well. It's life.'

'You mean those women your father married,' Katy murmured, distracted, thinking that on some level their approaches to life had been similarly tarnished by unfortunate experiences with the opposite sex. It was easy to think that, because you came from a wildly different background from someone, the things that affected the decisions you made had to be different, but that wasn't always the case. Money and privilege had been no more guarantee of a smooth ride in his case than a stable family background had been in hers.

Lucas shrugged. 'I have no more time for the gold-diggers,' he gritted. 'At least a guy with his head screwed on has a fighting chance of recognising them for what they are and can take the necessary precautions. You, I'm guessing, had no chance against a skilled predator. Continue.'

'I'd confided in my best friend,' Katy said, with a grimace. 'I felt such a fool. Claire was far more experienced than me, and she was livid when I told her about the messages I'd accidentally seen on his phone from his wife. He'd made a mistake in leaving it on the table while he vanished off to the toilet when we'd been having a meal out. Up popped a reminder to phone the kids to say good night and to remember some party they were going to on the weekend. He'd told me he was going to be away on business. Weekends, he'd always said, were tricky for him because he was trying to kick-start a photography business and they were the only times he could do whatever he had to do—networking and the like—because he was at the bank during the week.'

'A skilled excuse,' Lucas said drily. 'The man obviously came with form.'

'That was what Claire said. She told me that I was

probably not the first, which needless to say didn't make me feel at all better.'

It was as though she was looking at a very young, very naïve stranger from the advantageous position of someone who was much older and wiser. And she had Lucas to thank for that.

'Anyway, she started doing a little digging around. The world's a small place these days.' Katy grimaced. 'She found that he was a serial womaniser and she went to see his wife.'

'Ah.'

'I had no idea at the time that that was her plan, and afterwards she confessed that she didn't quite know what had prompted her to take such drastic action. But she was upset on my behalf and, in a weird way, upset on behalf of all the other girls he had conned into sleeping with him. His marriage fell apart on the back of that, so...'

'I'm getting the picture loud and clear. The ex who hates you and holds you responsible for the breakdown of his marriage now has the perfect vehicle for revenge put into his hands.'

'If I had told you the whole story in the first place, you would have realised that there was no chance I could have been any kind of mole. Then we wouldn't have ended up here and none of this would be happening now.'

Lucas smiled wryly. 'Really think that would have been how it would have worked?'

'No,' Katy answered honestly. 'You wouldn't have believed me. I would have been guilty until proven innocent.' At that point in time, he'd been a one-dimensional autocrat—ruthless, suspicious, arrogant. At this point in time…

She didn't know what he was and she didn't want to think too hard about it. They had a situation and she began to see all the nooks and crannies of it. If Duncan decided to take his revenge by publicising a tale of some sordid love tryst between Lucas and herself, not only would Lucas's deal be ruined but he would have to face the horror of the world gossiping about him behind his back. His reputation would be in tatters because, however much a lie could be disproved, mud inevitably stuck. He was the sort of guy who would claim to shrug off the opinions of other people, but that would be a heck of a lot to shrug off.

And it would all have been *her* fault.

Could she allow that to happen?

And then, aside from Lucas, there was the matter of her and her parents. They would never live it down. She felt sick thinking about their disappointment and the whispers that would circulate around the village like a raging forest fire blazing out of control. When she returned to see them, people would stare at her. Her parents would shy away from discussing it but she would see the sadness in their eyes.

She would be at the heart of a tabloid scandal: 'desperate virgin in sordid tryst with billionaire happy to use her for a few days before discarding her'. 'Sad and gullible innocent lured to a villa for sex, too stupid to appreciate her own idiocy'.

'Marry me!' she blurted out and then looked at him with wide-eyed dismay.

She jumped to her feet and began pacing the veranda, before curling onto the three-seater wicker sofa and drawing her knees up.

'Forget I said that.'

'Forget that I've received a marriage proposal?' Lucas drawled, strolling over to the sofa and sitting down, body angled towards her. 'It's the first I ever have…'

'It wasn't a marriage proposal,' Katy muttered, eyeing him with a glower, her cheeks tinged with heated colour.

'Sure about that? Because I distinctly heard the words "marry me".'

'It wasn't a *real* marriage proposal,' Katy clarified, hot all over. 'It just seemed that…if Duncan does what he's threatening to do—and I guess he will, if he's already started dropping hints to your client—then it's not just that your deal will be jeopardised—'

'Ruined,' Lucas elaborated for good measure. 'Shot down in flames…dead in the water and beyond salvation…'

'All those things,' Katy mumbled, guilt washing over her with tidal force. She breathed in deeply and looked him directly in the eyes. 'It's not even a marriage proposal,' she qualified. 'It's an *engagement* proposal. If we're engaged then Duncan can't spread any rumours about sordid trysts and he can't take your reputation away from you by implying that you're the sort of womaniser who's happy to take advantage of… of…an inexperienced young girl…'

He wasn't saying anything and she wished he would. In fact, she couldn't even read what he was thinking because his expression was so shuttered.

'Your deal can go ahead,' she plunged on. 'And you

won't have to worry about people gossiping about you behind your back.'

'That sort of thing has never bothered me.'

Katy almost smiled, because that was just *such* a predictable response, then she thought about people gossiping about him and her heart clenched.

'What's in it for you?' Lucas asked softly.

'Firstly,' Katy told him with absolute honesty, 'You're here because of me, so this is pretty much my fault. Secondly, I know how much this deal means to you. Thirdly, it's not just about you. It's also about me. My parents would be devastated and I can't bear the thought of that. And *you* might not care about what other people think of you, but *I* care what other people think of me. I wouldn't be able to stay on at either of my jobs because of the shame, and I would find it really hard to face people at home who have known me all my life.'

It was slowly dawning on her that there had been something in his softly spoken words when he had asked her what would be in it for her, something she hadn't registered immediately but which she was registering fast enough now.

'It would work.' She tilted her chin at a defiant angle to rebut the hidden insinuation she had read behind his words. She might have been wrong in her interpretation but she didn't think so. 'And it would work brilliantly because there's no emotional bond between us. I mean, there's no danger that I would get it into my head that I was doing anything but role-playing. You could get your deal done, we could defuse a potential disaster and I would be able to live with myself.'

'You're presenting me with a business proposition, Katy?' He dealt her a slashing smile that threatened to knock her sideways. 'You, the ultimate romantic, are presenting me with a business proposition that involves a phoney engagement?'

'It makes sense,' she defended.

'So it does,' Lucas murmured. 'And tell me, how long is this phoney engagement supposed to last?' He couldn't help but be amused by this from the girl who typified everything that smacked of flowers, chocolates, soul mates and walks up the aisle in a frothy, meringue wedding dress. Then he sobered up as he was struck by another, less amusing thought.

Had he changed her into something she was never meant to be? He had shown Katy the marvels of sex without strings because it was something that worked for him, but had he, in the process, somehow *changed* her? For reasons he couldn't explain, he didn't like the thought of that, but he pushed those uneasy reservations to one side, choosing instead to go for the straightforward explanation she had given, which was that it was a solution that would work for her as well as it would work for him.

Katy shrugged. 'You still haven't said whether you think it's a good idea or not.'

'I couldn't have come up with something better myself.' Lucas grinned, then looked at her seriously. 'But you should know that I wouldn't ask you to do anything you feel uncomfortable about.'

Katy's heart did that weird, clenching thing again. 'I feel very comfortable about this and, as for how long it would last, I haven't given much thought to that side of things.'

'You'd be deceiving your parents,' Lucas pointed out bluntly.

'I realise that.' She sighed and fiddled with the ends of her long hair, frowning slightly. 'I never thought that the ends justified the means, and I hate the thought of deception, but, between the devil and the deep blue sea, this seems the less hurtful option.'

Lucas looked at her long and hard. 'So we're a loved-up couple,' he murmured, his dark eyes veiled. 'And in fact, so irresistibly in love with one another that we escaped for some heady time to my yacht where we could be together free from interruption from the outside world. Your colleagues at work might find it a little hard to swallow.'

'You'd be shocked at how many people believe in love at first sight.' Katy smiled. 'You know, just because *you're* such a miserable cynic when it comes to love, doesn't mean that the rest of us are as well...'

'So now I'm a miserable cynic,' Lucas drawled, reaching out to tug her towards him. 'Tell me how likely it is that you would fall head over heels for a miserable cynic?'

'Not likely at all!' Katy laughed, looking up at him, and her heart did that funny thing again, skipping a beat, which made her feel as though she'd been cruising along quite nicely only to hit a sudden patch of violent turbulence. 'I'm afraid what you have is a girl who could only fall head over heels for someone as romantic as she is!' She frowned and tried to visualise this special person but the only face to fill her head was Lucas's dark and devastatingly handsome one.

'If we're going to be engaged, then we need to get

to know one another a whole lot better,' Lucas told her, still admiring the very practical streak which had led her to propose this very practical solution. Although, why should he be that surprised? She was a whizz at IT and that, surely, indicated a practical side to her that she herself was probably not even aware of.

He stood up, his fingers still linked with hers, and led her back through the villa and in the direction of his bedroom.

'What are you going to do with me once the engagement is over?' he murmured, toeing open his bedroom door, and then propelling her backwards to his bed while she tried to contain her laughter. 'I mean…' he lowered his head and kissed her, flicking his tongue into her mouth and igniting a series of fireworks inside her '… I'm assuming that, since you are the one with the clever plan to stage a fake engagement, you'll likewise be the one with the clever plan when it comes to wriggling out of it. So how will you dispose of me?'

He slid his hand under her tee-shirt and the warmth of her skin sent his body immediately into outer orbit. She wasn't wearing a bra, and he curved his big hand over her breast and gently teased her nipple until it was ripe and throbbing between his skilful fingers. They tumbled onto the bed, he settled her under him and straddled her so that he could see her face as he continued to tease her.

As usual, Katy's brain was losing the ability to fire on all cylinders, especially when he pushed up the tee-shirt and lowered himself to suckle her nipple. He looked up and caught her eyes, then flicked his tongue over the stiffened bud before devoting his attention to her pouting lips, kissing her again until she felt as though she was coming apart at the seams.

'Well?' He nuzzled the side of her neck and she wriggled and squirmed underneath him, hands on his waist, pushing into the waistband of his trousers and feeling his buttocks.

'Oh, I think we'll just drift apart,' Katy murmured. 'You know the sort of thing. You'll be working far too hard and you'll be spending most of your time in the Far East because of the deal you've managed to secure. I'll grow lonely and…who knows?…maybe I'll find some hunky guy to help me deal with my loneliness…'

'Not if I have any say in the matter,' Lucas growled, cupping her between her legs and rubbing until the pressure of his hand did all sorts of things through the barrier of her clothes.

'No,' Katy panted, bucking against his hand as she felt the stirrings of an orgasm building. 'I have to admit,' she gasped, her fingers digging into his shoulders, 'That finding another man wouldn't work, so perhaps you'll have to tire of me not being around and find someone else instead…'

And how she hated the thought of that although, she laughed shakily to herself, in the game of make-believe, what was the big deal? 'Let's not talk about this.' She tugged apart the button on his trousers and awkwardly tried to pull down the zipper. She looked at him and met his eyes. 'We can be engaged…for two months. Long enough to find out that we're not really compatible and short enough for no lasting damage.'

'You're the one calling the shots.' Lucas nipped her

neck, reared up and yanked off his shirt, before proceeding to undress her very, very slowly and, when she was completely naked, pushing apart her thighs and gazing down for a few charged seconds at her stupendous nudity. 'And I like it… Now, stop talking. It's time for action, my wife-to-be…'

CHAPTER EIGHT

KATY HAD A week to think about what would happen when they arrived back in London. The surprise announcement of their engagement had hit the headlines with the fanfare of a royal proclamation. Sitting in the little square in the island's town, whilst they sipped coffees in the sunshine, she had scrolled through the newspapers on her phone and read out loud some of the more outrageous descriptions of the 'love at first sight' scenario which Lucas had vaguely hinted at when he had called, firstly, the anxious Ken Huang and then his personal assistant, who had been instructed to inform various elements of the press.

Lucas had been amused at her reaction to what, for him, was not entirely surprising, considering the extent of his wealth and eligibility.

Now, finally on the way back to London, with the helicopter that had delivered them to his super-yacht due to land in under half an hour, the events of the past few days no longer felt like a surreal dream that wasn't quite happening.

It was one thing to read the centre pages of the tabloids and marvel that she was actually reading about herself. It was quite another to be heading straight into the eye of the hurricane where, she had been warned by Lucas, there might still be some lingering press attention.

'At least there's been some time for the story to calm down a bit,' he had told her. 'Although there's nothing the public loves more than a good, old-fashioned tale of romance.'

'Except,' Katy had quipped, 'A good, old-fashioned tale of a break-up.'

Lucas had laughed but, now that the story was out in the open, now that her parents had been told and had doubtless told every single person in the village and beyond, Katy was beginning to visualise the fallout when the phoney engagement came to an end. In short, her theory about the end justifying the means was beginning to look a little frayed at the edges.

She had spoken to her parents every single day since the announcement and had played fast and loose with fairy stories about the way her heart had whooshed the minute she had clapped eyes on Lucas, the second she had *known* that it was the real thing. They had wanted details and she had given them details.

Katy knew that she would have to face all sorts of awkward questions when this charade was over. No doubt, she would be an object of pity. Her parents would be mortified that yet again she had been short-sighted enough to go for the wrong guy. If they ever happened to meet Lucas in the flesh, then they would probably suss that he was the wrong guy before the fairy tale even had time to come crashing down.

The world would feel sorry for her. Her friends would shake their heads and wonder if there was something wrong with her. And, inevitably, there would be malicious swipes at her stupidity in thinking that she could ever have thought that a relationship with someone like Lucas Cipriani could ever last the distance.

Who did she think she was?

And yet she was happy to close the door on reality because the thrill of living for the moment was so intense. It ate everything up. All her incipient doubts, and all her darkest imaginings about what lay beyond that two-month time line they had agreed upon, were swept aside and devoured by the intensity of appreciating every single second she had with him.

The timer had been set and every feeling, every sensation and every response was heightened to an excruciating pitch.

'I have something to tell you.' Lucas pulled her towards him. It still surprised him the way he couldn't get enough of her. 'Tonight we will be the main event at a black-tie ball.'

Katy stared at him in consternation. 'Tonight?'

'The Chinese company's throwing it. It seems that Ken Huang is keen to meet you, as are all the members of his family—and, in all events, with signatures now being put to paper, it's a fitting chance to celebrate our engagement publicly as well as the closing of the deal. Your parents, naturally have been invited to attend, as have your friends and other family members. Have you got any other family, as a matter of interest?'

Katy laughed. 'Shouldn't you know that?'

'I should,' Lucas said gravely, 'But these things sometimes get overlooked in a hectic whirlwind romance.' She was wearing a little blue top and some faded cut-off jeans and, if they had been anywhere remotely private, he would have enjoyed nothing better than getting her out of both items of clothing.

'I've never been to a ball in my life before,' Katy confided, brushing aside her unease because not only would she have to mix with people she had no experience of mixing with but she would also be *on show*. 'It would be nice if Mum and Dad came, but honestly, I doubt they will. It wouldn't be their thing at all, and my dad's calendar is so packed with community stuff that he will struggle to free up the time without more advance warning.' She sighed and looked at him a little worriedly.

Lucas was overwhelmed by a sudden surge of protectiveness that came from nowhere and left him winded. He drew back slightly, confused by an emotion that had no place within his vocabulary. 'It's no big deal.'

'It's no big deal *for you*,' Katy told him gently. 'It's a huge deal *for me*.'

Lucas frowned. 'I thought everyone liked that sort of thing,' he admitted. 'There'll be a host of well-known faces there.'

Katy laughed because his self-assurance was so deeply ingrained that it beggared belief. 'Part of me didn't really think about how this would play out when we returned to London,' she admitted. 'It felt very… unreal when we were in Italy.'

'Yes it did,' Lucas agreed. 'Yet surely you would have expected a certain amount of outside attention focused on us…?'

He knew that this very naivety was something he

found intensely attractive about her. Having experienced all the trappings of extreme wealth for the past fortnight, she still hadn't joined the dots to work out what came as part and parcel of that extreme wealth, and intrusive media coverage at a time like this was one of those things. Not to mention a very necessary and unfortunately inevitable black-tie event. He decided that it would be unwise to mention just how much attention would be focused on her, and not just from reporters waiting outside the venue.

'You're going to tell me I'm an idiot.'

'I've discovered I quite like idiots.' He touched her thigh with his finger and Katy shivered and came close to forgetting all her apprehensions and doubts. They might be acting out a charade when it came to an emotional involvement with one another, or at least the sort of emotional involvement that came under the heading of 'love', but when it came to physical involvement there was no reporter who wouldn't be convinced that what they had was the real deal.

'When we get to the airfield, don't be surprised if there are one or two reporters waiting and just follow my lead. Don't say anything. I've given them enough fodder to be getting on with. They can take a couple of pictures and that'll have to do. In a week, we'll be yesterday's salacious gossip. And don't worry—you'll be fine. You never run yourself down, and you're the only woman I've ever met who gets a kick out of telling me exactly what she thinks of me. Don't be intimidated by the occasion.' He laughed and said, only partly in jest, 'If you're not intimidated by me, then you can handle anything.'

Buoyed up by Lucas's vote of confidence, Katy

watched as the door of the helicopter was pushed open to blue sky, a cooler temperature than they had left behind and a fleet of reporters who flocked towards them like a pack of wolves scenting a fresh kill.

Katy automatically cringed back and felt his arm loop through hers, gently squeezing her reassuringly as he batted aside questions and guided her towards the black car waiting for them.

A reporter yelled out asking to see the engagement ring. Katy gazed in alarm at her ring-free finger and began stumbling out something vague when Lucas cut into her stammering non-answer, drawing briefly to a halt and smoothly explaining that the jeweller's was going to be their first stop as soon as they were back in the city.

'But it won't be, will it?' she asked as soon as they were settled into the back of the car with the glass partition firmly shut between the driver and them.

'Do you think you're going to be able to get away without a ring on your finger at the ball?' Lucas said wryly. 'Brace yourself for a lot more attention than you got from those reporters back there at the air field.' He settled against the door, inclining his big body towards her.

She was waking up to life in *his world*. Not the bubble they had shared in the villa, and even more so on his yacht, where they'd been secluded and tucked away from prying eyes, but the real world in which he moved. She was going to be thrown into the deep end and it couldn't be helped. Would she be able to swim or would she flounder?

He had told her that she would be fine and again he felt it—that strong streak of protectiveness when he thought about her lost and trying to find her way in a world that was probably alien to her. He knew from experience that the people who occupied his world could be harsh and critical. He disliked the thought of seeing her hurt, even though the practical side of him knew that the disingenuousness that he found so intensely appealing would be a possible weakness under the harsh glare of real life, away from the pleasant bubble in which they had been cocooned.

'We can stop for a bite to eat, get freshened up at my place and then head out to the jeweller's, or else we can go directly there. And, on the subject of things to be bought, there'll be a small matter of something for you to wear this evening.'

'Something to wear…'

'Fancy. Long.' He shrugged. 'Naturally you won't be expected to foot the bill for whatever you get, Katy.' He wondered whether he should go with her, hold her hand.

Katy stilled and wondered how the insertion of money into the conversation could make the hairs on the back of her neck stand on end. It felt as though something was shifting between them, although she couldn't quite put her finger on what that *something* was.

'Of course.' Politeness had crept into her voice where before there had only been teasing warmth, and she didn't like it. But how could she pretend that things hadn't changed between them? They had embarked on a course of action that wasn't *real* and perhaps that was shaping her reactions towards him, making her prickly and on edge.

Yes, she was free to touch, but there were now in-built constraints to their relationship. They were supposed to project a certain image, and that image would require her to step out of her comfort zone and do things she wasn't accustomed to doing. She was going to be on show and Lucas was right—she wasn't in the habit of running herself down and she wasn't going to start now. If she was hesitant and apprehensive, then that was understandable, but she wasn't going to let sudden insecurities dictate how she behaved.

'I think I'd rather get the ring and the outfit out of the way, then at least I can spend the afternoon relaxing, although I don't suppose I'll have much time to put my feet up.' She sighed and said with heartfelt honesty, 'I never thought I'd be getting an engagement ring under these circumstances.' She looked at her finger and tried to think back to those days when she had stupidly believed that Duncan was the man for her. Then she glanced across at Lucas and shivered. He was so ridiculously handsome, so madly self-assured. He oozed sex appeal and her body wasn't her own when she was around him. When she was around him, her body wanted to be his and only his.

What if this were a real engagement, not some crazy charade to appease other people?

She was suddenly filled with a deep, shattering yearning for a real relationship and for everything that came with it. This time it wasn't just for a relationship to rescue her from making decisions about her future, which had been the reason she'd allowed herself to be swept away by fantasies about tying the knot with Duncan.

Time slowed. It felt so right with Lucas and yet he was so wrong. How was that possible? She had proposed a course of action that had made sense, and she had imagined she could handle it with cool and aplomb because what she felt for Lucas was lust and lust was a passing fever. But looking at him now, feeling his living, breathing warmth next to her... The time they had spent together flickered like a slow-motion movie in her head: the laughter they had shared; the conversations they had had; their lazy love-making and the soaring happiness that had engulfed her when she had lain, warm and sated, in his arms.

Katy was overcome with *wanting more*. She transferred her gaze blindly down to her finger and pictured that ring on it, and then her imagination took flight and she thought of so much more. She imagined him on bended knee...smiling up at her...wanting her to be his wife *for real* and not a pretend fiancée for two months...

She loved him. She loved him and he certainly didn't love her. Sick panic filled her at the horror that she might have opened the door for hurt, and on a far bigger scale than Duncan had delivered. Indeed, next to Lucas, Duncan was a pale, ineffectual ghost and obviously one who had not taught her any lessons at all.

Lucas noted the emotions flickering across her face and instantly barriers that had been carefully crafted over many years fell back into place. He didn't do emotion. Emotions made you lose focus, sapped your strength, made you vulnerable in ways that were destructive. Gold-diggers had come close to destroying his business, but it had been his father's own emotions that had finally let him down. Lucas could feel himself mentally stepping back and he had the oddest feeling that just for a while there he had been standing too close to an inferno, the existence of which he had been unaware.

He leaned forward, slid the glass partition to one side and instructed the driver to deliver them to a jeweller Katy had never heard of but which, she guessed, would be the sort of place to deal with very, very exclusive clients.

'Where are we?' she asked forty-five minutes later, during which time Lucas had worked on his computer, catching up on transactions he had largely ignored while they had been in Italy, he'd told her without glancing at her.

'Jeweller's,' he said. 'Stop number one.'

'It doesn't look like a jeweller's...'

'We wealthy folk like to think that we don't frequent the sort of obvious places every other normal person does,' Lucas said, back in his comfort zone, back in control.

'Interesting story here,' he expanded as the car drew to a smooth halt and the driver stepped out to open the door for her. 'The woman who owns the place, Vanessa Bart, inherited it from her father and employed a young girl to work here—Abigail Christie. Long story but, to summarise, it turned out that she had a child from my friend Leandro, unbeknown to him, and like star-crossed lovers they ended up meeting again quite by chance, falling in love and getting married a while back.'

'The fairy tale,' Katy said wistfully as they were allowed into a shop that was as wonderful as Aladdin's cave. 'It's nice that it happens now and again.' She smiled and whispered, 'There's hope for me yet.'

'Wrong sentiment for a woman on the verge of wearing an engagement ring from the man of her dreams.' Lucas's voice was less amused than he would have liked. He laughed shortly and then they were being ushered into the wonderful den of exquisite gems and jewels, tray after tray of diamond rings being brought out for her to inspect, none of them bearing anything so trashy as a price tag.

Lucas watched her down-bent head as she looked at the offerings. He was a man on the verge of an engagement and, whether it was phoney or not, he suddenly had that dangerous, destabilising feeling again…the sensation of getting close to a raging inferno, an inferno he couldn't see and therefore could not protect himself against. He shifted uneasily and was relieved when she finally chose the smallest, yet as it turned out one of the dearest, of the rings.

'Rest assured,' Katy said quietly as they were once again passengers in the back seat of the car, 'That I won't be taking the ring with me when this is all over.'

'Let's just live a day at a time.' Lucas was still unsettled and frankly eager now to get to his office where he wouldn't be inconvenienced by feelings he couldn't explain. 'Before we start deciding who gets what when we're dividing the spoils.'

'Where do we go for the dress?'

'Selfridges. I've already got my PA to arrange a personal shopper for you.'

'A personal shopper…'

'I have to get to my office, so will be unable to accompany you.'

As their eyes tangled, Katy felt the thrill of being

here next to him, even if that thrill was underlain with the presence of danger and the prospect of unhappiness ahead. 'I wouldn't expect you to come with me. I don't need you to hold my hand. If you let me have the name of the person I'm supposed to meet, then I can take it from there. And, after I've done all the other stuff I'm supposed to do, then I think I'm going to head back to my place and get changed there.'

Begin stepping away, she thought sadly. *Begin a process of detachment. Protect yourself.*

Lucas was already putting the romance of Italy behind him. There would be a ring on her finger, but he wasn't going to be hankering for all that un-diluted time in each other's company they had had at his villa. He was slipping back to his reality and that involved distancing himself from her; Katy could sense that.

'Why?' Lucas realised that he didn't want her not to be around when he returned to his apartment. He wanted her to be there for him and he was irritated with himself for the ridiculous gap in his self-control.

'Because I want to check on my place, make sure everything's in order. So I'll meet you at the venue. You can text me the details.' She sounded a lot brisker than she felt inside. Inside, she wanted so much more, wanted to take without consequence, just as she wanted to give without thought. She wanted him to love her back and she wanted to shove that feeling into a box and lock it away to protect her fragile heart.

'You'll be nervous.' Lucas raked his fingers through his hair, for once on the back foot with his legendary self-control. 'There'll be reporters there.

You won't know what to do. You'll need me to be there with you, by your side.'

Where had that come from?

'But…' His voice as smooth as silk, he regained his footing. 'I see that you might want to check your place and check your mail.' He was back on familiar ground and he relaxed. 'We've got our lives to be getting on with.' He smiled wryly. 'Why kid ourselves otherwise? Don't worry. In a few weeks' time, this will be little more than something you will one day laugh about with your kids.'

'Quite,' Katy responded faintly, sick with heartache, for which she knew that she had only herself to blame. 'I'll see you later.' She forced herself to smile and marvelled that he could be so beautiful, so cool, so composed when she was breaking up inside. But then, he hadn't crossed the lines that she had.

Katy had no idea where to start when it came to looking for something to wear to a black-tie event because she had never been to one in her life before, and certainly, in her wildest imagination, had never dreamt that she would be cast in the starring role at one. She had phoned her mother but, as predicted, it had been impossible at short notice, what with her father's community duties. She had promised that she would send lots of pictures. Now, suddenly, she felt quite alone as she waited for her personal shopper to arrive.

It took over two hours for a dress to be chosen and, no matter how much she told herself that this was all an act, she couldn't help wondering what it would feel like to be trying these clothes on for real, to parade for a man who returned her love, at an event that would celebrate a union that wasn't a charade.

The dress she chose was slim-fitting to the waist, with a back scooped so low that wearing a bra was out of the question, but with an alluringly modest top half that fell in graceful layers to the floor. When she moved, it swirled around her like a cloud, and, staring at the vision looking back in the mirror, she felt the way Cinderella might have felt when the wand had been waved and the rags had been replaced with the ball gown that would later knock Prince Charming off his feet.

Prince Charming, however, had left her thoroughly to her own devices. He was back in the real world and already distancing himself from her without even realising it.

The Fairy Godmother would have to come up with more from her little bag of tricks than ever to turn Lucas into anything more than a guy who had fancied her and had talked her into having sex with him. He would happily sleep with her until the designated time was over, and then he would shove her back into the nearest pumpkin and head straight back to the women he was accustomed to dating, the women who slotted into his lifestyle without causing too many ripples.

She had expected the car from earlier to collect her but when the driver called for her at home, punctual to the last second, and when she went outside, it was to find that a stretch limo was waiting for her.

She felt like a princess. It didn't matter what was real or what was fake, she was floating on a cloud. But that sensation lasted just until they arrived at the hotel and she spotted the hordes of reporters, the beautiful people stopping to smile and pose for photos and the crowds milling around and gaping, as though they were being treated to a live cabaret. The limo pulled to a slow stop and nerves kicked in like a rush of adrenaline injected straight into her blood system. She feared that she wouldn't be able to push her way through the throng of people.

Then, like magic, the crowd parted and she was looking at Lucas as she had never seen him before. Her eyes weren't the only ones on him. As one, everyone turned. He had emerged from the hotel and was impeccably dressed in his white dress shirt and black trousers, everything fitting like a dream. He was so breathtakingly beautiful that Katy could scarcely bring herself to move.

The scene was borderline chaos, with guests arriving, cameras snapping, reporters jostling for prime position, but all of that faded into the background for Lucas as his eyes zeroed in on the open door of the limo and the vision that was Katy stepping out, blinking but holding her own as cameras flashed all around her.

Lucas felt a surge of hot blood rush through him. Of course she was beautiful. He knew that. He had known it from the very first minute he had set eyes on her in his office, but this Katy was a feast for sore eyes, and she held him captive. Their eyes met and he was barely aware of walking towards her, hand outstretched, gently squeezing her small hand as she placed it in his.

'You look amazing, *cara*,' he murmured with gruff honesty.

Nerves threatening to spill over, and frantically aware of the popping of camera bulbs and the rapt attention of people who were so far removed from her world that they could have been from another planet, Katy serenely gazed up at him and smiled in her most confident manner.

'Thank you, and so do you. Shall we go in?'

CHAPTER NINE

KATY HAD TO call upon every ounce of showmanship and self-confidence acquired down the years to deal with the evening.

Blinded by the flash of cameras, which was only slightly more uncomfortable than the inquisitive eyes of the hundred or so people who had been selectively invited to celebrate the engagement of the year, she held on to Lucas's hand and her fixed, glassy smile didn't waver as she was led like a queen into the hotel.

Lucas had told her that she looked amazing, and that buoyed her up, but her heart was still hammering like a drum beating against her ribcage as she took in the flamboyant décor of the five-star hotel.

It was exquisite. She had no idea how something of this calibre could be rustled up at a moment's notice, but then money could move mountains, and Lucas had oodles of it.

In a daze, she took in the acres of pale marble, the impeccable line of waiting staff in attendance, the dazzling glitter of chandeliers and an informal bar area dominated by an impressive ice sculpture, around which was an even more impressive array of canapés for those who couldn't wait for the waitresses to swing by. There was a buzz of interest and curiosity all around them.

'You'll be fine,' Lucas bent to murmur into her ear. 'After an hour, you'll probably be bored stiff and we'll make our departure.'

'How can we?' Katy queried, genuinely bewildered. 'Aren't *we* the leading actors in the production?'

'I can do whatever I like.' Lucas didn't crack a smile but she could hear the rich amusement in his lowered voice. 'And, if you feel nervous, rest assured that you outshine every other woman here.'

'You're just saying that…they'll all be wondering how on earth you and I have ended up engaged.'

'Then we'd better provide them with an explanation, hadn't we?' He lowered his head and kissed her. His hand was placed protectively on the small of her back and his mouth on hers was warm, fleeting and, oh, so good. Everything and everyone disappeared and Katy surfaced, blinking, ensnared by his dark gaze, her body keening towards his.

She wanted to cling and carry on clinging. Instead, she stroked his cheek briefly with her fingers and then stepped back, recalling the way he had reminded her earlier that what was happening here was just a show.

'Perhaps you could introduce me to the man you're doing the deal with.' She smiled, looking around her and doing her best to blank out the sea of beautiful faces. 'And thanks,' she added in a low voice, while her body continued to sizzle in the aftermath of that kiss. 'That was an inspired way to provide an explanation. I think you're going to be far better at this than I could ever hope to be.'

'I'll take that as a compliment,' Lucas drawled, wanting nothing more than to escort her right back into his limo and take her to his bed. 'Although I'm not entirely sure whether it was meant to be. Now, shall we get this party started?'

Having been introduced to Ken Huang, who was there with his family and two men who looked very much like bodyguards, Katy gradually edged away from the protective zone around Lucas.

Curiosity warred with nerves and won. She was surrounded by the beautiful people you saw in the gossip magazines and, after a while, she found that she was actually enjoying the experience of talking to some of those famous faces, discovering that they were either more normal than she had thought or far less so.

Every so often she would find herself drifting back towards Lucas but, even when she wasn't by his side, she was very much aware of his dark gaze on her, following her movements, and that made her tingle all over. There was something wonderfully possessive about that gaze and she had to constantly stop herself from luxuriating in the fallacy that it was heartfelt rather than a deliberate show of what was expected from a man supposedly in love with the woman wearing his ring.

Katy longed to glue herself to his side but she knew that circulating would not only remind Lucas that she was independent and happy to get on with the business of putting on a good show for the assembled crowd, just as he was, but would also shore up the barriers she knew she should mentally be erecting between them.

Everything had been so straightforward when she had been living with the illusion that what she felt for him was desire and nothing more.

With that illusion stripped away, she felt achingly vulnerable, and more than once she wondered how she was going to hold on to this so-called relationship for the period of time they had allotted to it.

In theory, she would have her window, during which she could allow herself to really enjoy him, even if she knew that her enjoyment was going to be short-lived.

In practice, she was already quailing at the prospect of walking away from him. He would probably pat her on the back and tell her that they could remain good friends. The truth was that she wasn't built to live in the moment, to heck with what happened next. Investing in a future was a by-product of her upbringing and, even though she could admit to the down side of that approach, she still feverishly wondered whether she would be able to adopt the right attitude, an attitude that would allow her to live from one moment to the next.

Thoughts buzzing in her head like a horde of hornets released from their nest, she swirled the champagne in her glass and stared down at the golden liquid while she pictured that last conversation between them. She dearly wished that she had the experience and the temperament to enjoy what she had now, instead of succumbing to dark thoughts about a future that was never going to be.

From across the crowded room, Lucas found his fiancée with the unerring accuracy of a heat-seeking missile. No matter where she was, he seemed to possess the uncanny ability to locate her. She wasn't taller than everyone else, and her outfit didn't stand out as being materially different from every other fancy long, designer dress, but somehow she emanated a light that beckoned to him from wherever she was. It was as if he was tuned into her on a wave length that was inaudible to everyone except him.

Right now, and for the first time that evening, she was on her own, thoughtfully staring down into a flute of champagne as though looking for answers to something in the liquid.

Abruptly bringing his conversation with two top financiers to an end, Lucas weaved his way towards her, approaching her from behind.

'You're thinking,' he murmured, leaning down so that he could whisper into her ear.

Katy started and spun round, and her heart began to beat faster. *Thud, thud, thud.*

She had shyly told the three colleagues who'd been invited to the ball about Lucas, glossing over how they had met and focusing instead on how they had been irresistibly drawn towards one another.

'You know how it is,' she had laughed coquettishly, knowing that she was telling nothing but the absolute truth, 'Sometimes you get hit by something and, before you know it, you're going along for the ride and nothing else matters.'

Lucas's stunning eyes on her now really did make her feel as though she had been hit head-on by a speeding train and she had to look down just in case he caught the ghost of an expression that might alert him to the way she really felt about him.

'Tired?' Lucas asked, drawing her towards the dance floor.

A jazz band had been playing for the past forty-five minutes, the music forming a perfect backdrop to the sound of voices and laughter. The musicians were on a podium, in classic coat and tails, and they very much looked as though they had stepped straight out of a twenties movie set.

'A little,' Katy admitted. His fingers were linked through hers and his thumb was absently stroking the side of hers. It made her whole body feel hot and she was conscious of her bare nipples rubbing against the silky fabric of her dress. The tips were stiff and sensitive and, the more his thumb idly stroked hers, the more her body went into melt down.

This was what he did to her and she knew that if she had any sense at all she would enjoy it while she had it. Instead of tormenting herself with thoughts of what life would be like when he disappeared from it, she should be relishing the prospect of climbing into bed with him later and making love until she was too exhausted to move a muscle.

'It's really tiring talking to loads of people you don't know,' she added breathlessly as he drew her to the side of the dance floor and turned her to face him.

The lighting had been dimmed and his gorgeous face was all shadows and angles.

'But you've been doing a pretty good job of it,' Lucas assured her with a wry smile. 'And here I was imagining that you would be a little out of your depth.'

Katy laughed, eyes dancing as she looked up at him. 'That must have been a blessed relief for you.'

'What makes you say that?' After spending the

past hour or so doing the rounds, Lucas felt relaxed for the first time that evening. No one had dared ask him any direct questions about the engagement that had sprung from nowhere, and he had not enlightened anyone, aside from offering a measured explanation to Ken Huang and his wife, both of whom, he had been amused to note, were full of praise for the romance of the situation. He had thought them far too contained for flowery congratulations but he'd been wrong on that point.

Under normal circumstances, he would have used the time to talk business. There were a number of influential financiers there, as well as several political figures with whom interesting conversations could have been initiated. However, his attention had been far too taken up with Katy and following her progress through the room.

People were keen to talk to her; he had no idea what she'd told them, but whatever it was, she had obviously struck the right note.

With women and men alike. Indeed, he hadn't failed to notice that some of the men had seemed a lot busier sizing her up than listening to whatever she had had to say. From a distance, Lucas had had to swallow down the urge to muscle in on the scene and claim his property—because she wasn't his and that was exactly how it ought to be. Possessiveness was a trait he had no time for and he refused to allow it to enter into the arrangement they had between them.

But several times he had felt his jaw tighten at the way her personal space had been invaded by men who probably had wives or girlfriends somewhere in the room, creeps with fancy jobs and flash cars who figured that they could do what they wanted with whomever they chose. Arrangement or no arrangement, Lucas had been quite prepared to land a punch if need be, but he knew that not a single man in the room would dare cross him by overstepping the mark.

Still.

Had she even noticed the over-familiarity of some of those guys? Should he have warned her that she might encounter the sort of men who made her odious ex pale in comparison?

'I can't imagine you would have wanted to spend the evening holding my hand,' she teased with a catch in her voice. 'That kiss of yours did the trick, and I have to say no one expressed any doubt about the fact that the most unlikely two people in the world decided to get engaged.'

'Even the men who had their eyes on stalks when they were talking to you?'

Katy looked at him, startled. 'What on earth are you talking about?'

'Forget it,' Lucas muttered gruffly, flushing.

'Are you *jealous*?'

'I'm not the jealous type.' He downed his whisky in one long swallow and dumped the empty glass, along with her champagne flute, on a tray carried by one of the glamorous waitresses who seemed to know just where to be at the right time to relieve important guests of their empty glasses.

'No.' Katy was forced to agree because he really wasn't, and anyway, jealousy was the domain of the person who actually *felt* something. She smiled but it was strained. 'No need to point out the obvious!'

Lucas frowned even though she was actually saying all the right things. 'That kiss, by the way,' he murmured, shifting his hand to cup the nape of her neck, keen to get off a subject that was going nowhere, 'Wasn't just about making the right impression.'

'It wasn't?'

'Have you stopped to consider that I might actually have wanted to kiss you?'

Katy blushed and said with genuine honesty, 'I thought it was more of a tactical gesture.'

'Then you obviously underestimated the impact of your dress,' Lucas delivered huskily. 'When I saw you get out of the back of my limo, my basic instinct was to get in with you, slam the door and get my driver to take us back to my apartment.'

'I don't think your guests would have been too impressed.' But every word sent a powerful charge of awareness racing through her already heated body. He was just talking about sex, she told herself weakly. Okay, so he was looking at her as though she was a feast for the eyes, but that had nothing to do with anything other than desire.

Lucas was excellent when it came to sex. He was just lousy when it came to emotion. Not only was he uninterested in exploring anything at all beyond the physical, but he was proud of his control in that arena. If he had foresworn involvement on an emotional level because of one bad experience with a woman, then Katy knew that somehow she would have tried to find a way of making herself indispensable to him. A bad experience left scars, just as Duncan had left her with scars, but scars healed over, because time moved on and one poor experience would always end up buried under layers of day-to-day life.

But Lucas wasn't like that. He wasn't a guy who had had one bad experience but was essentially still interested in having a meaningful relationship with a woman. He wasn't a guy who, even deep down, had faith in the power of love.

Lucas's cynicism stemmed from a darker place and it had been formed at so young an age that it was now an embedded part of his personality.

'Do I look like the kind of man who lives his life to impress other people?' he asked, libido kicking fast into gear as his eyes drifted down to her breasts. Knowing what those breasts looked like and tasted like added to the pulsing ache in his groin. 'Quite honestly, I can't think of anything I'd rather do than leave this room right now and head back to my apartment. Failing that, rent a bloody room in the hotel and use it for an hour.'

'That would be rude.' But her eyes were slumberous as she looked at him from under her lashes. 'We should dance instead.'

'You think that dancing is a good substitute for having mind-blowing sex?'

'Stop that!' She pulled him onto the dance floor. The music's tempo had slowed and the couples who were dancing in the half-light were entwined with one another.

It was almost midnight. Where on earth had the time gone? Lucas pulled Katy onto the dance floor and then held her so close to him that she could feel the steady beat of his heart and the pressure of his body, warm and so, so tempting.

She rested her head on his chest and he curled his fingers into her hair and leant into her.

This was heaven. For the duration of this dance, with his arms around her, she could forget that she wasn't living the dream.

Lucas looked down and saw the glitter of the diamond on her finger. The ring had fitted her perfectly, no need to be altered. He had slipped it onto her finger and it had belonged there.

Except, it didn't. Did it?

They had started something in full knowledge of how and when it would end. Katy had proposed a course of action that had been beneficial to them both and at the time, which was only a matter of days ago, Lucas had admired the utter practicality of the proposal.

She had assured him that involvement was not an issue for either of them because they were little more than two people from different planets who had collided because of the peculiar circumstances that had hurled them into the same orbit.

They had an arrangement and it was an arrangement that both of them had under control.

Except, was it?

Lucas didn't want to give house room to doubt, but that ring quietly glittering on her finger was posing questions that left him feeling uneasy and a little panicked, if truth be known.

The song came to an end and he drew away from her.

'We should go and say goodbye to Huang and his family. I've spotted them out of the corner of my eye and they've gathered by the exit. Mission accomplished, I think.'

Katy blinked, abruptly yanked out of the pleasant little cloud in which she had been nestled.

For all that common sense was telling her to be wary of this beautiful man who had stolen her heart like a thief in the night, her heart was rebelling at every practical step forward she tried to take.

She should pull back, yet here she was, wanting nothing more than to linger in his arms and for the music to never end.

She should remember Duncan and the hurt he had caused because, however upset she had been—and she now realised it had been on the mild end of the scale—whatever she had thought at the time, it would be nothing compared to what she would suffer when Lucas walked away from her. But nothing could have been less important in that moment than her cheating ex. In fact, she could barely remember what he looked like, and it had been that way for ages.

She had weeks of this farce to go through! She should steel herself against her own cowardly emotions and do what her head was telling her made sense—which was appreciate him while she could; which was gorge herself on everything he had to offer and look for no more than that.

But her own silly romanticism undermined her at every turn.

She gazed up at him helplessly. 'Mission accomplished?'

'We did what we set out to do,' Lucas said flatly. 'You only spent a short while with Ken Huang and his family, but let me tell you that he was charmed by our tale of love at first sight.'

'Oh, good.' He had already turned away and she

followed him, hearing herself say all the right things to the businessman while sifting through her conflicting emotions to try and find a path she could follow. In a show of unity, Lucas had his arm around her waist lovingly, and she could see how thrilled Ken Huang and his wife were by the romance.

Mission accomplished, indeed.

'Time to go, I think.' Lucas turned to her the second Huang had departed.

'Where?'

'Where do you think? We're engaged, Katy. Getting my driver to deliver you back to your flat is a sure-fire way of getting loose tongues wagging.'

'We're going back to your place?'

'Unless you have a better idea?' He shot her a wolfish smile but this time her blood didn't sizzle as it would have normally. This time she didn't give that soft, yielding sigh as her body took over and her ability to think disappeared like water down a plughole.

Mission accomplished. It was back to business for Lucas, and for that read 'sex'. They would go to his apartment, like the madly in love couple they weren't, and he would take her to his bed and do what he did so very, very well. He would send her pliant body into the stratosphere but would leave her heart untouched.

'We need to talk.' Nerves poured through her. She couldn't do this. She'd admitted how she felt about Lucas to herself and now she couldn't see a way of continuing what they had, pretending that nothing had changed.

'What about?'

'Us,' Katy told him quietly, and Lucas stilled.

'Follow me.'

'Where are we going? I mean, I'd rather not have this conversation in your apartment.'

'I'm on nodding acquaintance with the manager of this hotel. I will ensure we have privacy for whatever it is you feel you need to talk about.'

The shutters had dropped. Katy could feel it in his body language. Gone was the easy warmth and the sexy teasing. She followed him away from the ball room, leaving behind the remaining guests. He had said his goodbyes to the people who mattered and, where she would have at least tried to circulate and make some polite noises before leaving, Lucas had no such concerns.

She hung back as he had a word with the manager, who appeared from nowhere, as though his entire evening had been spent waiting to see if there was anything he could do for Lucas. There was and he did it, leading them to a quiet seating area and assuring them that they would have perfect privacy.

'Will I need something stiff for this *talk*?' Lucas asked once the door was closed quietly behind them. On the antique desk by the open fireplace, there was an assortment of drinks, along with glasses and an ice bucket. Without waiting for an answer, he helped himself to a whisky and then remained where he was, perched against the desk, his dark eyes resting on her without any expression at all.

Katy gazed helplessly at him for a few seconds then took a deep, steadying breath.

'I can't do this.' She hadn't thought out what she was going to say but, now the words had left her mouth, she felt very calm.

'You can't do what?'

'This. *Us.*' She spread her arms wide in a gesture of frustration. His lack of expression was like an invisible force field between them and it added strength to the decision she had taken impulsively to tell him how she felt.

'This is as far as I can go,' she told him quietly. 'I've done the public appearance thing and I've had the photos taken and I… I can't continue this charade for any longer. I can't pretend that…that…'

Lucas wasn't going to help her out. He knew what she was saying, he knew why she was saying it and he also knew that it was something he had recognised over time but had chosen to ignore because it suited him.

'You love me.'

Those three words dropped like stones into still water, sending out ripples that grew bigger and bigger until they filled the space between them.

Stressed out, stricken and totally unable to tell an outright lie, Katy stared at him, her face white, her arms folded.

'I wish I could tell you that that wasn't true, but I can't. I'm sorry.'

'You knew how I felt about commitment…'

'Yes, I knew! But sometimes the heart doesn't manage to listen to the head!'

'I told you I wasn't in the market for love and commitment.' He recalled what he had felt when he had seen other men looking at her and then later, when his gaze had dropped to that perfect diamond on her finger, and something close to fear gripped him. 'I will *never* love you the way you want to be loved and the way you deserve to be loved, *cara*. I can desire you but I am incapable of anything more.'

'Surely you can't say that?' she heard herself plead in a low, driven voice, hating herself, because she should have had a bit more pride.

Lucas's mouth twisted. In the midst of heightened emotions, he could still grudgingly appreciate her bravery in having a conversation that was only ever going to go in a pre-ordained direction. But then she *was* brave, wasn't she? In the way she always spoke her mind, the way she would dig her heels in and defend what she believed in even if he was giving her a hard time. In the way she acted, as she had at an event which would have stretched her to the limits and taken her far out of her comfort zone.

'I can't feel the way you do,' Lucas said, turning away from her wide, green, honest eyes and feeling a cad. But it wasn't his fault that he just couldn't give her what she wanted, and it was better for him to be upfront about that right now!

And maybe this was a positive outcome. What would the alternative have been—that a charade born of necessity dragged on and on until he was forced to prise her away from him? She had taken the bull by the horns and was doing the walking away herself. She was rescuing him from an awkward situation and he wondered why he wasn't feeling better about that.

He hated 'clingy' and he didn't do 'needy' and a woman who was bold enough to declare her love was both. He should be feeling relieved!

'I've seen how destructive love can be,' he told her harshly. 'And I've sworn to myself that I would never allow it to enter my life, never allow it to destroy me.' He held up one hand, as though she had interrupted him in mid-flow when in fact she hadn't said a word.

'You're going to tell me that you can change me. I can't change. This is who I am—a man with far too many limitations for someone as romantic and idealistic as you.'

'I realise that,' Katy told him simply. 'I'm not asking you to change.'

Suddenly restless, Lucas pushed himself away from the desk to pace the room. He felt caged and trapped—two very good indications that this was a situation that should be ended without delay because, for a man who valued the freedom of having complete control over his life, *caged and trapped* didn't work.

'You'll meet someone…who can give you what you want and need,' he rasped, his normally graceful movements jerky as he continued to pace the room, only stopping now and again to look at her where she had remained standing as still as a statue. 'And of course, you'll be compensated,' he told her gruffly.

'I'm not following you.'

'Compensated. For what you've done. I'll make sure that you have enough money so that you can build your life wherever you see fit. Rest assured that you will never want for anything. You will be able to buy any house you want in any part of London, and naturally I will ensure that you have enough of a comfort blanket financially so that you need not rush to find another job. In fact, you will be able to teach full-time, and you won't have to worry about finding something alongside the teaching because you won't have to pay rent.'

'You're offering me money,' Katy said numbly, frozen to the spot and stripped bare of all her defences. Had he any idea how humiliating this was for her—

to be told that she would be *paid off* for services rendered? She wanted the ground to open up and swallow her. She was still wearing the princess dress but she could have been clothed in rags because she certainly didn't feel like Cinderella at the ball.

'I want to make sure that you're all right at the end of this,' Lucas murmured huskily, dimly unsettled by her lack of expression and the fact that she didn't seem to hear what he was saying. The colour had drained from her face. Her hair, in contrast, was shockingly vibrant, hanging over her shoulders in a torrent of silken copper.

'And of course, you can keep the ring,' he continued in the lengthening silence. 'In fact, I insist you do.'

'As a reminder?' Katy asked quietly. 'Of the good old days?'

The muscles in her legs finally remembered how to function and she walked towards him stiffly.

For one crazy, wild moment, Lucas envisaged her arms around him, but the moment didn't last long, because she paused to meet his eyes squarely and directly.

'Oh, Lucas. I don't want your money.' She felt the engagement ring with her finger, enjoying the forbidden thought of what it would feel like for the ring to be hers for real, and then she gently pulled it off her finger and held it out towards him. 'And I don't want your ring either.'

Then she turned and left the room, noiselessly shutting the door behind her.

CHAPTER TEN

BEHIND THE WHEEL of his black sports car, Lucas was forced to cut his speed and to slow down to accommodate the network of winding roads that circled the village where Katy's parents lived like a complex spider's web.

Since leaving the motorway, where he had rediscovered the freedom of not being driven by someone else, he had found himself surrounded on all sides by the alien landscape of rural Britain.

He should be somewhere else. In fact, he should be on the other side of the world. Instead, however, he had sent his next in command to do the honours and finalise work on the deal that had been a game changer.

Lucas didn't know when or how the thing he had spent the better part of a year and a half consolidating had faded into insignificance. He just knew that two days ago Katy had walked out of his life and, from that moment on, the deal that had once upon a long time ago commandeered all his attention no longer mattered.

The only thing that had mattered was the driving need to get her back and, for two days, he had fought that need with every tool at his disposal. For two days, Lucas had told himself that Katy was the very epitome of what he had spent a lifetime avoiding. She lived and breathed a belief in a romantic ideal that he had always scorned. Despite her poor experience, she nurtured a faith in love that should have been buried under the weight of disappointment. She was the sort of woman who terrified men like him.

And, more than all of that put together, she had come right out and spoken words that she surely must have known would be taboo for him.

After everything he had told her.

She had fallen in love with him. She had blatantly ignored all the 'do not trespass' signs he had erected around himself and fallen in love with him. He should have been thankful that she had not wept and begged him to return her love. He should have been grateful that, as soon as she had made that announcement, she had removed the engagement ring and handed it back to him.

He should have thanked his lucky stars that she had then proceeded to exit his life without any fuss or fanfare.

There would be a little untidiness when it came to the engagement that had lasted five seconds before imploding, and the press would have a field day for a week or so, but that hadn't bothered him. Ken Huang would doubtless be disappointed, but he would already be moving on to enjoy his family life without the stress of a company he had been keen to sell to the right bidder, and would not lose sleep over it because it was a done deal.

Life as Lucas knew it could be returned to its state of normality.

Everything was positive, but Katy had left him and, stubborn, blind idiot that he was, it was only when that door had shut behind her that he had realised how much of his heart she was taking with her.

He had spent two days trying to convince himself that he shouldn't follow her, before caving in, because he just hadn't been able to envisage life without her in it, at which point he had abandoned all hope of being able to control his destiny. Along with his heart, that was something else she had taken with her.

And now here he was, desperately hoping that he hadn't left everything too late.

His satnav was telling him to veer off onto a country lane that promised a dead end, but he obeyed the instructions and, five minutes later, with the sun fading fast, the vicarage she had told him about came into view, as picturesque as something lifted from the lid of a box of chocolates.

Wisteria clambered over faded yellow stone. The vicarage was a solid, substantial building behind which stretched endless acres of fields, on which grazing sheep were blobs of white, barely moving against the backdrop of a pink-and-orange twilit sky. The drive leading to the vicarage was long, straight and bordered by neat lawns and flower beds that had obviously taken thought in the planting stage.

For the first time in his life, Lucas was in a position of not knowing what would happen next. He'd never had to beg for anyone before and he felt that he might have to beg now. He wondered whether she had decided that replacing him immediately would be a cure for the pain of confessing her love to a guy who had sent her on her way with the very considerate offer of financial compensation for any inconvenience. When Lucas thought about the way he had responded to her, he shuddered in horror.

He honestly wouldn't blame her if she refused to set eyes on him.

He drove slowly up the drive and curled his car to the side of the vicarage, then killed the engine, quietly opened the door and got out.

'Darling, will you get that?'

Propped in front of the newspaper where she had been scouring ads for local jobs for the past hour and a half, Katy looked up. Sarah Brennan was at the range stirring something. Conversation was thin on the ground because her parents were both so busy tiptoeing around her, making sure they didn't say the wrong thing.

Her father was sitting opposite her with a glass of wine in his hand, and every so often Katy would purposefully ignore the look of concern he gave her, because he was worried about her.

She had shown up, burst into tears and confessed everything. She had wanted lots of tea and sympathy, and she had got it from her parents, who had put on a brave face and said all the right things about time being a great healer, rainbows round corners and silver linings on clouds, but they had been distraught on her behalf. She had seen it in the worried looks they gave one another when they didn't think she was looking, and it was there in the silences, where before there would have been lots and lots of chat and laughter.

'I should have known better,' Katy had conceded the evening before when she had finally stopped crying. 'He was very honest. He wasn't into marriage, and the engagement was just something that served a purpose.'

'To spare us thinking you were...were...' Her mother had stumbled as she had tried to find a polite way of saying *easy*. 'Do you honestly think we would have thought that, when we know you so very well, my darling?'

Katy could have told them that sparing them had only been part of the story. The other part had been her concern for Lucas's reputation. Even then, she must have been madly in love with him, because she had cared more about his reputation than he had.

She also didn't mention the money he had offered her. She felt cheapened just thinking about that and her parents would have been horrified. Even with Lucas firmly behind her, she still loved him so much that she couldn't bear to have her parents drill that final nail in his coffin.

The doorbell rang again and Katy blinked, focused and realised that her mother was looking at her oddly, waiting for her actually to do something about getting the door.

Her father was already rising to his feet and Katy waved him down with an apologetic smile. She wondered who would be calling at this time but then, for a small place it was remarkably full of people who urgently needed to talk to her parents about something or other. Just as soon as the cat was out of the bag, the hot topic of conversation would actually be *her*, and she grimaced when she thought about that.

She was distracted as she opened the door. The biggest bunch of red roses was staring her in the face. Someone would have to have wreaked havoc in a rose garden to have gathered so many. Katy stared down, mind blank, her thoughts only beginning to sift through possibilities and come up with the right answer when she noted the expensive leather shoes.

Face drained of colour, she raised her eyes slowly, and there he was, the man whose image had not been out of her head for the past two agonising days since they had gone their separate ways.

'Can I come in?' Unfamiliar nerves turned the question into an aggressive statement of fact. Lucas wasn't sure whether flowers were the right gesture. Should he have gone for something more substantial? But then, Katy hated ostentatious displays of wealth. Uncertainty gripped him, and he was so unfamiliar with the sensation that he barely recognised it for what it was.

'What are you doing here?' Katy was too shocked to expand on that but she folded her arms, stiffened her spine and recollected what it had felt like when he had offered to pay her off. That was enough to ignite her anger, and she planted herself squarely in front of him, because there was no way she was going to let him into the house.

'I've come to see you.'

'What for?' she asked coldly.

'Please let me in, Katy. I don't want to have this conversation with you on your doorstep.'

'My parents are inside.'

'Yes, I thought they might be here.'

'Why have you come here, Lucas? We have nothing to say to one another. I don't want your flowers. I don't want you coming into this house and I don't want you meeting my parents. I've told them everything, and now I just want to get on with my life and pretend that I never met you.'

'You don't mean that.'

'Yes. I do.'

Her voice was cold and composed but she was a mess inside. She badly wanted her body to do what her brain was urgently telling it to do, but like a runaway train it was veering out of control, responding to him with frightening ferocity. More than anything in the world, she wanted to creep into his arms, rest her head against his chest and pretend that her life wasn't cracking up underneath her; she hated herself for that weakness and hated him for showing up and exposing her to it.

She glanced anxiously over her shoulder. In a minute, she knew her father would probably appear behind her, curious as to who had rung the doorbell. Lucas followed her gaze and knew exactly what she was thinking. He was here and he was going to say what he had come to say and, if forcing his way in and flagrantly taking advantage of the fact that she wouldn't be able to do a thing about it because it would create a scene in front of her parents was what it took, then so be it.

What was the point of an opportunity presenting itself if you didn't take advantage of it?

So he did just that. Hand flat against the door, he stepped forward and pushed it open and, caught unawares, Katy fell back with a look that was part surprise, part horror and part incandescent rage.

'I need to talk to you, Katy. I need you to listen to me.'

'And you think that gives you the right to barge into my house?'

'If it's the only way of getting you to listen to me...'

'I told you, I'm not interested in anything you have to say, and if you think that you can sweet talk your way back into my bed then you can forget it!' Her voice was a low, angry hiss and her colour was high.

His body was so familiar to her that she was responding to him like an engine that had been turned on and was idling, ready to accelerate.

From behind, Katy heard her mother calling out to her and she furiously stepped aside as Lucas entered the house, *her sanctuary,* with his blasted red roses, on a mission to wreck her life all over again. No way was she going to allow her parents to think that a bunch of flowers meant anything, and she took them from him and unceremoniously dumped them in an umbrella stand that was empty of umbrellas.

'I should have bought you the sports car,' Lucas murmured and Katy glared at him. 'That wouldn't have fitted into an umbrella stand.'

'You wouldn't have dared.'

'When it comes to getting what I want, there's nothing I won't do.'

Katy didn't have the opportunity to rebut that contentious statement because her mother appeared, and then shortly after her father, and there they stood in the doorway of the kitchen, mouths round with surprise, eyes like saucers and brains conjuring up heaven only knew what. Katy shuddered to think.

And, if she had anticipated Lucas being on the back foot, the wretched man managed, in the space of forty-five minutes, to achieve the impossible.

After *everything* she had told her parents—after she had filled them in on her hopeless situation, told them that she was in love with a man who could never return her love, a man whose only loyal companion would ever be his work—she seethed and fumed from the sidelines as her parents were won over by a display of charm worthy of an acting award.

Why had Lucas come? Shouldn't he have been in China working on the deal that had ended up changing *her* life more than it had changed his?

He didn't love her and, by a process of common sense and elimination, she worked out the only thing that could possibly have brought him to her parents' house would be an offer to continue their fling. Lucas was motivated by sex, so sex had to be the reason he was here.

The more Katy thought about that, the angrier she became, and by the time her parents began making noises about going out for supper so that she and Lucas could talk she was fit to explode.

'How *dare* you?' That was the first thing she said as soon as they were on their own in the comfortable sitting room, with its worn flowered sofas, framed family photos on the mantelpiece and low coffee table groaning under the weight of the magazines her mother was addicted to. 'How *dare you* waltz into my life here and try and *take over*? Do you think for a moment that if you manage to get to my parents that you'll get to me as well?'

She was standing on the opposite side of the room to him, her arms folded, the blood running hot in her veins as she tried her hardest not to be moved by the dark, sinful beauty that could get to her every time.

It infuriated her that he could just *stand there,* watching her with eyes that cloaked his thoughts, leaning indolently against the wall and not saying anything, which had the effect of propelling her into hysterical, attacking speech. She was being precisely the sort of person she didn't want to be. If she wasn't careful, she would start throwing things in a minute, and she definitely wasn't going to sink to that level.

Lucas watched her and genuinely wasn't sure how to proceed. Where did you start when it came to talking about feelings? He didn't know because he'd never been there before. But she was furious, and he didn't blame her, and standing in silence wasn't going to progress anything.

'I really like your parents,' Lucas said, a propos of nothing, and she glared at him as though he had taken leave of his senses.

'You've wasted your time,' she told him flatly. 'I'm not interested in having another fling with you, Lucas. I don't care whether my parents fell in love with you. I want you to leave and I don't want to see you ever again. I just want to be left in peace to get on with my life.'

'How can you get on with your life when you're in love with me?'

Mortification and anger coursed through her, because just like that he had cut her down at the knees. He had taken her confession and used it against her.

'How can *I* get on with my life when I'm in love with *you*?' Lucas realised that he was perspiring. Sealing multi-million-pound deals were a walk in the park compared to this.

Thrown into instant confusion, Katy gaped, unwilling to believe him. If he'd loved her, he wouldn't have let her go, she thought painfully. He would have tried to stop her. He wouldn't have offered her money to compensate for all the other things he couldn't provide.

Lucas noted the rampant disbelief on her face, and again he couldn't blame her.

'You don't believe me and I understand that.' His voice was unsteady and he raked his fingers through his hair in an unusually clumsy gesture. 'I'd made it clear that I could never be interested in having the sort of relationship I knew you wanted. You were so…so *different* that I couldn't get my head around ever falling for you. I'll be honest—I could never get my head around falling for *anyone*. I'd always equated love with vulnerability, and vulnerability with being hurt.'

'Why are you telling me this?' Katy cried jerkily. 'Don't you think I don't know all that?' But the uncertainty on his face was throwing her off-balance, and hope was unfurling and blossoming fast, yanking the ground from under her feet and setting up a drumbeat inside her that was stronger than all the caution she was desperate to impose on herself.

'What you *don't* know is that you came along and everything changed for me. You made me feel…different. When I was around you, life was in Technicolor. I put it down to the incredible sex. I put it down to the fact that I was in a state of suspended animation, far from the daily demands of my office. I never put it down to the truth, which was that I was falling for you. I was blind, but then I'd never expected to fall in love. Not with you, not with any woman.'

'You mean it? Please don't say anything you don't mean. I couldn't bear it.' Was this some ploy to try and talk her into bed? He was right, the sex *had* been incredible. Was he working up to an encore by flattering her? But, when she looked at him, the discomfort on his face was palpable and it made her breathing shallow and laborious.

'You confused me. There were times when I felt disorientated, as though the world had suddenly been turned upside down, and when that happened I just told myself that it was because you were a novelty, nothing like what I was used to. But I behaved differently when I was around you. You made me say things I've never said to anyone else and I felt comfortable doing it.'

'But you didn't try and stop me,' Katy whispered. 'I told you how I felt and you…you let me walk away. No, worse than that, you offered me money.'

'Please don't remind me,' Lucas said quietly. Somehow, he had closed the gap between them, but he was still hesitant to reach out and touch her even though he badly wanted to do just that.

'You have to understand that money is the currency I'm familiar with, not love. My father was derailed after my mother's death. I grew up watching him get carried along on emotional riptides that stripped him of his ability to function, and that taught me about the importance of self-control and the need to focus on things that were constant. Relationships, in my head, were associated with frightening inconsistency and I wanted no part of that. The only relationship I would ever consider would be one that didn't impact on the quality of my life. A relationship with a woman who wanted the same sort of thing that I did.' He smiled wryly. 'Not an emotional, outspoken and utterly adorable firebrand like you.'

Katy liked all of those descriptions. She liked the expression on his face even more, and just like that her caution faded away and her heart leapt and danced and made her want to grin stupidly at him.

'Keep talking,' she whispered, and he raised his eyebrows and smiled at her.

'So here I am,' Lucas said simply. 'I'd worked like the devil for a deal that, in the end, won't mean anything if you aren't by my side. I think that was when I was forced to accept that the only thing that mattered to me was *you*. I should have guessed when I realised how protective you made me feel and how possessive. You make me the best person I could be, and that means someone who can be hurt, who has feelings, who's willing to wear his heart on his sleeve.' He pulled her towards him and Katy sighed as she was enveloped in a hug that was so fierce that she could feel the beating of his heart. He curled his fingers into her hair and tilted her face to deliver a gentle kiss on her lips.

'I never expected to fall in love with you either,' she admitted softly. 'I was so certain that I knew the sort of guy I should end up with, and it wasn't a guy like you. But it's like you fill in the missing pieces of me and make me complete. It's weird, but when I met Duncan I was looking for love, looking for that *something else*, but I wasn't looking for anything at all when I met you—yet love found me.'

'I know what you mean. I was comfortable *wanting* you because I understood the dynamics of desire. Strangely, loving you has made me understand how my father ended up becoming entangled in a series of inappropriate relationships. He was deeply in love with my mother and he wanted to replicate that. Before I met you, I just didn't get it, but then I never understood how powerful love could be and how it can turn a black-and-white life into something filled with colour and light.'

'And when I returned home,' Katy admitted, 'And I saw the interaction between my parents, I knew that I could never settle for anything less than what they have. I was so upset when you showed up because I thought you'd come to try and persuade me into carrying on with what we had. Maybe because of the deal, or maybe because you still fancied me, even though you didn't love me.'

'Now you know the real reason I turned up with those flowers that you dumped out of sight—you want the fairy-tale romance and I want to be the lucky person who gives it to you. Will you do me the honour of marrying me, my darling? For real and for ever?'

'Just try and stop me…'

EPILOGUE

KATY PAUSED AND looked at Lucas, who was standing staring out to the sea, half-naked because he enjoyed swimming at night, something he had yet to convince her to try.

There was a full moon and the light threw his magnificent body into shadow. To think that a little over a year ago she had come aboard this very yacht, kicking and screaming and accusing him of kidnapping her.

She smiled because that felt like a lifetime ago and so much had happened since then. The engagement that wasn't an engagement had turned into the real thing and they had been married, not once, but *twice*. There was a lavish affair, held a week after the actual wedding, where reporters had jostled for prime position and celebrities had emerged from limos dressed to kill for the event of the century. But first had come something altogether smaller, in her home village, where they had married at a ceremony officiated by her father at the picturesque local church. The reception there had been warm, small and cosy.

Lavish or cosy, Katy just knew that she was the happiest person in the world.

They had had their honeymoon in Italy, where they

had stayed with Lucas's father for a few days. Katy knew that she would be seeing a great deal more of Marco Cipriani, because he had got along with her parents like a house on fire, and plans were already afoot for him to discover the joys of the northern countryside at its finest at Christmas.

And she knew that during the festive season there would certainly be reason for a great deal of celebration.

'Lucas…'

Lucas turned, and his heart stopped just for a second as he watched the woman who had so taken over his life that contemplating an existence without her was unthinkable. He smiled, held his hand out and watched her walk towards him, glorious in a casual, long dress which he knew he would be removing later.

Katy walked straight into his open arms and then looked up at him with a smile. 'I have something to say… We both have eight months to start thinking of some names…'

'Names?'

'For our baby, my darling. I'm pregnant.' She tiptoed to plant a kiss on his very sexy mouth.

'My darling, perfect wife.' Lucas closed his eyes and allowed himself to be swept away in the moment before looking down at her with love. 'I never thought that life could get any better, but I do believe it has…'

* * * * *

MILLS & BOON®

MODERN™

POWER, PASSION AND IRRESISTIBLE TEMPTATION

MILLS & BOON®

EXCLUSIVE EXTRACT

Charlotte Adair has spent her life locked away – but once freed, she finds the one man she's ever loved, billionaire Rafe Costa, is now blind, believes she betrayed him, and is bent on a vengeful seduction! Weeks after their scorching encounter he learns she's pregnant—with twins! Rafe steals Charlotte away, but she is a far from biddable prisoner. She is irresistible, defiant—and Rafe must seduce her into compliance!

Read on for a sneak preview of Maisey Yates's book
THE ITALIAN'S PREGNANT PRISONER
The final part of her Once Upon a Seduction... trilogy

Charlotte hadn't touched a man since Rafe. She'd had no interest.

She needed to find some interest. Because she was going to have a normal life. Whatever she did, it would be her choice. And that was the point.

She didn't know what answers she had expected to find here. Right now, the only clear answer seemed to be that her body, her heart, was still affected by him.

He excused himself from the group, and suddenly, he was walking her way. And she froze. Like a deer caught in the headlights. Or rather, like a woman staring at Rafe Costa.

She certainly wasn't the only woman staring. He moved with fluid grace, and if she didn't know better, she would never have known his sight was impaired at all.

He was coming closer, and as he did her heart tripped over itself, her hands beginning to shake. She wished she could touch him.

Oh, she wanted it more than anything. In that moment, she wanted it more than her next breath. To put her hands on Rafe Costa's face one more time. To kiss those lips again. To place her hand over his chest and see if she could still make his heart race.

It was easy to forget that her stepmother had told her how Rafe had left, taking an incentive offered by her father to end his tenure there earlier. It was easy to forget that and remember instead the way it had felt when he had kissed her. Touched her. The way she had pleaded with him to take her virginity, to make her his in every way.

Really, he had never wanted her. He had simply been toying with her.

She should remember that. Her treacherous, traitorous body should remember that well. But it didn't. Instead, it was fluttering. As if a host butterflies had been set loose inside her.

Suddenly, he was there. So close that if she wanted to she could reach out and touch the edge of his sleeve with her fingertips.

Could bump into him accidentally, just to make contact. He wouldn't know it was her. He couldn't.

Suddenly, he turned. He was looking past her, his dark eyes unseeing, unfocused. But then, he reached out and unerringly grabbed hold of her wrist, dragging her toward his muscular body.

"Charlotte."

Don't miss
THE ITALIAN'S PREGNANT PRISONER
By Maisey Yates

Available October 2017

www.millsandboon.co.uk

Join Britain's BIGGEST Romance Book Club

50% OFF your first parcel

- **EXCLUSIVE offers** every month
- **FREE delivery direct** to your door
- **NEVER MISS a title**
- **EARN Bonus Book** points

Call Customer Services
0844 844 1358*

or visit
llsandboon.co.uk/subscriptions

OVERHEARD IN DUBLIN AGAIN

DUBLIN WIT FROM OVERHEARDINDUBLIN.COM

Gill & Macmillan

827

Dedicated to Phyllis

Gill & Macmillan Ltd
Hume Avenue, Park West, Dublin 12
with associated companies throughout the world
www.gillmacmillan.ie
© Gerard Kelly and Sinéad Kelly 2007
978 07171 4204 1

Print origination by TypeIT, Dublin
Illustrations by Eoin Coveney
Printed and bound by Nørhaven Paperback A/S,
Denmark

This book is typeset in 10pt Garamond Book on 11pt.

The paper used in this book comes from the wood pulp
of managed forests. For every tree felled, at least one
tree is planted, thereby renewing natural resources.

A CIP catalogue record for this book is available from
the British Library.

5 4 3 2

Spelling it out

In Ireland we have this weird habit of spelling words out loud when children are present, so that they don't understand us, you know, like, 'I'll call ya later when the child is in B-E-D.'

Well, I was in McDonald's a couple of weeks ago and a couple and their daughter were at the counter ordering. The husband orders something, and when told they didn't have it, he says 'F**k'. Then the wife turns to him and shouts,

'How many times do I have to tell you not to say fuck in front of the C-H-I-L-D?'

Overheard by PONCHO, Micky D's
Posted on Friday, 16 March 2007

How much is the bus?

A friend of mine had an accident years ago with a chainsaw in which he lost one finger and part of another. We were in a bar one night, about to get a bus to another disco, and a guy shouts

across the bar to him enquiring how much the bus would cost. He put up his hands to signify €10 and the guy shouts back at him, 'What, €8.50?!'

Overheard by Anonymous, pub
Posted on Friday, 16 March 2007

Rough justice

In court a few years back the usual traffic violations were being called up. A man wearing a Dublin Bus uniform and carrying a Dublin Bus bag gets called. The judge asks the prosecuting Garda what he has him here for. 'Driving in a bus lane, your honour,' explains the Garda.

After the courtroom stops laughing the judge says to him, 'You should know better than most as you're a bus driver.'

The accused replies, 'I'm sorry, your honour, but I taut I was in me bus.'

Overheard by Phil, the Four Courts
Posted on Thursday, 15 March 2007

Bono speaks

At the U2 concert in Croke Park, Bono asks the audience for some quiet. Then in the silence, he starts to slowly clap his hands. Holding the audience in total silence, he says into the microphone, 'Every time I clap my hands, a child in Africa dies.'

A voice from near the front of the audience pierces the silence:

'Fookin' stop doin' it, then!'

Overheard by Anonymous, Croke Park, 2005
Posted on Wednesday, 14 March 2007

Sex education gone wrong

While travelling home on the Luas recently, I heard a group of four young girls speak about a class they had that day in school. One announces to the group,

'Oh my God, that was terrifying wasn't it? Who do you think has one, I'd say it's you Amanda, like you were with your man and everyone knows he's been with everyone.'

Amanda: 'The cheek of you, it's not me. Ya heard what Miss said, one in four of your age group have an STI. It could be anyone.'

I think they may have needed less sex education and more Mathematics!

Overheard by Anonymous, on the Luas
Posted on Tuesday, 13 March 2007

8 December

Getting on to a bus on O'Connell Street one day, and there were a few other people getting on. Just before it was my turn, the guy before me shouted, '1.20 please' to the driver, in a country accent. The bus driver nodded with his head towards the box where you throw the money in. The young lad from the country then leaned over and shouted into the box, '1.20 please!'

Overheard by Anonymous, O'Connell Street
Posted on Tuesday, 13 March 2007

The trouble with neighbours

My cranky no-kids neighbour had a major problem with us unruly brats when we were young (I'm the youngest of seven). After years of listening to her complaints, my older brother had had enough. Calling one day to complain about the family dog she says to my brother, 'My husband is going mad, your dog is always chasing him in the car,' to which my brother replies,

'I'm sorry, Mrs Quinn, my dog doesn't have a car.'

Overheard by Anonymous, at home on the doorstep
Posted on Saturday, 10 March 2007

At the cleaners

Waiting for my turn in a dry-cleaners recently, a man was having difficulty in getting his suit back.

'It's a Giorgio Armani,' said the customer patiently.

'A wha'?' said the assistant.

'A Giorgio Armani!' he replied rather haughtily.

'Hey, Monica, can you find a George O'Malley suit down there?'

Overheard by Anonymous, south Dublin dry-cleaners
Posted on Wednesday, 7 March 2007

Horse on bus

Got on the no. 27 bus into town one morning, and the bus driver was in such a state of convulsive laughter at something he was hearing over the bus radio that he couldn't take my fare. When he eventually calmed down he said,

'There's a horse after getting on the bus in Darndale and they can't get him off!'

Overheard by Anonymous, on the no. 27 bus
Posted on Tuesday, 6 March 2007

One is not amused

On the bus, couldn't help overhearing two old dears …

Old Dear #1: 'So have ya the place ready for the christening?'

Old Dear #2: 'I have. I was scrubbing all week. It's fit for the Queen now.'

Old Dear #1: 'I hear she's a fussy bitch alright.'

Overheard by Cabra Joe, on the no. 121 bus into town
Posted on Monday, 5 March 2007

Haircut?

Girl: 'Hey, how are you? Did you get a haircut?'

Boy: 'What? Are you serious!? Of course I did!'

Girl: 'Jeez, calm down, I wasn't sure.'

Boy: 'What do you mean you're not sure!? I used to have an afro!'

Overheard by Anonymous, Grafton Street
Posted on Saturday, 3 March 2007

Lunatic!

A crowd of us outside Café en Seine on Dawson Street on Saturday night, watching the lunar eclipse, when I overheard a D4 girl answering her mobile phone and exclaiming excitedly,

'Hi Nicola! We're outside watching the moon orbit the sun!'

Nobody bothered correcting her!

Overheard by Pete, Café en Seine on Dawson Street
Posted on Monday, 5 March 2007

Who knew Dublin Bus drivers had chauffeur training?

On the bus home from work before Christmas, absolutely lashing rain. The bus pulls up at a stop, obviously a few feet from the footpath. Doors open but no one gets on, then I hear a roar from outside,

'Can ya move da bus in closer, I'm wearin' sandals!'

… and the driver did!

Overheard by Ali, on the no. 65B bus
Posted on Tuesday, 6 March 2007

Save the moles!

I was in Dublin Airport and I was buying a pack of notebooks for my daughter. They were really thin and bound in cardboard, but it said 'moleskin', so up at the till the lady said, 'Dat'll be €17 there now, love, dat's very spensive isn't it?'

'I know … it's because they are moleskin,' I replied.

Then she said under her breath — not even to me, 'Ah, de poo-ur moles!'

Overheard by Lorcan, Dublin Airport
Posted on Wednesday, 7 March 2007

Fraddles

A friend of my Dad's was going on holiday and wanted to buy some clip-on sunglasses to attach to his specs. He went into a chemist and asked the girl behind the counter if they sold any.

'Fraddles?' asked the shop assistant.

'Yeah, Fraddles, is that what they're called? I'll have a pair of Fraddles, please.'

'No,' said the shop assistant, 'Do you want them FOR ADULTS or children?!'

Overheard by Anonymous, in an unnamed Dublin chemist
Posted on Wednesday, 21 March 2007

Child running for bus

As I am a bus driver for many years with Dublin Bus, I come across some very funny incidents. A woman with two small children was running for the no. 3 bus at Westland Row, so I waited for them. The youngest of the small kids was called (I can only guess) Chantelle. As the mother was calling the child to hurry up, she mouthed,

'Chanfuckintelle, will you hurry up!'

I'm still laughing about it ten years on.

Overheard by Dave, on the no. 3 bus at Westland Row
Posted on Thursday, 8 March 2007

Taxing the lion ...

On O'Connell Street, a charity worker had stopped a pedestrian.

Charity worker: 'Would you like to buy a line, sir?'

Guy: 'I'm from the country, why would I want to buy a lion, sure he'd eat all the sheep ...'

Overheard by Michael, O'Connell Street
Posted on Thursday, 8 March 2007

8

Happy talk

This is probably one of those 'ya had to be there' things but it still makes me laugh.

Happened about seven years ago, was working in a hotel in the city centre as night manager. I had a night porter on with me who was a lovely fella but had a dreadful stammer. I ordered a taxi for some people leaving a function and this taxi driver comes in and roars, 'Did y-y-youse order a Teh-teh-teh-TAXI?'

With that the night porter appears from the back office with this big, angry head on him and says,

'Are you tay-tay-tay-takin' de p-p-p-piss owra m-m-m-me?'

Overheard by Snow White, hotel in city centre
Posted on Friday, 9 March 2007

Tony O'Toole's fault!

While waiting for my luggage at carousel no. 3 at Dublin Airport, a voice over the intercom:

'Whoever's waiting at carousel no. 3, move to no. 5, 'cos Tony O'Toole broke it!'

Overheard by Anonymous, baggage at Dublin Airport
Posted on Wednesday, 7 March 2007

Safe as houses

My slightly superior neighbour was boasting to my Mam about how fantastic her precious youngest son was doing since emigrating to New York. She said, 'Oh he's doing brilliant, he's living in one of the condoms that they're all living in over there.'

My mother just smiled smugly.

Maybe I'm out of touch but I think she meant condominium …

Overheard by my Mam, Finglas
Posted on Monday, 5 March 2007

Kids can sometimes be too honest!

I used to work in a well-known 5-star D4 hotel. I took a fancy to their lovely china cups with the hotel's initials printed on them. I didn't think a couple would be missed.

One day I treated my Mam and eight-year-old sister to afternoon tea there. As my colleague served them, my little sister says in a loud voice to my Mam,

'Hey Mam, they have the same cups as us!'

Overheard by Anonymous, D4 hotel
Posted on Saturday, 3 March 2007

I hit a Pole

Last week I was walking in Sandyford near the Mint. A woman driver had her car parked on the path with the hazard lights on. Coming closer it was clear that she had hit a Yield sign when going through a left slip road. She was on the phone telling someone about her accident.

'I hit a pole, luckily there's not much damage to the car ...'

'No! A Yield sign, not a Polish person!'

Overheard by Southsider, Sandyford
Posted on Thursday, 1 March 2007

Bring on the harassment lawsuit ...

Coming up to the counter in McDonald's, I heard the middle-aged manager say to the tired-looking girl sweeping the floor, 'Go on, sweep me off my feet.'

I had to bite my lip ...

Overheard by Anonymous, McDonald's, Blackrock
Posted on Monday, 26 February 2007

Huh?

Standing waiting with five others for the no. 18 bus in Rathmines. A guy walks by, recognises a familiar face amongst the group and says,

'Ah there yeh are again, Charlie. I saw yeh the other day on O'Connell Street, but by the time I caught up with yeh, you were gone.'

Overheard by Seamus, Rathmines
Posted on Sunday, 25 February 2007

Inspiration for the day

After a long slog all the way from Tallafornia into town on the no. 65 bus, the bus driver pulled up on Dame Street where the majority of people got out, and the bus driver yelled at everybody, 'Fly my pretties, FLY!'

Overheard by Twister, on the no. 65 bus
Posted on Thursday, 22 February 2007

Always in the last place you look

On the no. 111 bus (single decker), we were travelling along behind a no. 7 bus (double decker). They both follow the exact route for 20 minutes or so.

Both buses were pulling up towards a bus stop. The no. 7 lets people off and a fairly scum-baggish looking chap is one of them. He goes to his jeans pocket and it seems like he has lost something.

In the meantime he hasn't noticed the no. 7 leave and the no. 111 pull into the stop to let people off.

He pushes through the people getting off, has a sudden realisation halfway down the bus and says,

'What happened to the f**kin' stairs?'

Overheard by Anonymous, on the no. 111 bus
Posted on Thursday, 22 February 2007

Law abidin'

On a train from Dublin to Galway, August 2006. One very drunk man was causing no end of trouble, to the extent that the train had to be stopped so he could be thrown off. His very embarrassed friend was trying to calm him down, so Mr Drunk roars at him, in a very strong Dub-el-in accent,

'Wha' are yous getting law abidin' on me for? I'll law abide you in a min-a!'

If only …

Overheard by Sweary, train, Dublin to Galway
Posted on Wednesday, 21 February 2007

All 'fore' Americans

Coming into Dublin, cabin crew distribute cards to non-EU passengers, which for many provides some good entertainment. On one such occasion an American lady proclaimed, 'Excuse me, Mam, this card is looking for four names and I've only got three.'

Rather than getting into the technicalities of the word 'forename', I smiled and told her three names would do nicely.

Overheard by Karen, Aer Lingus flight
Posted on Wednesday, 21 February 2007

Young at heart

Not so much heard as seen.

Was standing in a queue for a bank machine on O'Connell Street beside one of the Londis shops when out bursts this young lad, with a security guard chasing after him. The guard catches up with him and pins him on the ground, and the young lad throws away about six dirty mags that he had stolen.

The security guard proceeds to beat him and this old man on a walking stick walks over and picks up the mags, like he's helping the security guard. Then he abandons his walking stick and runs down the road with one leg trailing behind him.

Some smart-arse shouts after him, 'Run, Forrest, run!' leaving myself in hysterics and a much bemused Asian tourist!

Overheard by Anonymous, O'Connell Street
Posted on Friday, 2 February 2007

Spit

Was in Ballyfermot a few years ago and was waiting to cross at the traffic lights. A young mother was standing beside me and was holding her young son's hand. The boy spat into the pedestrian crossing button, looked up at his mother and exclaimed, 'Mah! Sumwuns goin' teh press dah!'

Overheard by James, traffic lights near Ballyfermot church
Posted on Thursday, 1 February 2007

Late-night Luas

Whilst standing on a late-night Luas to Tallaght, a drunken couple were having a row. The husband, who was crippled, seemed unfazed at the distress he was causing the other passengers. At St James's Hospital, another drunken man stepped on and began accosting the drunken husband for the way he was treating his wife. A verbal row ensued between the drunken trio.

The husband, clearly frustrated, claimed he was going to beat the man up and suggested they should take it outside at the next stop. At this point the wife leans in and whispers some words of advice that nobody in the carriage can hear. The husband responds,

'What do you mean I'm in a f**king wheelchair!?'

Overheard by Kevin, on the bleedin' Daniel Day
Posted on Wednesday, 31 January 2007

Early planning

26 January in Milosky's Woodworkers supply centre in Terenure. One of the staff was making some polite conversation with my father:

'You know, it's only 11 months until St Stephen's Day!'

Overheard by Leo, Milosky's in Terenure
Posted on Tuesday, 30 January 2007

Too much information

After asking the young assistant at the ice-cream stand in the Omni Centre for two ice-cream cones, she says, 'I'll be back in a minute, love, right?'

A lifetime later she comes back, hands me the

ice-creams and says, 'Sorrrreee bout dat, luv, I had te go to de toilet!'

Lovely!

Overheard by Philip, Omni Centre, Santry
Posted on Saturday, 27 January 2007

Final resting place

Some time ago a friend and I were at a funeral. It was cold and raining. On the way from the burial we pass an open grave: very mucky with water puddled at bottom. My friend looks in and says,

'Wouldn't you die if you had to go in there!'

Overheard by Bubbles, Glasnevin Cemetery
Posted on Friday, 26 January 2007

I don't know where she gets it

Heard on the no. 78A bus:

Woman #1: 'Yer little wan's getting awful big, how old is she now?'

Woman #2: 'Oh, Britney's going on four, oh, and you should hear the f**king language out of her. Tell Anto to f**k off, Britney!'

Britney: 'F**k off!'

Woman #2: 'Jaysus, I don't know where she gets the language outta.'

Overheard by Chuck, on the no. 78A bus
Posted on Friday, 26 January 2007

Ahh, Ma!

In a checkout queue behind mother and son (11+) with earphones in and he pipes up in a really loud voice,

'Ahhh, Ma, did you put this Barry Manilow co-pack-arama shite on my iPod?!?!?'

Overheard by Anonymous, Tesco, Clearwater
Posted on Friday, 26 January 2007

Take-away

Late Saturday in Burger King, O'Connell Street, I overheard a young fella ask for a 'BIG MAC', to which the assistant replies, 'Sorry, but that's a McDonald's burger.'

The young fella replies, 'I know, Bud, don't be long!'

Overheard by Frozenthumbs, Burger King
Posted on Thursday, 25 January 2007

Cup of tea

A guy from the inner city works for my uncle in a trophy shop on Marlborough Street. He was making tea for my uncle and a sales rep who had called in. He brings in the two cups of tea and forgets which cup he had put the sugar in, so he takes a slug out of one of the cups and says to the sales rep, 'Yep, that's yours.'

Overheard by Anand, Marlborough Street
Posted on Thursday, 25 January 2007

Extra vanganza!

On the bus coming home from town the other day, just going past Parkgate Motors. Two girls were sitting behind me. One of them turns to the other and asks, 'What is a vangaza?' The other says, 'Wat, why?' 'Well,' she says, 'that garage's cars have extra vangaza!' The other just goes, 'Don't know?'

I looked at the garage, and in big letters it said, 'Car Extravaganza'!

Overheard by Sam, on the no. 25A bus
Posted on Thursday, 25 January 2007

She was clearly confused!

I was walking along the canal beside Portobello College when a swan began to get out of the

canal. A young girl with her boyfriend notices this and says to him excitedly,

'Oh look, the big duck is gettin' out of the sea!'

Overheard by Lou, canal at Portobello
Posted on Thursday, 25 January 2007

National Development Plan me arse!

Overheard an old man in the Cherry Tree pub criticising the government's newly published National Development Plan in which €184 billion will be invested over the next seven years.

He moans, 'For jaysus sake, how am I gonna benefit from dat! Why don't dey just divide the €184 billion by four million people! Dat way we'd all get €46,000 each!?

How did he work that out in his head?

Overheard by Anonymous, Cherry Tree pub, Walkinstown
Posted on Thursday, 25 January 2007

Carnival time in Gort

Passenger #1: 'Did you see your woman from "Coronation Street" is on tonight, trying to trace her ancestors in Gort?'

Passenger #2: 'She'll have a job, the place is full of bleeding Brazilians.'

Overheard by Paddy, on the no. 19 bus to Rialto
Posted on Wednesday, 24 January 2007

A good catch

In Tamango's niteclub several years ago a guy kept asking my friend up to dance and she kept turning him down. After about an hour of him pestering her, we left the club.

As we were leaving, he turned and shouted, 'I didn't catch your name.'

To which my friend replied, 'I didn't f**king throw it at you!'

> Overheard by Amanda, Tamango's at the
> White Sands Hotel, Portmarnock
> Posted on Wednesday, 24 January 2007

Drunk as a skunk

Drunk girl: 'You are locked!'

Drunk man (practically being carried by the girl): 'I amn't!'

Drunk girl: 'Fifty euro says you wet the bed!'

> Overheard by Anonymous, outside the
> Foggy Dew on Dame Street
> Posted on Tuesday, 23 January 2007

Toilet break

Getting off the no. 16 bus in Terenure, I wonder why the driver is turning off the bus engine. As I'm stepping off the bus, the driver gets out of the driver's cab and I hear him say loudly to all the people on the bus,

'I'm running into the Spar to use the toilet, I'll

be back in a minute, but don't worry I'll get yous all ice-creams!'

I giggled all the way down the road!

Overheard by Clare, Terenure village
Posted on Sunday, 21 January 2007

Kids in pubs, what do you expect?

In the pub over Christmas one afternoon. There's a gang of lads in the corner, and one of them had his son with him. This kid, about four or five, suddenly gets up and grabs his coat.

'Where you going?' his dad asks.

'Out for a smoke,' the little fella answers.

Overheard by AG, Skerries
Posted on Thursday, 18 January 2007

Whiskey in the bar

A friend of mine was in a bar in Malahide and he asked the (Polish) girl behind the counter for a 'Paddy'. She went and filled him a glass of 'Powers'.

He said nothing the first time, but the second time, as she was heading for the 'Powers' again, he said, 'There's a bottle of Paddy on the shelf there.'

'Oh' she said, 'I thought they were the same. Everywhere I go I see "Paddy Powers"!'

Overheard by Stephen, Malahide
Posted on Wednesday, 17 January 2007

Oh dear

At the Zoo during the weekend, I was looking at the penguins, when I overheard a women telling her son, 'Ah, look at the ducks!'

Overheard by Jane, Dublin Zoo
Posted on Wednesday, 17 January 2007

Nick-Nack-Paddy-Wack-in-the-Ilac

In the Ilac Centre on Saturday, waiting at the ground floor for the lift to the car park. A large group of people were also waiting. As the lift doors open, we all wait for the lift to empty before piling on. Standing at the back of the lift that quickly became full, leaving a group of six or seven unable to fit on.

One woman about 50 years old, bloke's haircut, bleach blond/yellow, about 5 foot, typical wifeswap head on her, starts telling everyone to push back so she could fit on. Everyone looks around and sees there is no room. A man at the front tells the woman, 'There is no room.'

She says, 'Push back!'

He says, 'There is no room, just wait.'

Furiously, she says, 'Diya want me to drag ya out of da lift and ya can bleedin' wait?'

Everyone just sniggered at her muppet mentality and the lift doors closed in her face.

Classic.

Overheard by Stephen, Ilac Centre
Posted on Monday, 15 January 2007

Never wear a short skirt ...

I was out on Friday night with a couple of girls I used to work with. One of them, who shall remain nameless to spare her blushes, was wearing high heels and an incredibly short skirt. We were walking from one pub to another when a group of four lads, about fifteen years old, passed us and quick as a flash one pipes up,

'Jaysus, if I'd legs like that I'd walk on me hands!'

Overheard by Anonymous, Wexford Street
Posted on Monday, 15 January 2007

Anybody there?

I was in a pub toilet the other night and an obviously drunk woman stumbled in.

'Mary!' she called.

'Yeah?'

'Are you in here?'

A pause, as 'Mary' thought about this: 'Yeah.'

The rest of the queue was in stitches!

Overheard by Tina, ladies' toilets, Frazers
Posted on Sunday, 14 January 2007

Free green thingies

While shopping in Tesco, my girlfriend's mother is packing her bags while the girl behind the till is scanning her shopping. She picks up one of the items and holding it up says,

'Wha's dat?'

'It's an avocado.'

'Av-a-wha?'

'Avocado.'

'Ah f**k it,' she says and throws it into one of the bags — without scanning it.

Overheard by Anonymous, Tesco, Finglas
Posted on Saturday, 13 January 2007

Monkey magic

On entering Dublin Zoo not so long ago, there was a monkey swinging from his treehouse to a tree via rope and making — well — monkey sounds! Then I overhear a little girl about seven ask her mother, 'Maa, is that monkey real?'

Her bigger brother then interrupts: 'Nooo! It's a bleeding man in a monkey suit, ya thick ya!'

Then the mother clips the lad on the head and says, 'Don't f**king ruin it for her, ya little b*ll*x!'

Ahh, ignorance is bliss!

Overheard by Pips, Dublin Zoo
Posted on Friday, 12 January 2007

I'm on the night train — bottoms up!

The Sunday Waterford-to-Dublin rail service had recently banned alcohol on the service, prohibiting all alcohol on board, in addition to roving security patrols up and down the train. The reason for the Elliot Ness style clamp-down was gregarious hoards of anti-social commuters clambering aboard after a heavy weekend in Kilkenny, still pissed, smoking pot, drinking their voddy and fouling the air with their nasal tones and mangled grammar, not to mention their booze-infused flatus.

To copperfasten Irish Rail's no-nonsense intent, the announcer on the PA announced the following one evening:

'This is the five o'clock service from Plunkett Station Waterford to Heuston Station Dublin. THERE IS NO ALCOHOL PERMITTED ANYWHERE ON THIS TRAIN, there is no baggage permitted on seats, there is no smoking permitted anywhere on this service including toilets. Anybody found contravening this will be removed from the train by the Gardaí at the next station.'

There was a pause and then the mic was keyed again:

'Just stay quiet and you'll get there.'

Overheard by Jack, Waterford to Dublin train
Posted on Friday, 12 January 2007

Talk isn't cheap

Was standing outside the post office on Cork Street, waiting for it to open, when this auld one started chatting to me.

The conversation got around to the ever-increasing house prices. She told me that because it is so expensive to buy in Dublin, her daughter and her daughter's husband had to buy a house in Co. Meath but, 'Dey don't like it

ar all 'cos dey hafta commUUN-icate for two
hours a day.'

Overheard by Danixx, Cork Street
Posted on Friday, 12 January 2007

Bad manners

I was sitting on a bench in Malahide Castle when
a couple with a young girl came and sat on the
bench opposite me. The mother gave the little
girl an orange to keep her quiet.

The parents were in the middle of a
conversation when the child began to sob
loudly. Juice from the orange had squirted into
her face. When asked what was wrong, the little
girl tearfully stated,

'The orange spat at me!'

Overheard by Amy, Malahide Castle
Posted on Friday, 12 January 2007

Can you bring me the bill, please?

I was sitting in a coffee shop having lunch and a
mother and her young daughter were sitting at
the table next to me. On finishing their lunch,
the young girl went into the bathroom.

A few minutes later, obviously having had a bout
of diarrhoea, she came out and announced
loudly to her mother,

'Mommy, Mommy, my poo has melted!'

Overheard by Ann, coffee shop in Malahide
Posted on Friday, 12 January 2007

Chivalry me arse

I was out driving the car along Kevin Street when it broke down. Got out of the car and was looking at it when a young fella passing by shouted,

'Hey missus, do you wanta push?'

I said, 'Yes please.'

He said, 'Go ahead!'

Overheard by Ann, Kevin Street
Posted on Friday, 12 January 2007

Teddy bear's bum

Donegal teacher teaching in a Dublin school. She shows the children a map of Ireland and shows them where Donegal is. She tells them that Ireland is shaped like a teddy bear, so Donegal is the head i.e. the brains of the country.

A week later, Co. Wexford came up in conversation. A child asked where on the teddy bear was Wexford. When they were shown, one wee fella said,

'Ah jaysus, Miss, I wouldn't go there on me holidays!'

Overheard by Anne (I was the teacher), in a Dublin school
Posted on Friday, 12 January 2007

The science of alcohol

In Pravda, Thursday night, outside having a smoke. This couple are on their way inside. She turns around and says to him, 'It's not as cold as it was earlier.'

Guy behind them: 'That's 'cos you're locked.'

Thought it was classic.

Overheard by Big Al, outside Pravda pub
Posted on Friday, 12 January 2007

A youthful imagination

On the bus last Thursday and this mother gets on with her four-year-old daughter. The daughter sits down first and then the mother beside her. Immediately the child starts crying.

When her mother asks her what the problem is, she replies, tearfully, 'You sat on Jalu!'

I can only assume 'Jalu' was an imaginary friend …

Overheard by Sean, on the no. 16 bus, Rathfarnham
Posted on Thursday, 11 January 2007

Nothing in life is free, not even the Herald!

Walking past the start of the Luas line at St Stephen's Green. A man is selling the *Evening Herald*. A young woman walks past and takes a newspaper from him. She then proceeds to walk away. He looks at her, puzzled and says, 'Eh, one euro please.'

She hands it back to him: 'Sorry I thought it was free.'

Overheard by Ciara-Ann, outside St Stephen's Green
at the Luas stop
Posted on Thursday, 11 January 2007

Inflation nation

A New York friend of mine was in Dublin over the Christmas and New Year period. He had finally got to grips with Dublin's confusing transport system and had even got the hang of the exact change fare on the buses (having been stung with getting no change on more than one occasion).

On New Year's Day he got on a bus with his exact change, only to discover the fare had gone up by 5c. He says to the driver,

'Geez man, it was €1.35 yesterday, what the hell is goin' on?'

To which the driver replies, dead pan, 'Happy New Year!'

Overheard by Anna, on Dublin bus
Posted on Thursday, 11 January 2007

Do It Yourself

I used to work in a B&Q hardware store. A woman walked in one day and I overheard her ask,

'Do you know anywhere around here where I can get nailed?'

Overheard by Miley, B&Q, Airside Retail Park, Swords
Posted on Thursday, 11 January 2007

Painful passing experience

In the local pub one evening, decided to use the toilets (once the seal is broken, have to go every half hour).

Picture the scene: three urinals and the one in the middle is the only one free. I tend to suffer from stage fright and the fact that two guys were standing on either side of me didn't help matters. The guy on my left said,

'Jaysus, I'll have to pay a visit to the doctor, this is now beyond a joke.'

I asked was everything ok, to which came the reply,

'I don't think so … I keep pissing these Blue Lumps.' (Channel Blocks)

Needless to say, I almost wet myself!

Overheard by Keith, Tolka House
Posted on Wednesday, 10 January 2007

Real Dublin poetry

At the Dublin versus Mayo match last autumn, a mate of mine on the Cusack Stand overheard another supporter say,

'Ah jaysus, dere's a great sight … the hill wavin' like a showal a' mackerill!'

A truly beautiful simile!

Overheard by Rob, Croke Park
Posted on Wednesday, 10 January 2007

Sarky security

Standing in Arnotts a few weeks back, I overheard some 'chung wan' ask the security man where the bargain basement was.

He was on the ball and replied, 'First floor.'

Overheard by Biffo, Arnotts
Posted on Wednesday, 10 January 2007

A hard pill to swallow

Years ago, a group of us, while returning from college on the DART, were yapping away as students are wont to do. One member of the group was going on a bit much about some academic nonsense — in fact we had all tuned out with boredom — when an auld fella on the seat beside us turned to him and said,

'Hav yez got a Disprin or a Anadin?'

We shrugged and the auld fella pointed at our boring friend and said,

'Cos I have a pain in me b*llix listenin' to tha'
shite!'

Overheard by Rob, on the DART
Posted on Wednesday, 10 January 2007

All you need is love

Waiting for the train yesterday at Pearse Station,
when I overheard a girl beside me (a real
Howaya) trying to get her boyfriend to stop
grabbing her.

Or, as she put it, 'Stop feelin' me bleeedin'
hole!'

Overheard by Count Dooku, Pearse Station
Posted on Wednesday, 10 January 2007

Terminology crisis

In a training class today in the office, the trainer
apologised in advance, explaining that the
course material was new and that we were the
first class she was going to train on it, so we
would be her …

Before she could say it, the loo la Spanish bird
in the office that has not been able to manage
English pronunciation despite four years in
Dublin, shouts out …

'We will be Guinness Pigs!'

Priceless, never a truer word said, I pondered.

Overheard by Swissoff, in the office
Posted on Wednesday, 10 January 2007

Lift of sardines ... and one tomato

In a lift at Arnotts in town a few weeks ago. Quite squashed. The lift stops on the first floor and this couple are waiting to get in, but nobody gets out. This guy gets in and says, 'Ah, come on, Mary, there's enough room here, these people will shift!'

When she still shows reluctance, and obvious embarrassment, some guy shouts from the back, 'C'mon, Mary!'

Soon everyone's saying, 'C'mon, Mary!'

She gets on with a face like a tomato!

Overheard by Sean, Arnotts in town
Posted on Tuesday, 9 January 2007

Olden days

I was walking through town the other day and an old gent in front of me tripped and fell. Naturally, I helped him up, and in doing so he said,

'Jaysus, they don't make paths like they use to, that wouldn't have happened in my day, damn foreigners.'

Of course, I agreed with the aul' racist!

Overheard by Mike, city centre
Posted on Tuesday, 9 January 2007

He ain't heavy ...

Guy#1: 'How's that brother of yours?'

Guy#2: 'He is still a miserable f**ker.'

Guy#1: 'Ah c'mon, he's not dat bad.'

Guy#2: 'I only talk to him in case I need a transplant, or bone marrow.'

Overheard by P, McDonald's, Dublin Airport
Posted on Tuesday, 9 January 2007

He actually had to think about that

Hanging around the old Dundrum Shopping Centre last Sunday, I overheard these guys talking:

Guy#1: 'Yeah, I had salmonella dere a few years ago.'

Guy#2: 'Did yeh die?'

Silence for a few seconds.

Guy#1: 'Nope.'

Overheard by Sean, the old Dundrum Shopping Centre
Posted on Monday, 8 January 2007

The sandwich maker

In O'Brien's Sandwich bar the other day and the girl who was about to make my sandwich turns to her work mate and says,

'I f**kin' hate makin' sandwiches.'

Overheard by Janine, O'Brien's, Blanchardstown
Posted on Monday, 8 January 2007

The common language

Bus from Phoenix Park to town, heading up the quays. Two Dublin girls sitting behind me.

34

Dublin Girl: 'Why do all deese forddinerts come over heeor?'

To which her friend replied, 'Dey learn de English langwitch.'

Dublin Girl: 'Why do dey wan teh learn deh English langwitch?'

Response: 'Cos it's deh most comminist langwitch in da world.'

With that, the younger of the two young women responds, at the top of her voice for the whole bus to hear (you know the type) …

'I speak English and I don't go arowind braginn dah im BALEEEDIN' COMMIN!'

The looks she got from tourists was priceless and of course, the rest of us Irish on the bus were nearly in tears.

Overheard by Magillycuddyreeks, bus from Phoenix Park

Posted on Monday, 8 January 2007

D4

This was in a lecture in UCD and the lecturer was trying to determine how many D4 heads were in the class (for some reason).

Lecturer: 'So, hands up who thinks they might be considered a D4 type.'

No response until after five minutes of silence.

Some student: 'Well, it's not very D4 to say you're a D4.'

Overheard by Stephen, lecture in UCD

Posted on Sunday, 7 January 2007

Mistaken identity

A few weeks ago walking past the statue of Phil Lynott I noticed an American couple. The wife (I presume) said,

'Quick, George, take a photo of me beside Michael Jackson!'

Overheard by Higgs, Grafton Street
Posted on Friday, 5 January 2007

Late buses

Several years ago, I was on the no. 123 Imp bus in Dublin. It was a dark and rainy day and the traffic was mad. The buses were all running late. The crowded bus I was on stopped at Eason's on O'Connell Street to let two people off and two on, when a distraught lady soaking wet at the bus stop said to the driver,

'This is a disgrace, you're really late, I've been waiting here for ages in the rain, there's supposed to be a bus here every 20 minutes,' to which the driver replied,

'Every eight minutes, luv!' closed the door — and drove on.

Overheard by DuffMan, no. 123 bus
Posted on Friday, 5 January 2007

Plastic bag required at back of bus

Recently while taking the no. 16 bus home I had one of the funniest encounters with a Dublin Drunk.

I was sitting upstairs on the back seat with a friend. At one of the stops the drunk got on, and managed to get up the stairs and stumble down to the back seat. The bus was jammers as usual and the only seats left available were the two between me and the drunk.

A couple of minutes later he suddenly turned to me and asked for a plastic bag. Which I didn't have. He turned back around to face the corner of the bus and started urinating.

Well, I've never seen the top of a bus empty so fast, and to this day I've been wondering would a plastic bag really have helped.

Overheard by Paul, on the no. 16 bus
Posted on Friday, 5 January 2007

Doggie bag optional

A friend of mine lives in an exclusive gated compound in Foxrock — from the outside it looks like one huge enormous mansion.

One night she took a taxi home. Upon approaching the security gate and surveying the 'estate', the taxi driver appraised the swanky property as follows:

'Shur this is the dog's b*llix!'

Overheard by VooDoo, Foxrock dinner party
Posted on Friday, 5 January 2007

Discover Ireland

While on a bus trip from Galway to Dublin, a group of friends were sitting behind me.

Girl: 'Sorry, driver, where are we now?'

Driver: 'Moate.'(Westmeath)

Girl (to her friends): 'We're in Howth, lads, deadly, sure we're nearly home.'

Overheard by Anonymous, bus from Galway to Dublin
Posted on Thursday, 4 January 2007

In times of crisis listen to your stomach

I was on a rugby tour to Milan a couple years ago and as the plane took off from Dublin, an Italian man up the front got into difficulty. There was a big commotion and the stewards laid him on the floor. After a minute the pilot came on and announced the man was having heart trouble and that we were returning to Dublin to get him to a hospital. Then, as the guy lies there, one of the old boys travelling with the team (who had been in the airport bar prior to departure) shouts out,

'If he DIES, can I have his BREAKFAST?!'

Practically the whole plane broke into highly inappropriate laughter. I don't think any Italians got it though.

Overheard by Garrett, Aer Lingus flight EI737 to Milan
Posted on Thursday, 4 January 2007

The ice-cream house

Standing outside Áras an Uachtarain and a woman is standing beside us with her child. The little girl asks, 'Mammy, what's the name of that house?'

The mother informs her child that the name of the house is 'Áras an uactar reoite' (the ice-cream house)!

Overheard by Niamh, in the Phoenix Park
outside Áras an Uachtarain
Posted on Tuesday, 2 January 2007

Boxing Day

Many moons ago one St Stephen's night I was walking down Swords Main Street and overheard two teenage girls discussing the Christmas TV.

'Did ye see "Michael Collins" last night?' enquired one.

The other, with completely the wrong end of the stick, replies, 'No, me Ma HATES boxing!'

Overheard by Hugh, Main Street, Swords
Posted on Tuesday, 2 January 2007

You couldn't make it up

Old couple queuing for the last bus on Abbey Street, 11.30, 1 January:

Woman: 'Very cold, isn't it?'

Man: 'Yes, I'd say it's the coldest night this year.'

Overheard by Bren, queuing for last bus on 1 January

Posted on Saturday, 2 January 2007

Buy drinks but you can't smoke

Was at Centra of Stoneybatter during the Christmas holidays, where two kids not more than seventeen years old were buying two bottles of Jack Daniels and two six-packs of beer. Once they paid for all the drinks, one of the kids returns to the cash point and asks for 20 Silk Cut Purple. The reply of the cashier was, 'You are too young to buy cigarettes.'

Old enough to drink, but not old enough to smoke?

Overheard by C&P, Centra in Stoneybatter

Posted on Tuesday, 2 January 2007

It's a clean machine

A few years ago, a woman, recently returned from Germany where they like things neat and pristine, boarded a no. 7 bus. Looking around the bus, she saw the discarded tickets and other litter on the floor. She turned to the bus driver and said, 'This bus is filthy.'

To which he replied without a moment's

hesitation, 'Well, get off and wait for a clean one then.'

Overheard by Anonymous, on the no. 7 bus
Posted on Monday, 1 January 2007

Dubliners' sympathy for the Yanks

Sitting in a bar in town listening to an Irish trad band with a group of American tourists. They were all really into the music and everything was nice and relaxed. After a while a young Dublin couple sat down very close to a few of the Yanks and struck up a conversation.

Dublin couple: 'So how do ye like it here?'

Yanks: 'Yes, very enjoyable.'

Dublin couple (man): 'September 11th must have been pretty shite?'

Yanks: 'Oh yes …' interrupted by Dublin couple (woman):

'Forget that, what about the Smoking Ban …'

Overheard by Lucy, pub in Dublin city
Posted on Friday, 29 December 2006

Ah bless

I was on the no. 17A bus last week when an old man and his grandson got on. We were stuck in traffic outside a school. The little boy looked out the window and saw three girls that looked very similar, so he shouts out,

'Grandda, are they three little twins?'

Overheard by Pauline, on the no. 17A bus
Posted on Friday, 29 December 2006

Losing weight in Finglas

Two women were chatting on leaving the local community centre after attending a weight-loss meeting.

'I don't like that instructor,' said the first woman.

'Why?' replied her friend.

'I prefer the one we had last week — she weighs you lighter!'

Overheard by Emer, outside a weight-loss meeting in Finglas
Posted on Friday, 29 December 2006

The photographer

I was on the no. 39 bus the other night, and overheard three girls, one of whom had a camera. There was a bit of a discussion as to who would take a photo.

One said to the others, 'Look, I'll take the bleedin' photo, after all I AM the photographicis!'

Overheard by Paddy, on the no. 39
bus coming from Blanchardstown
Posted on Friday, 29 December 2006

BLT without the LT please

I was in a sandwich shop in town recently. There's a guy ahead of me in the queue — didn't look like the sharpest knife in the drawer — anyway, he proceeds to order a BLT baguette.

However, he wanted it 'without lettuce or tomato' …

Overheard by Tav, sandwich shop
Posted on Friday, 29 December 2006

Holy God!

Sitting in a church on the northside of Dublin last Christmas Eve. It was the children's Christmas mass, so full of excited kiddies. We were early so were waiting for the mass to begin and one little girl in front kept asking her Dad, 'Daddy, where's Holy God?' to which he replied, 'He'll be out in a few minutes.'

She repeated the question numerous times, while the father was getting less and less patient with her. Eventually she said, one last time,

'Daddy, where's Holy God?' to which he replied loudly,

'HE'S AWAY IN A MANGER!'

The first three rows of the church were in fits!

Overheard by Fiona, Lisa & Jamie, St Canice's Church
Posted on Tuesday, 12 December 2006

Greetings

Was strolling down O'Connell Street when three teenage skanger birds were walking by me. One of their mobiles goes off. It was obviously one of her friends and she answered affectionately, 'Howareya slu'?'

Overheard by Anonymous, O'Connell Street
Posted on Friday, 29 December 2006

The great escape

My aunt and uncle are quite strict on their children. One of the rules was that the front garden gate must not, under any circumstances, be open in case their four-year-old son got out.

I was babysitting him one day and he rushed into the room where I was watching TV, a look of sheer horror on his face:

'Patrick, come quick! The gate is open and I might get out!'

Overheard by Froosh, uncle's house
Posted on Tuesday, 26 December 2006

An ecumenical matter

While waiting in A&E in St Vincent's Hospital, people naturally have to give some personal details. I overheard a girl replying to the question 'What religion are you?' with 'Normal'!

Overheard by Anonymous, A&E department, St Vincent's Hospital
Posted on Friday, 29 December 2006

What a return!

During the summer, while Bushy Park skate park was still under construction (right beside the tennis courts), some skateboarders were kicked off the site and decided to play tennis. One of the boys was using his board as a racket.

An old posh woman who was playing with her husband/partner a few courts away came over and said, 'I don't like the way you're playing tennis with that skateboard.'

Skateboarder quickly and wittily replied,

'Well, I don't like the way you're playing tennis with tha racket!'

Overheard by Brian, Bushy Park
Posted on Tuesday, 26 December 2006

Austin Powers for kids

A couple of years ago, when *Austin Powers* first came out on DVD, I was working in Chartbusters (Phibsboro). One evening I was out on the floor tidying up the DVD display. A concerned woman came up to me with a copy of *Austin Powers*. Pointing to the age certificate, which happened to be 15s, she asked,

'Excuse me, do you have this in 12s?'

Overheard by Ciarán, Chartbusters, Phibsboro
Posted on Monday, 25 December 2006

Last chance

Best ever flight I was on was with Go Airlines a few years back. Just before take-off the air hostess was getting ready for her safety routine, when the pilot came over the mic saying,

'Ladies and gentlemen, please pay attention to the safety instructions as this may be the last chance you ever get …'

Overheard by Eileen, Go Airlines, Dublin Airport
Posted on Friday, 22 December 2006

Cosmic Lady

Was on the Nitelink home from town last night and a woman who looked a bit crazy turned around to me and asked, 'Excuse me, do you have today's date?'

'It's the 21st of December,' I said, 'shortest day of the year.'

'Oh yes,' she replied, 'The world splits into two today doesn't it.'

What could I say to that?!

Overheard by Podge, Nitelink
Posted on Friday, 22 December 2006

Money

In the barber's the other day the barber was trying to make conversation with a young lad of about thirteen or fourteen.

Barber: 'Are you getting anything for Christmas?'

Young Lad: 'Money.'

Cue a few laughs from the people under their breath who were waiting.

Barber: 'Is that it?'

Young Lad: 'Yeah, I wouldn't trust me Ma to buy anything for me!'

Cue more laughs.

Overheard by Paul, Shaves, Balbriggan
Posted on Friday, 22 December 2006

El radio

My auntie was over in the Canaries and brought a load of stuff back for the family. She bought my Gran a small stereo for her kitchen. My Gran said she couldn't possibly have it in the house.

'Why not?' says my auntie.

'I'll buy one here ... all this thing will do is play Spanish radio stations, and I like listening to Gerry Ryan in the morning!'

Overheard by Simon, family home
Posted on Friday, 22 December 2006

Birdman of Finglas

I was in the local day care centre, collecting my mother-in-law, when I noticed a man holding a Zimmer frame, slowly walking past the room I was in. He stops at the door and shouts, 'CUCKOOOOOO', then waddles off, breaking his shite laughing all the way down the corridor!

Overheard by Philip, day care centre, Finglas West
Posted on Thursday, 21 December 2006

Little cutie

Mother wheeling pram with cute one-year-old boy in Smithfield. Along comes her friend Mary (she hasn't seen her for some time):

Mother: 'Howya, Mary, this is little Paddy.'

Mary: 'Jazsus, he's a lovely little b*ll*x.'

Overheard by Brian, Smithfield
Posted on Thursday, 21 December 2006

Flying without brains

Two D4 girls at Dublin Airport, going through security. One girl walks through detectors. It beeps and she gets all afraid.

Security: 'Remove your boots, please.'

D4 girl #1: 'Oh, sorry.'

She walks through again with the BOOTS IN HER HAND! She seems surprised when it beeps again! DOPE!

D4 girl #2 goes through fine.

Security: 'Have you any fluids in your bag?'

D4 girl #2: 'No … just water.'

Overheard by Eadz nd Natz, Dublin Airport
Posted on Wednesday, 20 December 2006

Carol singers slacking off!

I was walking up Grafton Street, past some carol singers taking a rest from singing on a cold night. Two lads walked past me, and one goes to the other in a really disgruntled Dublin accent,

'Jaaaysus, I thought dey were supposed to sing for me money!'

He'd work 'em to the bone!

Overheard by John, Grafton Street
Posted on Wednesday, 20 December 2006

Interior decorating?

Having lunch with the lads while working in Dublin Airport, the conversation turns to the mots.

First Bloke: 'So how's the new mot, what's she like?'

Second Bloke: 'Ah jaysus yeah, she's lovely, has red hair!'

First Bloke: 'Really, and does the carpet match the curtains?'

Second Bloke: 'I don't bleedin' know, I was never in her gaff!'

Overheard by G, lunchtime at Dublin Airport
Posted on Tuesday, 19 December 2006

I wonder if he passed?!

I was walking past the Driving Test Centre in Finglas. There was a Dublin Bus trainee and his tester walking side by side, towards the red learner bus, obviously to do his test. I overheard the trainee saying to the tester,

'Did ya ever drive a bus yerself, Boss?'

Overheard by Bob, Finglas Test Centre
Posted on Monday, 18 December 2006

Dub uses poetic licence

Had to go to hospital the other night. I was sitting in A&E when this guy who looked like Lorcan from *Fair City* came in, shouting and roaring. The nurse asked what was wrong, and he pointed at his blood-soaked leg and said,

'Hurry up, will yiz, I'm bleeeeeeedin' bleedin'!'

Overheard by Paulie, St Vincent's
Posted on Monday, 18 December 2006

Have you ever ordered a sandwich before?

Standing in the queue for a sandwich in O'Brien's in the Omni Centre:

Customer: 'Can I have a sandwich, please?'

O'Brien's Girl: 'Brown or white?'

Customer: 'What?'

O'Brien's Girl: 'Brown or white bread?'

Customer: 'White.'

O'Brien's Girl: 'Butter or mayo?'

Customer: 'What?'

O'Brien's Girl: 'Butter or mayo?'

Customer: 'Eh, butter.'

O'Brien's Girl: 'What would you like?'

Customer: 'Chicken.'

O'Brien's Girl: 'That all?'

Customer: 'Eh … cheese.'

O'Brien's Girl: 'That it?'

Customer: (silence)

O'Brien's Girl: 'Anything else?'

Customer: 'Lettuce. Oh, and coleslaw.'

O'Brien's Girl: 'Anything to drink?'

Customer: 'Tea.'

O'Brien's Girl: 'Medium or large?'

Customer: 'What?'

And so on. Needless to say, when he got to the counter to pay for it, he couldn't remember what he'd ordered!

Overheard by The Dude, Santry
Posted on Monday, 18 December 2006

A long way from home

League final 2005, Armagh versus Wexford. Was sitting in front of about six fellas from Wexford, having the craic before throw in. There was an announcement over the tannoy:

'Could the parents of a little girl who is lost please make their way to the First Aid room. Her name is Kimberley and she's from New York.'

Quick as lightning, one of the Wexford fellas says,

'New York!? Feck me, she *is* lost!'

Overheard by Lorraine, Croke Park
Posted on Monday, 18 December 2006

The complexity of shopping these days

In Dunnes Stores on Saturday, the girl in front of me at the checkout asks the checkout operator, 'How much are yizzer 30c bags?'

Overheard by Jess, Dunnes Stores, The Square
Posted on Monday, 18 December 2006

What they teach them in school nowadays

While dropping my son to school the other day, wc passed by the school's large crib with the nativity scene.

My son pipes up: 'I know about baby Jesus!'

Dad: 'Really? Who was he?'

Son: 'Baby Jesus is a sheep.'

Dad: 'No, he's not!'

Son: 'Yes, he is! He's the Lamb of God!'

There's really no response to that, is there?

Overheard by Shay, at my son's school
Posted on Friday, 15 December 2006

In the bookies

Recently while putting on a bet for a mate, I heard two guys talking and the conversation went like this.

First Guy: 'Well Mick, any luck on the 2:45?'

Second Guy: 'Do you know the expression —

beat on the post by a head?'

First Guy: 'Yeah.'

Second Guy: 'Well my horse was … beat on the head by a post.'

Needless to say, his horse came nowhere.

Overheard by Keith, betting shop
Posted on Thursday, 14 December 2006

The backwards man

A drunken, old (but jolly) man gets on the bus and sits in the wheelchair-user carer's seat, i.e. facing us all. After a few blasts of banter with a woman and her baby, he loudly asks us all, 'Why are you all sitting backwards anyway?' then continues laughing away to himself …

Overheard by Podge, on the no. 19 bus on the way to town
Posted on Thursday, 14 December 2006

Mass circumcision

Two oul' fellas discussing the inadequacies of the Luas.

Oul' fella #1: 'They should've linked up the Luas lines.'

Oul' fella #2: 'And the DART.'

Oul' fella #1: 'And have a circle line.'

Oul' fella #2: 'They should have it circumcise the entire city …'

Overheard by Owen, Connolly Luas stop
Posted on Thursday, 14 December 2006

What a cabbage!

Two lads get on the no. 79 bus on Aston Quay, with McDonald's food. One says to the other as he takes the lettuce out of his burger,

'Jaysus, I hate all this cabbage in me booorgar!'

Overheard by Paul, on the no. 79 bus on the way to Ballyfermot
Posted on Tuesday, 12 December 2006

Laughing in the moonlight

It was late Saturday evening and I was queuing for the AIB pass machine off Grafton Street. I noticed two tourists — a couple — asking a slightly drunk man to take their photo with the Phil Lynott statue. As they posed for the photo they asked him, 'Who is this by the way?' to which he replied,

'Oh, that's Phil Lynott — he was the first black man in Ireland!'

Overheard by Anonymous, Grafton Street
Posted on Monday, 11 December 2006

First time on public transport?

D4 girl getting on the Westport to Dublin bus. She didn't have any change so she said to the driver, 'Can I pay by Laser?'

Overheard by John, on the Westport to Dublin bus
Posted on Sunday, 10 December 2006

Get with it, Santa!

In a hairdresser in Swords last week. There was a woman with her little girl, about four, talking about writing her letter to Santa.

Little girl: 'Can we not just send Santa a text?'

Mam: 'I don't think Santa has a mobile phone.'

Little girl: 'Ah, Mam, sure everyone has a mobile phone these days.'

Overheard by JT, hairdresser in Swords
Posted on Friday, 8 December 2006

Anyone for da mouse?

Christmas time about three or four years ago, myself and a few mates were walking down Henry Street, checking out all the stalls and listening to them shouting out all their Christmas offers: 'Geta ur rapin papor three for a eura,' and so on.

Out of the blue, some auld one with a bread-board that's full of wind-up toy mice for cats on top of an old pram starts to shout, 'Anyone der for da Mouses?'

Didn't know what was funnier — the Mouses, or the fact she was selling them at Christmas. Only in Dublin!

Overheard by Hick, Henry Street
Posted on Friday, 8 December 2006

Mixed doubles

In the local on Sunday afternoon for dinner, the pub was packed with families. There were four lads playing doubles on a pool table. A little girl, about four, runs over to the pool table and starts to mess up their game. There's an almighty screech from the mother:

'Reebbeccaaaa, stop playing with those boys' balls!'

Overheard by Philip, the local
Posted on Thursday, 7 December 2006

Battle of the supermarkets

I was in the South Terrace at a soccer match in Lansdowne Road a few years ago. Niall Quinn had made top goal scorer, and a chant of 'Superquinn, Superquinn, Superquinn!' started. Just as the chant was ending, a man at the back of the crowd shouts,

'Up Tesco!'

The whole crowd burst into laughter.

Overheard by Mick, Lansdowne Road
Posted on Wednesday, 6 December 2006

Ciúnas!

Saw a sign in Image beauty salon in Ballymun:

'Noisy children will be sold as slaves!'

Overheard by Anonymous, Ballymun
Posted on Tuesday, 5 December 2006

Mc Breakfast

While in McDonald's early one morning, a customer asked the cashier, 'What do you have for breakfast?'

To which she replied, 'Ah, usually just a cup of coffee and a slice of toast.'

Customer was not impressed!

Overheard by Anonymous, McDonald's, Donaghmede
Posted on Sunday, 3 December 2006

He knows when you've been bad or good ...

Walking into the Blanchardstown Shopping Centre last week, saw this little kid, about three years old, running in front of me, with his mum and granny pushing a pram behind him.

Little kid twirls around and falls flat on his back. Picks himself up, no bother, but then his Granny breaks into raucous laughter.

'AHAHAHAHAAAA! That's what you get for not holding your Nana's hand. Santy did that to ya!'

Who knew Father Christmas was so vindictive?!

Overheard by TD, Blanchardstown Shopping Centre
Posted on Friday, 1 December 2006

Ah, Dublin logic ...

Two women standing at a bus stop, apparently discussing what to wear on a night out. One says to the other,

'Well, if it's cold, you can always wear those fishnet tights ... you know, the ones with the holes in them.'

Don't ya just love Dublin logic?

Overheard by Ali, at a bus stop on Westmoreland Street
Posted on Tuesday, 28 November 2006

D'yerknowharimean, Bud?

Skanger telling his friend (in a nasal whiney voice) how he fools his ma:

'Sure I smoke away in the front room when me Mudder's on a bingo. When she comes back I do have me runners off and I'm after rubbin me feet t'geder, so I am, so the smell of me fee covers up the smell of the hash. D'yerknowharimean?'

Overheard by Beatrice, queuing in the chip shop
Posted on Monday, 27 November 2006

Toilet talk

Sitting in the bog in a city-centre pub after a few scoops, the bloke in the next cubicle says, 'Howya, how's it goin'?' to which I reply, 'Ah, not too bad!' Then he says, 'Sorry!' and I say again, 'Not too bad!' Then he says,

'Listen I'll ring you back, there's some lunatic in the jacks next to me!'

I cringed — and waited 'til he left!

Overheard by Peter, Knightsbridge, Bachelors Walk
Posted on Monday, 27 November 2006

New advances in English dictation

Closing time outside a city centre pub. Argy-bargy between a group of my friends and a bunch of skangers; scuffles followed by skangers taking flight. One skanger temporarily detained and pinned to ground by friend. The skanger refutes all and any involvement in said ruckus by screaming … wait for it …

'I didn't do nuthin to no-one never!'

A double double negative!

Overheard by Anonymous, outside city centre pub
Posted on Friday, 24 November 2006

This DART will terminate in …

On the DART between Bray and Greystones, three Loreto Dalkey schoolgirls walk through the carriage. An announcement is made:

'This train will terminate at the next station.'

One of the girls lets out a little yelp, starts flapping her arms, then says loudly,

'Oh my God! Does that mean the train is broken?'

Private school education, eh?

Overheard by Alan, DART from Bray to Greystones
Posted on Thursday, 23 November 2006

Brainbox of the year

In the local boozer after work, and in the corner the *Weakest Link* was on the box.

'What's the capital of Spain?' asks Anne Robinson.

One of the locals shouts out, 'BARCELONA, ye gobshite!'

Overheard by Tony, Bottom of the Hill, Finglas
Posted on Saturday, 18 November 2006

Barbed-wire top

I was recently working at a high-class fundraiser that a good-looking woman with a big pair of breasts and a top with a low cleavage was organising. She was introduced to a new contributor (an old man):

Old Man: 'Can I compliment you on your Barbed-Wire top.'

The woman looked blank …

Old Man continues: 'It protects the property — but doesn't obstruct the view.'

Overheard by Richie, at a fundraiser
Posted on Wednesday, 15 November 2006

The Dublin chipper

Drunk guy goes in to a chipper (real Dublin accent) and approaches the counter where a guy of possibly Indian or middle-eastern descent is working:

Drunk Dub: 'Giz a ray and chips dere.'

Counter guy (in thick foreign accent): 'Flat ray?'

Drunk Dub: 'Ah jaysus no, pump er up a bih for me, will ya!'

Overheard by Abey-baby, chipper near Parkgate Street
Posted on Wednesday, 15 November 2006

Catholic guilt

On Halloween night, I was standing at my bus stop beside three guys who were off to a fancy dress party and were all dressed as priests. When the bus finally came, the three get on and ask how much. The driver tells them 95c each, only to be met with one of the lads replying,

'I remember when Dublin Bus were a friend to the clergy!'

Overheard by Jamie, on the no. 50 bus, Drimnagh
Posted on Tuesday, 14 November 2006

I'm a celebrity, get me outta here!

A few years back, I was having a conversation with a work mate. He began telling me about a party he was at that weekend. He said he arrived and knew everyone there except this one girl. He asked a friend who she was and was told that she was a bit of a smug, snobby bitch who had some claim to fame and was full of herself because of this fact.

He at some opportunity spoke to her during the night, initiating the conversation with, 'Hey, I know you somehow, I recognise your face.'

Apparently the girl began to glow with self obsession until he said,

'Did you …? Did you …? Did you serve me in Boots the other day?'

Needless to say she was disgusted …

Overheard by Stephen, Glasnevin
Posted on Tuesday, 14 November 2006

Fire safety

At work, in our previous offices, we had a sign outside the lifts advising the safety precautions to be taken in using them — fairly normal, except that, under 'In case of fire', some smart-arse had written,

'Bring marshmallows.'

Overheard by Seamus, Booterstown
Posted on Tuesday, 14 November 2006

No speekee Ingrish

Walking along Grafton Street, couple of D4 girls talking about somebody they knew who had adopted a Chinese baby. One of them perplexedly asked,

'Loike, when he grows up, will he think in English?'

Hmmmm …

Overheard by John, Grafton Street
Posted on Tuesday, 14 November 2006

Dreamland …

Sitting at home at the weekend, my girlfriend and my Mam are having a conversation about what's happening at the moment in *Eastenders*.

My Girlfriend: 'She's putting the baby up for adoption.'

My Mam: 'Yeah, it's terrible, the poor child.'

My Dad: 'It's not real life, it's only a television programme.'

My Mam (I love this bit!): 'Ah, get a life!'

Overheard by SB, at home at the weekend
Posted on Monday, 13 November 2006

The northside diet

During the summer I was driving to the airport and stopped at the traffic lights at the back of the Custom House. An Eastern European couple cross the road in front of me, holding hands. The girl was very slim and was dressed in figure-hugging white pants.

I had my window rolled down, and a taxi driver parked in the next lane shouts across in a thick northside accent,

'Jaysus, would ya look at da, all our birds do is stuff their bleedin' faces with burgers and chips!'

Overheard by Paddy, outside the Custom House
Posted on Monday, 13 November 2006

Axe-wielding bus driver

I was on the no. 65 bus to Blessington, and the top deck of the bus had been cordoned off with a bus ticket roll (much like a crime scene). Kids had smashed the upstairs windows.

Upon passing the Jobstown Inn pub, a drunk

proceeded on and stood beside the driver, talking to him through the security screen. Within the first three stops, he had asked the bus driver 101 stupid questions, which the driver was clearly getting angered by.

The drunk then asked the driver, 'What happened upstairs?'

The driver said, 'There was a murder up there earlier.'

The man clearly shocked said, 'What happened?'

The driver then said, 'On the last run there was some drunk asking me stupid questions. So I took me axe out and chopped him up! Now, have ya any more questions?'

The drunk — petrified at this stage — stutters, 'No, next stop's mine thanks.'

Overheard by Gary, on the no. 65 bus

Posted on Sunday, 12 November 2006

Apple tart

A friend of mine ordered a slice of apple tart in the Kylemore café.

'Do ya wanna eat it?' asked the girl behind the counter.

'Pardon?' said my friend.

'I said do ya wanna eat it?' repeated the girl.

'Well, yes,' he said, rather confused.

With that she threw the apple pie in the microwave:

'Ten cent extra.'

Overheard by Exdub, Kylemore café
Posted on Friday, 10 November 2006

Cinders

I was standing outside Burger King on Grafton Street at about four o'clock on a Sunday morning, one shoe in my hand because my feet were killing me.

This lad wearing a white tracksuit comes up to me and asks me can he have my shoe.

'What do ya want my shoe for?' I asked.

'So I can find ya in de mornin!'

Overheard by Ali, Grafton Street
Posted on Friday, 10 November 2006

Guinness is good for you ...

Saw a Guinness truck go down Parnell Street yesterday, with 'EMERGENCY RESPONSE UNIT' written in large letters in the dirt on the back.

Overheard by Anonymous, Parnell Street
Posted on Friday, 10 November 2006

Plan B

At Croke Park. All-Ireland Hurling Final 2006, Kilkenny versus Cork. Before the end of game, an announcement comes over the tannoy about spectators staying off the pitch, and for stewards to take up their positions.

The game ends. As expected, hundreds of fans start to run on the pitch to congratulate their heroes. Over the tannoy, 'Plan B, Plan B, Plan B'.

To add to the hilarity of the moment, 'PLAN B' was displayed in huge letters on the big screen!

Overheard by the Cat, Croke Park
Posted on Friday, 10 November 2006

Know it all

Worked with a severely irritable and thick French barman in Temple Bar some time back. Because of his demeanour he was a constant target for teasing from the other staff. One afternoon he could take no more and snapped at us,

'You tink dat I know f**k nothing! I tell you dat I know f**k all!'

We died …

Overheard by Barman, Temple Bar
Posted on Friday, 10 November 2006

Brothers are great

My daughter was going to her debs. They were meeting at the Assumption Secondary School in Walkinstown to get on the coach to the hotel, so the whole family went down to the school to see her off and have a look at the dresses.

When you walk up the drive, there is a sign saying, 'Slow Pupils Crossing'. Her brother looks at the sign and says,

'I can see why you sent her here!'

Overheard by JDub12, Assumption Secondary School, Walkinstown

Posted on Thursday, 9 November 2006

Supermacs – a family restaurant

Late at night, sitting in Supermacs, I see a large biker guy walk in who is absolutely locked. He proceeds up to the counter and says,

'Gimme a family box — without the father!'

Overheard by Bob, Supermacs

Posted on Thursday, 9 November 2006

Think bigger

A little boy was in the toy shop where I work, begging for a toy. The conversation went like this:

Boy: 'Mom, can I get something small?'

Mom: 'No you can't.'

Boy (thinks for a second): 'Can I get something BIG!?'

Overheard by Brian, toy shop

Posted on Tuesday, 7 November 2006

Throwing her weight around

On the Westport to Dublin train on Sunday after the Ireland versus Australia International Rules disaster. Middle-aged woman with giant (I mean the size of a small country) rear end has just gotten on the train and is bashing into everyone as she attempts to find a seat, then throwing herself around as she tries to get her luggage onto the overhead storage shelf.

With much huffing and puffing, she eventually sits down. A young fella smartly quips,

'Coulda done with you against the Ozzies today, Mrs!'

Overheard by Gerry, Westport to Dublin train
Posted on Monday, 6 November 2006

Aussie does indeed rule

While we were getting hockeyed by Australia in the International Rules match on Sunday, there was an Ozzie woman up on the Hill who kept waving her huge flag whenever her team scored, and the people behind her were getting annoyed since it was in the way.

Then in the 4th quarter when Ireland managed to score one mighty singular point, and she kept her flag down, a voice roared after the clapping,

'Where's your flag now?'

Overheard by Bozboz, Hill 16
Posted on Monday, 6 November 2006

Tight jeans

Me and my sister were walking down Thomas Street when a woman walked by wearing extremely tight jeans. My sister is stunned for a second then just says,

'Jaysus, she must've had to jump off the top of de wardrobe to get into dose ...'

Overheard by Anonymous, Thomas Street
Posted on Sunday, 5 November 2006

Righteous indignation

My mother was doing her weekly shopping in Dunnes. A married couple with their son of about four years of age were selecting a trolley. The small boy told his mother, 'Don't pick that one, Mammy — it's f**ked.'

The mother told the child off for using bad language, only to be told in reply,

'But Daddy SAID it was f**ked.'

Overheard by Seamus, Dunnes Stores, Kilnamanagh
Posted on Saturday, 4 November 2006

Cops and robbers

I had a week off work and was washing my car in my driveway. Two boys, not more than ten years old, were playing cops and robbers on bikes. Everything seemed normal until the 'cop' stopped talking on his imaginary walkie-talkie and informed the robber,

'I don't give a f**k about my job, I'm gonna kick your bleedin' head in.'

Overheard by Seamus, Tallaght
Posted on Saturday, 4 November 2006

Long way to go

On the steps of a church after the funeral of an elderly lady.

One mourner: 'That was very sad.'

Second mourner: 'It was. I'm so depressed I just want to find a nice quiet pub and drink meself into Bolivia.'

Overheard by Anonymous, in Clondalkin
Posted on Saturday, 4 November 2006

Why townies shouldn't do agriculture

Just before the Leaving Cert, I was giving grinds to two D4 girls in Agricultural Science. One of the short questions on the paper was, 'Why would the weather forecast be important to potato farmers in Ireland?'

I would have presumed that everybody who did history in primary school would have learned of the potato famine and blight caused by the unusual muggy weather, but apparently not, as one of the girls replied to me,

'So that farmers will know when to put on sun screen?'

God be with the next generation …

Overheard by K, giving grinds
Posted on Friday, 3 November 2006

World Vision

While walking through Temple Bar with my mother, this guy approached and asked would she like to hear more about 'World Vision'. She replied,

'No tanks, luff, I don't need any glasses.'

She didn't cop on until long after the man had walked by that he wasn't talking about Vision Express …

Overheard by Rosso, Temple Bar
Posted on Thursday, 2 November 2006

Wise words from a Finglas head

I saw this overweight middle-aged guy out power-walking on Ballygall Road in Finglas. A youngfella from the other side of the road shouts over,

'Hey mister, you'd want to do less of the power eatin!'

Fair play to the big guy, he just laughed and kept booting along.

Overheard by S, Finglas
Posted on Friday, 27 October 2006

That'll learn him

Overheard on Hill 16:

Dublin were all over Roscommon but were failing to hit the target and were running up a high amount of wides. After the tenth or so such wide, some well-mannered educated chap (clearly out of place on Hill 16) pipes up and says,

'Come on, Dublin, let's convert our superiority into scores!'

A reply came from a cider-drinking yobbo,

'Do yiz hear f**king Shakespeare down dere!'

Overheard by Diego, from Hill 16 A5 section
Posted on Wednesday, 25 October 2006

Happy birthday

I was in a pub in town at the weekend, a pretty rowdy pub, when two female guards walked in to verify a reported disturbance. A girl sitting near the door shouts out,

'Whose birthday is it? Get yezer kits off, girls!'

Overheard by Jayo, the International Bar
Posted on Wednesday, 25 October 2006

Edible underwear

The Southern Cross Business Park in Bray. A company called 'The Butlers Pantry' (a food manufacturer) had recently moved in to the estate. The driver of a delivery truck comes over and asks us smokers outside,

'Sorry lads, can you tell me where I can find the Butlers Panties?'

Overheard by Barney, Bray
Posted on Wednesday, 25 October 2006

The cheek!

Walking to work this morning on Dawson Street, spotted a Garda standing beside an illegally-parked van, writing a ticket. Van owner runs out of a local shop and says, 'Is there a problem, Garda?'

Garda: 'Yeah, would you look at that, some eejit is after putting a footpath and double yellow lines under your van — the cheek of them!'

Overheard by Aine, Dawson Street
Posted on Wednesday, 25 October 2006

Feckin' immigrants

I'm Aussie, but lived in Dublin for a few years. Anyway, two weeks or so after I arrived, I got a job, and having walked out of said successful interview at about 2 p.m., thought that I should celebrate with a few jars.

Went into a pub near Aungier Street and ordered a pint. It was almost empty so I started chatting with the barman. A few pints later, he's having one or two himself and we've become new-found best mates. He's going on about how great Australia is, and congratulations on gettin' de job, young lad, and you keep your nose clean now. He even buys me a pint to 'celebrate ye gettin yer start in Dooblin'. Grand.

Then this Polish girl comes in and asks, in fairly broken English, 'Do you hev job I can take, yes?'

He rudely tells her no, and as soon as she leaves, he throws her CV in the bin and says to me, in all seriousness ...

'Feckin' immigrants, comin' here and takin' all our jobs.'

Utter genius!

Overheard by Rory, an unnamed pub
Posted on Saturday, 21 October 2006

BIMBO

Sitting chatting with the gurlies. We were talking about Heather Mills, and one of my friends said, 'Oh yeah, that's the one married to Paul McCartney with the PROSTATE leg!'

Overheard by Wen, straight from a mad mate's mouth!
Posted on Friday, 20 October 2006

Decimalisation

Walking through Phibsboro on the North Circular, a small old woman shouts to a rather large black man, 'I have tha' two shillin's for ya!'

He looks at her confused and shrugs.

'The two shillins — the euro I owe ya!'

Overheard by Gar, Phibsboro

Posted on Friday, 20 October 2006

What's wrong with a Knife?

Earlier this year I was working in Habitat. This very southside Dublin girl in her late teens, dressed in designer clothes, walked up to me and asked,

'Do you sell bagel slicers?'

I said I didn't even know such a thing existed and, no, the store never stocked them. She said in all seriousness, as if I had been living in the Dark Ages and the store was some throwback to 50s Ireland,

'Well, like, they have them in *The OC* ...' and then turned and walked away.

Television really is warping this generation's minds!

Overheard by Anonymous, at work in Habitat

Posted on Friday, 20 October 2006

Bright spark!

Whilst in Woodie's wandering about, as is a handyman's wont, I came across a salt-of-the-earth Dublin family. They had just passed a stand with solar power lamps on display when the mother got rather excited:

Mother: 'Ah Tom, wouldn't dem lamps be lovel-illy out by de roses in de drive?'

Tom: 'Not bad alright, how much are dey?'

Mother: 'Only €9.99 each.'

Son: 'Ah here, dem solar-powered lamps, I heard 'bout dem, they're a scam.'

Mother: 'Why, what's wrong wit 'em?'

Son: 'Sure dey don't work … der's no bleedin' sun at night …'

Overheard by Hick, Woodie's DIY
Posted on Thursday, 19 October 2006

Talking to yourself!

My boyfriend was upstairs on a bus to work one morning. A little girl and her father got on and sat right up the front. The little girl started to talk at the top of her voice, 'Dis is grea, Da, ya can see everythin up here, Ma never lets me si up here!'

The father, looking a bit embarrassed by the daughter's loudness, says, 'Der's no need to shout, I'm sittin righ beside you.'

The little girl replies as loudly as before, 'Righ so, I'll just talk to meself in me own head den.'

Overheard by CS, on a bus to Rathfarnham
Posted on Thursday, 19 October 2006

At the dogs

Many years ago I was at the Dogs in Harold's Cross with my parents — it was my mother's first visit.

Before the fifth race starts, my Ma has a pained expression and says, 'Ah, the poor dog, he must be tired.'

'Which one, Ma?'

'The one with the stripey jacket on, this is his fifth race!'

Overheard by Jinho, at the Dogs, Harold's Cross
Posted on Thursday, 19 October 2006

Just folly me directions

Outside a nightclub on Harcourt Street, I overheard a young fella beside me giving directions to someone how to get there. He says,

'Jaysus, will you just tell the taxi driver it's on "HARD CORE STREET"!'

Bless! These people are the future?

Overheard by Alanjo, Harcourt Street
Posted on Thursday, 19 October 2006

Hot weather, wouldn't you say!

One of those nice hot summer nights, I picked up three girls around the Ringsend area. Nice girls, chatting away on the way to Stephen's Green. In the middle of the conversation one turns to the others and says,

'Jaysus, I'm roasting tonight, this weather is killing me.'

One of the others agrees with her, and to express her feelings on the point replies,

'Yeah, I'm boiling, me knickers are wringing!'

Ahhh, Dub girls — where would you get it!

Overheard by Anonymous, in my taxi in Ringsend
Posted on Thursday, 19 October 2006

Ribena man

Drunk man on the no. 150 bus holding a carton
of Ribena turns around to me and says, 'That
can't be true, 95% of Irish blackcurrants grow up
to be Ribena berries?'

How can you respond to that?

Overheard by Timmy, on the no. 150 bus
Posted on Wednesday, 18 October 2006

Bleedin' embolisms

Coming home from Clonshaugh Industrial
Estate the other day, my pal Damo overheard
two auld ones talking about multicultural
Dublin:

'… Jaysus, there's bleedin' Chinese embolisms
everywhere …'

Trying hard not to picture haemorrhaging on a
city-wide scale, he hid his laughter and
presumed she meant symbols.

Overheard by Babs, from a pal returning
from Clonshaugh Industrial Estate
Posted on Wednesday, 18 October 2006

Ferocious language

I went to Argos to buy a pocket-sized electronic
thesaurus. Upon arriving I located one in the
catalogue, filled in the little paper slip with the
Argos code and then joined the queue. I handed
the paper slip to the cashier who was a middle-
aged Dublin lady, and the name of the item
popped up on her screen, along with the price.

'So it's an Oxford … The … Thes …
Tyrannosaurus rex at €29.99. Now would you
like to insure him for an extra €3 for three
years?'

I shook my head and said no thanks.

"No, OK, so you don't want to insure him, no
problem love, that's grand, here's your order
number.'

Overheard by Karen, Argos
Posted on Wednesday, 18 October 2006

Friends for Less

Working for Vodafone years ago, had a
promotion called Friends For Less, basically
nominate three 087 numbers you ring the most
to save money. Anyway, we'd always ask
customers at the end of the call do they want to
register three numbers. Had some muck savage
on who replied, 'Ya, sure, I'll go for 2, 6 and 8!'

!?!?!?

Overheard by Will, while working at Vodafone
Posted on Monday, 16 October 2006

Preparing for an evening of culture

In Molloys off-licence in Clondalkin last Saturday
night about eight o'clock.

This girl and her Ma came in. The Ma, of course,
was wearing her pyjamas and slippers. They
picked up a couple of bottles of Black Tower
and were looking at the crisps. The daughter
picks up a packet of fancy Thai spicy crisps with
pictures of red peppers on the bag.

'Wharrabouh dem, Ma?'

'Ah, no way. Dey look like dey'd burn yeh.'

Overheard by Austo, Molloys, Clondalkin
Posted on Monday, 16 October 2006

Monkey magic on the no. 10 bus

After waiting over 45 minutes on the NCR for a no. 10 from the Phoenix Park, the bus finally pulls up to the stop. When the door opens the old woman, a real Dub, at the front of the queue says to the driver,

'What were ye doin up there? Feedin' the bleedin' monkeys!'

The driver replies, 'Yeah, and takin' on some bleedin' monkeys as well!'

Only in Dublin!

Overheard by Joxer, North Circular Road
Posted on Friday, 13 October 2006

A T-ahem

Waiting in an ATM queue on Georges Street one weekend and one person seems to be taking quite a long time to use the machine. Man behind me shouts up to the girl at the machine,

'What are you gettin up there, a bleedin' mortgage!'

Overheard by Seán, Georges Street
Posted on Friday, 13 October 2006

Only something a Dub would say!

The day of the Liffey Swim a few weeks back, my friends and I were heading in to town on the no. 25A bus. Of course everyone was curious to see what was happening, so whilst stuck in traffic on the quays this Dublin girl got up and went over to the other side of the bus to see what everyone was staring at.

She turned around and said to her boyfriend (and everyone else on the bus),

'Jeysus, one a dem is gonna get stuck in a bleeding shopping trolley!'

Overheard by Penelope, on the no. 25A bus

Posted on Wednesday, 11 October 2006

That rhino's bleedin' sweatin!

Overheard by a friend of mine, who was recently at a circus on the northside of Dublin. Show was in full swing, animals and everything, including a rhino which was mounted by one of the performers.

Beside him was a young couple. Conversation is as follows:

Young one: 'That's f**king horrible!'

Young fella: 'What is?'

Young one: 'Him riding that rhino, it's bleedin' sweating!'

Overheard by Moz, at the circus

Posted on Wednesday, 11 October 2006

Making it up?

Overheard the announcer on an open-top Dublin Tour bus going by Burdock's chipper.

'To your right we have Burdock's, Dublin's most famous fish and chip shop. An array of celebrities have eaten in this famous chip shop, from Molly Malone right up to U2.'

Molly Malone?

Overheard by Willy, Werburgh Street
Posted on Tuesday, 10 October 2006

Off da ...

Crowd of young lads sitting in McDonald's, possibly just back from a trip to the US, or maybe just talking about a DVD they'd seen. Phrases such as 'off da hook' and 'off da ...' one thing and the other etc. are being bandied about.

The analyst of the group pronounces, 'Off da hook is the most famous of all the offdas.'

Overheard by Mozzer, McDonald's, Ranelagh
Posted on Monday, 9 October 2006

The joy of childbirth

A while back the sister-in-law of a mate of mine had her first child. It was a big baby and had to be delivered by Caesarean section. I'm translating here, because the text I got from my mate read:

'She had a baby boy this morning. Big fella. Came out the sun roof.'

Overheard by Diego, by text
Posted on Monday, 9 October 2006

Top prize?

Watching the Ireland versus Cyprus game on Saturday in the Bankers pub in town.

Coming near the end of the game, Ireland losing 5-2, the commentator says that after the game they will be doing their 'Man of the Match' competition. He said, 'The top prize is two tickets to Ireland's next match.'

Cue somebody shouts out,

'Yeah more a f**kin' booby prize!'

Overheard by Mac, Bankers in town
Posted on Monday, 9 October 2006

A G.S.O.H. essential

Two scobie types sitting on the no. 78A bus behind me, talking about a pet dog they used to have.

Scobie 1: 'Ye'd miss him around though, wouldn't ye?'

Scobie 2: 'Ah yea, he was a mad little b*stard, wasn't he?'

Scobie 1: 'Yeah. D'ya remember the time he left a shite on the bed and then when you were cleaning it he took another shite on the floor?'

Scobie 2: 'Yeah, he was gas . . .'

Overheard by Sue, on the no. 78A bus
Posted on Thursday, 5 October 2006

Rural resettlement

Picked up two women in my taxi in Ballymun. One asked to go to the City Council buildings at Wood Quay. They got talking on the way in, and one says to the other,

'Jaysus, I'm going in here to see about rural resettlement. I'm goin to tell them I want a dormant bungalow in Carlow, no upstairs …'

Overheard by Terry, in my taxi
Posted on Tuesday, 3 October 2006

True love

On the no. 150 bus going into town, a drunk couple get on and sit down the back. A few minutes pass, then the guy stands up and shouts, 'Excuse me, ladies and gentleman, I'd just like to say I love this woman!'

The woman turns her head away from him and says, 'Ah jaysus, will ye stop, you're makin' me scarlet!'

And he says, 'Shut up, ye stupid bitch!'

Overheard by JohnG, on the no. 150 bus
Posted on Monday, 2 October 2006

Where's de justice in dat?

One day while working in Dun Laoghaire
Shopping Centre, one annoyed 'head-the-ball'
comes running up to one of the security guards
and screams at him,

'Yer man is down there accusing me of
robbin ...'

The security guard looks back and the 'head-the-
ball' says,

'... I wouldn't mind but I haven't robbed in here
in weeks!'

Overheard by Cobs, Dun Laoghaire Shopping Centre
Posted on Friday, 29 September 2006

Never get a rickshaw in Dublin

I was getting on a rickshaw (drunk) going back
to a girl's house one Saturday evening. We were
in a passionate embrace and full of lust. As we
passed a couple of lads on a corner, one of them
shouted, 'De ye's want a knife and fork!'

Overheard by Karl, Rathmines
Posted on Thursday, 28 September 2006

Lost and found?

Overseen actually. Was walking past the Bleeding
Horse on Camden Street when my boyfriend

brought my attention to a small sticker on a lamp-post:

'Lost nail clippers, this is urgent, you have no idea how long my toe-nails are, information, please contact ...'

You can see it for yourselves, it's on a lamp-post near the smoking area on the street!

Overheard by Leona, outside the Bleeding Horse
Posted on Wednesday, 27 September 2006

Can I take your order?

A drunk goes into the local chipper after a few scoops and orders a shark burger and chips. The disgruntled worker ignores him but the man keeps shouting up his order. Eventually the chippy shouts back, 'We don' do dem!'

Your man responds, 'Ye don' do dem? Just a shark burger so!'

Overheard by Larry, northside chipper
Posted on Wednesday, 27 September 2006

Final destination

As the Luas was approaching the Red Cow, there was the following announcement over the loudspeaker:

'All passengers will be terminated at Abbey Street.'

Overheard by Helen, Luas (Red Cow)
Posted on Wednesday, 27 September 2006

Show must go on

Queuing for a p*ss in the pub, drunk guy at urinal beside me announces, 'I have stage fright. I can't go, and I am bursting!'

Overheard by Paul, The Old Mill pub, Tallaght
Posted on Monday, 25 September 2006

What's the craic

In passport control coming back from Thailand, my boy's passport had been stolen by a prostitute. He only had an emergency passport from the embassy (which was a green piece of paper, might I add).

The passport officer kindly told us, 'Believe me, it will turn up in a few days with a foreigner coming through in an Ireland jersey, asking me what the craic is!'

Overheard by Anonymous, Dublin Airport
Posted on Friday, 22 September 2006

Balanced diet

A young boy and his mother in the Centra in Bray. The young lad picks up a carton of milk and when seen by his mother is told to, 'Put it back, don't you know you are having a can of coke with your chips!'

Overheard by Barney, Centra, Bray
Posted on Thursday, 21 September 2006

800-year struggle

Spray-painted on a wall at the entrance of my mate's estate in Donabate:

'BIRTS OUT!'

It's been there for years, uncorrected!

Overheard by Rory, Donabate
Posted on Wednesday, 20 September 2006

Euclid would be proud

I was on the ferry from Holyhead to Dun Laoghaire and I got talking with an ould pair from Limerick. It was the first time they had travelled abroad. The ould one said to me,

'We usually go on holidays to Lahinch. It's grand. It's only 50 miles from home and only 50 miles back again.'

Overheard by John, Stena Line ferry
Posted on Wednesday, 20 September 2006

Talking fruit

Girl: 'So where are you from, you sound Australian?'

Guy: 'Wales, but I do have a bit of a kiwi accent.'

Girl (laughing hysterically): 'What?! Kiwis can't talk!'

Overheard by Anonymous, St Stephen's Green
Posted on Monday, 18 September 2006

EU or not EU

Arriving recently at passport control in Dublin Airport, I overheard two English girls debating whether they should be in the queue 'EU' or 'Non-EU'.

'I was never very good at geography in school,' one of them said, 'so I don't know if England is in the EU or not.'

'Well, we don't have the euro,' the other one replied, 'so we mustn't be.'

They then joined the non-EU queue.

Overheard by Sean, Dublin Airport
Posted on Monday, 18 September 2006

Small change

Got on the bus a couple of weeks ago, having decided to get rid of all the small coins in my change jar at home. I poured my €1.35 fare, all in coppers, into the machine.

'Robbin' the piggy bank again?' asked the bus driver.

'Something like that,' I laughed.

'Or else,' he said, grinning, 'you must be a terrible singer.'

Overheard by Aoibhlinn, on the no. 18 bus
Posted on Monday, 18 September 2006

Unhappy customer

On the crowded no. 39 bus from the city to Blanch at rush hour.

A little girl of maybe four years kept screaming and crying. Her mother was wondering what was bothering her.

'Why are you so upset?'

The little bugger replied, 'Mommy, I hate f**kin' Dublin Bus.'

Overheard by Mr Winterbottom, on the no. 39 bus
Posted on Saturday, 16 September 2006

Irish Superbowl

On a recent flight from New York to Dublin, three elderly Yanks had the following discussion:

Yank 1: 'I believe it's Superbowl weekend in Ireland next weekend.' (clearly talking about the upcoming All-Ireland football final)

Yank 2: 'Wow, they play (American) football in Ireland?'

Yank 1: 'No, Irish football.'

Yank 3: 'You mean soccer?'

Yank 1: 'No, Irish football, they play with a rugby-shaped ball and wear loads of padding.'

Had to bite my lip!

Overheard by Staffy, on a flight from New York to Dublin
Posted on Friday, 15 September 2006

Language barriers

A Dub in work is queuing for a sandwich. As it's being made up, he's answering all the questions — in pure Dub — from a Polish girl, who is using what English she has to try and understand what he wants. She's wearing a completely baffled expression because she has no idea what this fella is saying, but carries on as best she can:

'You want lettuce?'

'That's deadly!' (adds lettuce).

'Tomato?'

'Nice one … tomato' (adds tomato).

'Ok, you want mayonnaise or salad cream?'

'Aw sure, it's legend as it is.'

The Polish girl tries to put mayo on, to cries from Auld Dub, 'Nah, nah, it's legend, legend!'

Overheard by Anonymous, working in Dublin
Posted on Thursday, 14 September 2006

A Dub in London Zoo

At London Zoo, my friend's sister passes by an enclosure under construction. A Portakabin behind a fence had Mifflin & Co. printed on a yellow sticker near the roof of the cabin. She calls over her two kids,

'Tom and Liam, come and see the mifflins!'

Overheard by David, London Zoo
Posted on Thursday, 14 September 2006

I'll be back

A non-national was hit by a vehicle at the pedestrian crossing on O'Connell Street. It was a minor accident, but looked all the more dramatic as he rolled off the bonnet of the car

and continued walking briskly away. Cue a stunned Howya at the lights:

'Jaysus, it's the bleeding Terminator!'

Overheard by Vincent, O'Connell Street
Posted on Thursday, 14 September 2006

Time to go home

When I was leaving Electric Picnic on the Monday morning, a guy ahead of me said, 'You know you've been here too long when you start dancing to the sound of the generators!'

Overheard by Síle, Electric Picnic
Posted on Wednesday, 13 September 2006

Mental

My friend and I were sitting in a park having a cigarette, when an old drunken man approaches

92

us, asking for a 'spare smoke'.

Myself, whilst taking out a cigarette: 'I must warn you, they're menthol.'

Drunk: 'Ah, sure oim mental meself!'

Staying level headed

Going over the DART tracks on the upper floor of the no. 32 bus, it rocks and bounces over them, swaying dangerously. Old man who was trying to stand up gets pushed back into his seat by the movement, and mutters, 'Level crossing me HOLE!'

Terms of endearment

Walking down Henry Street, two young Dublin women chatting to each other while trying to keep their various kids from running too far ahead.

One woman hands her couple-of-months-old baby to the other in order to chase a toddler who is trying a great escape, with the immortal words:

'Hold this bundle o' f**ks, while I clatter yer man.'

Irish terror alert level

The day after the latest 'terror plot' panic in Britain, my Dad overheard a passenger who was waiting to board the ferry at Dun Laoghaire ask a harbour policeman,

'What state of alert are yis on?'

Quick as a flash the harbour policeman says, 'Barely awake.'

Overheard by Dub, Stena terminal, Dun Laoghaire
Posted on Tuesday, 5 September 2006

Anaesthesia! Bless you!

A few years ago, I had occasion to be in the casualty department of Blanchardstown Hospital, getting a cut stitched, as was the 'jaysis-howaya' chap in the next cubicle. He was being treated by a doctor of Asian origin, who had a very strong accent.

The youngfella says to the doctor as treatment started, 'Eh, d'ye moind if I don' look, pal?' to which the doctor says, 'Certainly.'

A blood-curdling scream followed, as well as every type of expletive you can think up. After this died down, the nurse that was treating me calmly called through the curtain,

'He said do you mind if I don't LOOK, not do you mind if I don't have a LOCAL!'

Overheard by Stillsick, James Connolly Hospital, A&E
Posted on Monday, 4 September 2006

Welcome to Ireland

An African gets on the no. 83 bus on Westmoreland Street, flashes his travel pass at the driver and sits down.

An auld one beside me says, '… and they've got the free travel as well …'

Overheard by Niall, on the no. 83 bus
Posted on Monday, 4 September 2006

The thin white line

My sister was driving to Dublin in the car and my father was the front-seat passenger; in the back was my three-year-old nephew. He suddenly asks, 'Mam, what are the white lines in the middle of the road for?'

My father and sister both explain the reason for white lines in the middle of the road.

There is silence in the back.

A couple of minutes later the nephew pipes up, 'But what happens when it snows?'

Overheard by Tappers, off me skin and blister
Posted on Sunday, 3 September 2006

Jesus was a joker

Two years ago when I was working in the city centre I used to meet a friend for lunch on the steps of St Mary's Pro-cathedral just off Marlborough Street (classy, I know!). So we'd sit there chatting and laughing our heads off, a little bit down from the main door where people would come out of Mass. So one day this old disgruntled pensioner woman comes over to scold us:

'You young wans have no respect, stop your laughing, this is a house of God!'

To which another woman says, 'Ah don't mind her, sure didn't Jesus enjoy a bit of messin in his day!'

Overheard by Liz, Marlborough Street
Posted on Wednesday, 30 August 2006

Get this man an atlas!

Some scumbag had been caught red-handed trying to lift cans out of the Centra/Spar at O'Connell Bridge by a 6' 10" security guard, clearly of African origin. Amidst the barrage of abuse he uttered whilst being ejected from the shop, he shouted,

'Get away from me, you big f**kin' Albanian asylum seeker b**tard, ye!'

Overheard by Hugh, Westmoreland Street
Posted on Wednesday, 30 August 2006

Love has its 'benefits'

Written on the sign at the front of the Social Welfare office on Tara Street:

'Noelle Call Me'

Only Dublin …

Overheard by Andy, Tara Street
Posted on Wednesday, 30 August 2006

Not such an easy pass

Driving down towards the M50 toll bridge with my Dad (in my sister's car, using her Eazy Pass). As my Dad pulls up to the barrier, he holds up the Eazy Pass in front of him. Nothing happens! He's going mad pointing the Eazy Pass in all directions, all over the windscreen. Still the barrier never moves.

He rolls down the window, says to the young lad in the booth, 'This poxy thing's not workin,' to which the young lad replies, 'Hold it up behind the rear view mirror, barcode facing out!'

My dad follows his instructions and — hey presto — the barrier lifts. Then the young lad says,

'Now you see dat, mister, they're Eazy Passes, not feckin' remotes!'

Overheard by Martin, M50 toll bridge
Posted on Monday, 28 August 2006

Cat tranquillisers

On the no. 7 bus coming through Sallynoggin, two lads sitting at the back of the bus with a cat:

'Where did ya get da cat?'

'I stroked it off me aunty.'

'For what?'

'Gonna take it to da mobile vet in Tesco car park and tell the vet the fecker's depressed, ye can get animal tranquillisers off them, piece of piss.'

'Ah yeah, nice one!'

This conversation went on for another five minutes — with the top of the bus in hysterics (under their breath of course)!

Overheard by Anonymous, on the no. 7 bus
Posted on Friday, 25 August 2006

More like Thick Lizzy

At a Thin Az Lizzy gig. Girl behind me mutters to her boyfriend (obviously didn't want to be there),

'Yeah, they are good, but why are they only playing Thin Lizzy stuff?'

… errr?

Overheard by Jimmy, Whelan's on Wexford Street
Posted on Thursday, 24 August 2006

Disability of Laziness

I was on the no. 77A bus one day, coming home from town. There was a foreigner selling newspapers at the traffic lights.

Two lads down the back, one of them comments, 'Jayz, you'd think he'd get a decent job like, ya know.'

The other one replies, 'What are you saying, you haven't even got a f**kin' job!'

'Yea well … I … I have a disability!'

Overheard by David, on the no. 77A bus
Posted on Wednesday, 23 August 2006

A taxi driver who cares

A friend of mine had just arrived home after a year studying abroad, and was in a taxi heading to town from Rathmines one summer evening. He had rolled down the window to get some air.

Coming down Wexford Street, traffic was slow as a lot of people were gathered outside Whelan's/ The Village and some had spilled onto the road.

As the taxi passed the crowd, someone reached into the car and slapped my mate across the face. As if this wasn't injury enough, after a few seconds the clearly unconcerned but amused driver enquired,

'Got a bit of a slap there, did ya?'

I'm not usually a fan of taxi drivers, but this one deserves a round of applause for his compassion …

Overheard by Dan, Wexford Street
Posted on Tuesday, 22 August 2006

Crystal balls

A friend of mine was getting on a no. 11 bus on O'Connell Street when a lady boarded, obviously irate at having waited so long. She asked the driver when the next no. 10 would be along. Quick as a shot, the driver turned to her and said,

'Missus, I've got two balls, unfortunately neither of them are crystal.'

Apparently this satisfied the lady and off she got,

laughing her head off!

Overheard by Kevin, on the no. 11 bus
Posted on Monday, 21 August 2006

Top quality food

I was in McDonald's with a few friends last week. One of my friends says, 'I'll have a milkshake and six nuggets please', to which the cashier replies, 'What flavour would you like?'

Quick as a flash, my other friend says, 'Chicken!'

The group of us cracked up laughing ... cashier didn't seem amused though.

Overheard by Anonymous, McDonald's, Stillorgan
Posted on Monday, 21 August 2006

Best birthday ever!

On the day of the infamous Dublin riots, I was crossing O'Connell Bridge when I passed two lads fresh from battle with the Gardaí (and presumably on their way to Leinster House). I overheard one say to the other,

'Jayse, Anto, this is the best birthday ya ever had!'

Overheard by Dan, O'Connell Bridge
Posted on Saturday, 19 August 2006

Advanced linguistics

Junior Cert French class, the fellow sitting in front of me turned around and started telling me about some match he'd been to at weekend, swearing every second word.

'Yeah, it was mad sh*t, the f**kin' defence was all over the f**kin' shop, they …'

'Jason, stand up!' the teacher says, 'How dare you use that language in my classroom!'

Jason turns around, genuinely outraged:

'What language? English?! Just 'cos it's a French class, we can't speak English?'

Overheard by Jay, Junior Cert French class
Posted on Friday, 18 August 2006

Super disturbing taxi driver

In a taxi the other day with a few friends. The Dubliner driver must have been 20 stone at least. Somehow the conversation turns to beds. Driver starts telling us that he's got a water bed at home. Cue a lot of, 'Oh right, what's that like then?' trying hard not to picture him.

After that he says, 'Ah, you have to try different things … y'know … experiment, like, did you ever try jumping off the wardrobe?'

Cue laughter as this sinks in, yet another disturbing sight.

'Yeah, jumping off the wardrobe, wearing a superman outfit, ya hafta try it.'

Man, we were in fits coming out of that cab. I hope he was joking, that poor woman …

Overheard by K, in a Dublin taxi
Posted on Tuesday, 15 August 2006

Would only happen in Dublin

About two months ago while getting the no. 27 bus home, I saw a 'head-the-ball' sitting upstairs at the back of the bus. He had an X-ray in his hands and was holding it up to the window, looking at it very curiously.

I hear some fluttering, and he was examining a totally different X-ray.

Hmmm, I began to grow curious and moved a seat or two back.

He had a pile of them, I could only guess 60+.

That's what I love about Dublin. A guy wanders into some hospital, decides he would like something to play with on the ride home, and tada — he has it!

Overheard by Graham, on the no. 27 bus
Posted on Thursday, 10 August 2006

The state of Kilbarrack

Was getting the no. 29A bus at Eden Quay the other day when two of our American friends boarded. The gentleman asked the driver, 'Excuse me, sir, where this does bus go?'

To which the driver replied, 'Kilbarrack, Bud.'

The American gentleman then enquired, 'What state is that in?'

To which our Dublin Bus hero replied, 'It's in an awful bleedin' state, mister.'

Overheard by Keith, on the no. 29A bus at Eden Quay

Posted on Tuesday, 8 August 2006

Six stabs = alrigh?

Young wan: 'How's Decco?'

Young fella: 'He's alrigh, got out of James's Monday.'

Young wan: 'What happened him?'

Young fella: 'Six stabs in the chest — he's alrigh — lucky b**tard.'

Overheard by Nicantuile, Tallaght

Posted on Sunday, 6 August 2006

Someone needs to spend more time in the office!

In Brown Thomas the other day looking at Chloé bags, and called over an official-looking woman to verify a price. Woman comes over and tells us a particular bag is €478.50, and €1,032 in the same colour but with a metallic sheen.

We ask why is it nearly double for a metallic colour and she launches into a big long discussion about it being this, that and the other and 'special metallic effect' and 'nearly impossible to get from any other designer'.

Then the husband came up behind her and asked if she was ready to go!

Couldn't believe she didn't even work there!

Overheard by Raychelle, Brown Thomas, Grafton Street

Posted on Friday, 4 August 2006

Hairy legs

Was in River Island on Grafton Street last week with my six-year-old niece, paying for a pair of jeans. The little brat roars out in front of a very long queue:

'Why are you buying jeans with holes in the legs of them? Sure isn't everyone going to see your hairy legs?!'

Overheard by Anonymous, River Island on Grafton Street

Posted on Wednesday, 2 August 2006

Animal noises

In Dublin Zoo last year I was walking by the farm animals. A little girl (about six) ran by us. Her Ma noticed a sheep and called after her daughter,

'Look, Kelly, a sheep ... moo ... or baah, whatever ...'

Overheard by Joey, Dublin Zoo

Posted on Tuesday, 1 August 2006

Destiny's Child

Walking past a chipper on Faussagh Avenue,
Cabra, I overheard two young girls, aged about
eleven, discussing one of their sisters:

'Ah sure me sister's been in a right mood since
the wedding was called off, her Beyonce was
doin the dirt on her!'

Overheard by Karen, Faussagh Avenue, Cabra
Posted on Sunday, 30 July 2006

Nuns Looking for heaven

I was walking down Nassau Street. Outside the
Kilkenny Showrooms, there were two elderly
nuns in habit, and an elderly lady looking at
what appeared to be a street map. Just at that
moment a middle-aged man, scruffy looking,
came out of the shop, looked at the group, and
spontaneously shouted across to them,

'What are you's looking for? The way to heaven?'

I laughed all the way back to work!

Overheard by Domer, outside the Kilkenny Showrooms
Posted on Thursday, 27 July 2006

Jaysis Jesus

Looking for a flat block in Dolphin's Barn
complex and stopped a local man, asking, 'Can
you tell me where flat 32G is, please?'

He responds, 'Is that G as in Jesus or J as in
jaysis?'

Overheard by Erica, Dolphin's Barn
Posted on Thursday, 20 July 2006

Bitten on the Supermacs

I was getting the bus in from the airport and sitting in front of me were two D4 girls, one telling the other about her friend who was attacked by a dog (or loike a massive wolf, as she put it). She said,

'And then the wolf cornered him and, loike, jumped on him and knocked him over, then it started biting him.'

Her mate goes, 'Oh my God! Where did it bite him?'

D4 girl: 'Outside Supermacs.'

Overheard by Ian, airport bus
Posted on Wednesday, 19 July 2006

Eagle-eye cops!

I was at the Dublin versus Offaly match, and just after a steward got hit with a bottle, I overheard two Gardaí talking. One pointed to the stands and said,

'Yer man there in the Dublin top threw the bottle!'

Overheard by Steve, Croke Park
Posted on Monday, 17 July 2006

It's a long way to the top!

On Hill 16 for the Dublin versus Offaly match, group of lads come along looking for a good spot to stand. Guy leading the group keeps going up higher towards the back, when one of the lads shouts out,

'For f**k's sake, we're not on a sponsored walk!'

Overheard by Anonymous, Hill 16
Posted on Sunday, 16 July 2006

Who needs the bank manager?

Guy looking for cash on the lane beside The George, lots of punters passing by in the evening. The usual, 'Any spare change?' to which I'm ashamed to say, you normally walk on.

Then, just as you reach this particular guy, he asks, 'Any chance of a loan of €50?'

I cracked up laughing. Gave him whatever change I had (well over a fiver) and he thanked me very much — before pointing out that it was 'grand' if I couldn't rise to a 50!

Overheard by M, Georges Street
Posted on Thursday, 13 July 2006

Results!

In school, our maths teacher was asking what results we got in our Christmas exams. He gets around to asking my mate who is clearly daydreaming:

Teacher: 'What did you get at Christmas?'

Mate: 'Liverpool jersey and a watch, Sir!'

Overheard by Daz, Ardscoil Rís, Griffith Avenue
Posted on Thursday, 13 July 2006

Weights and measures

Scruffy 'arty' type punter: 'Two pints of
Carlsberg, one with four inches of white
lemonade and the other with one inch of white
lemonade.'

Old style grumpy/sardonic Dublin barman: 'No
problem, I have me measuring tape out the
back.'

Overheard by DB, the Leeson Lounge
Posted on Wednesday, 12 July 2006

Small folk

My cousin's four-year-old daughter is very smart
and quick to pass comment loudly in public. She
was sitting on the bus with her mother when a
male midget wearing sports gear got on and sat
across the aisle from them. My cousin warned
her daughter not to say anything, even though
this was the first time she had seen a midget.

The little girl would not be frustrated, though, and after thinking about it for a few moments, said for all on the bus to hear,

'Mammy, that's the smallest tracksuit I've ever seen!'

Overheard by Erica, on the no. 10 bus
Posted on Wednesday, 12 July 2006

Free tour

Upstairs on the no. 38 bus coming into town. Old Dublin dear with headscarf, brown mac and sensible shoes, sitting behind a very tanned young girl with long black hair.

As we go by any landmark, the old dear leans slightly forward and whispers its name fairly loudly, 'The Phoenix Park', 'St Peter's Church', 'The Garden of Remembrance'. Girl is getting narked and finally turns round to old dear and says,

'I'm not a bleedin' foreigner! I just have a tan from me holidays!'

Overheard by Erica, on the no. 38 bus
Posted on Monday, 10 July 2006

KFnoChicken

About a year ago I went into KFC at lunchtime and asked for some sort of chicken meal. The assistant told me, 'We have no chicken today!'

KFC with no chicken … could only happen in Ireland!

Overheard by Nicola, KFC
Posted on Monday, 10 July 2006

A dishy name

My grandmother, a real Dub!

On the birth of my daughter Sorcha
(pronounced Sorsha):

'You're calling her what?'

'Saucer! What sort of name is that for a little girl,
she will never forgive you!'

Overheard by Paul, my Nan's house, Portmarnock
Posted on Monday, 10 July 2006

Little brown girl

A few years ago there was a street party on my
road. A woman was dancing with a load of
children in a ring! In the middle of the ring was
a little black girl. The woman enthusiastically
began to sing,

'Brown girl in the ring, tra-la-la-la-la …'

She suddenly realised what she was singing,
quickly stopped and went bright red!

Overheard by Will, Donnycarney
Posted on Sunday, 9 July 2006

I pity the fool …

In Down Under at Stephen's Green, wearing a
'Mr T' t-shirt with a picture of the man himself
saying, 'Ain't got no time fo jibba-jabba', or some
such catchphrase.

A girl approaches me by the bar, looks at the t-
shirt and says,

'So you're a big Mike Tyson fan?'

Overheard by Ciaran, Down Under bar, St Stephen's Green
Posted on Friday, 7 July 2006

Free-range

Middle-aged woman asks vegetable stall-holder on Moore Street,

'Are those onions free-range?'

Stall-holder looks at her and says,

'Yes, love, and I'm tellin' ye, they're very hard to catch!'

Overheard by Erica, Moore Street
Posted on Thursday, 6 July 2006

B.L.A.N.C.H.A.R.D.S.T.O.W.N.

Sitting in my car in southside retail park, two guys getting into car beside me. One has thick Dublin accent and the other guy was foreign:

Dublin Guy: 'No, we'll try Liffey Valley first.'

Foreign Guy: 'Not Blanchardstown?'

Dublin Guy: 'No, no, not Blanchardstown.'

Foreign Guy: 'Why not?'

Dublin Guy: 'Well … (trying to look for the words) … Blanchardstown is … eh … it's for (pronounced very carefully and slowly) s.c.u.m.b.a.g.s.'

The Dublin guy spots me smiling and, obviously worried, a minute later he goes,

'Excuse me, you're not from Blanchardstown are you?'

For the record, I don't think Blanchardstown is
for scumbags (I reckon he just didn't fancy
going through the toll!).

Overheard by Jo, Liffey Valley

Posted on Thursday, 6 July 2006

VH—not impressed

I was in ExtraVision a while back and two girls
came in asking the chap behind the counter
whether he sold video cassettes for a camera.
The bloke gave them a withering look and said,
'No'.

'Well, do you know where we can get some?' say
the girls.

'Try the 80s,' says the bloke as he turns his back.

Nice!

Overheard by Mugwumpjism, ExtraVision, Coolock

Posted on Tuesday, 4 July 2006

Muppetry

I was waiting to get on the bus on Dame Street,
feeling slightly under the influence. The bus
pulls up and the guy in front of me waves a €5
note and tries to stick it into the coin machine.
The bus driver looks past him, directly at me
and says, 'Once a muppet always a muppet,
that's what I always say!'

Overheard by Cole, Dame Street

Posted on Saturday, 1 July 2006

Foul-mouthed toddler

Walking into the Square in Tallaght yesterday, I was met by a woman walking backwards shouting, 'I'm leav-EN, come on Way-EN,' as she went out the door. I had a look to see who she was shouting at, and spotted a young lad of about two or three, starting to run all the way back at the escalators.

As he started to run, he began that frightened crying that only a lost child can do, and began roaring.

As he came closer I finally made out what he was saying:

'Fer f**k sake, MA! Fer f**k sake, MA!' … over and over.

Everyone within earshot was in knots!

Overheard by Ross, The Squa-AH
Posted on Friday, 30 June 2006

Not a fan of ice-cream

Picture this. Stuck in traffic on Amiens Street on a roasting hot day in June — going nowhere. Some poxy truck hit a car. I had the car windows down, getting some air. About four or five young ones were standing at a doorway across the road.

One had just thrown water at the others and there was the usual talk of, 'Tracey, ya b*ll*x!' etc.

I spotted this guy walking towards them and he was eating the biggest ice-cream I've ever seen. It looked like the ice-cream seller had thrown about eight scoops onto his cone.

As he walked passed, one of the girls shouts out,

'Here, youngfella, give us a lick of your balls!'

> Overheard by Damo, on Amiens Street
> Posted on Thursday, 29 June 2006

Health care crisis

Standing on Hill 16 during the Meath versus Dublin Leinster Championship game in 2005 when Meath pariah Graham Geraghty fell to the ground, badly injured. The motorised stretcher thing came to pick him up, and as he was being carted away in obvious pain to a chorus of BEE-BAH BEE-BAH, a little gurrier of no more than seven leapt up from behind me and roared,

'I hope you're waiting on a f**kin' bed!'

> Overheard by Hally, Croke Park
> Posted on Thursday, 29 June 2006

Extra time at the Ireland v. Chile game

Chile were winning 1-0, and it was coming towards the end of the game. The announcement came over the loudspeaker that there would be something ridiculous like six minutes of extra time (an unusual amount for a friendly game).

Anyhow, as it was announced, two typical Dubs were passing:

'Jaysus, Thommo, six minutes? He must be adding that much time for when we went for burgers!'

Overheard by John, Lansdowne Road
Posted on Wednesday, 28 June 2006

Cut down to size

Having a pint in Kehoes off Grafton Street. Quiet time, when three loud Americans come in from golf. Loudest guy is 6 foot 5 inches and is flanked by two nearly-7-footers. He says to the barmaid, 'These guys are nearly 7 foot tall, and I am 6 foot 5. Guess what they call me?'

Without drawing breath she replies,

'Billie Bob.'

Cue sniggering … and a return to the quiet of the pub.

Pure class. Wish I was that quick!

Overheard by Mark, Kehoes off Grafton Street
Posted on Tuesday, 27 June 2006

Moving statue

My mate and I were killing time by watching one of the human statue street performers on Grafton Street. Just as we were about to push off, a gruff voice came from the back,

'He'd move if you ran off with his box!'

Lovely stuff!

Overheard by Shane M, Grafton Street
Posted on Wednesday, 28 June 2006

Knowing where your priorities lie

(Irate) girl on mobile: '... So you're telling me I can't see you until after the World Cup?'

Overheard by Anonymous, St Stephen's Green
Posted on Friday, 23 June 2006

While Heimlich turns in his grave

While in the Cherry Tree pub recently, a man started to cough while eating peanuts. His female companion panicked and shouted,

'Quickly — somebody use the Heineken Manoeuvre!'

Overheard by Dick, Cherry Tree pub, Walkinstown
Posted on Wednesday, 21 June 2006

Miss Education

Walking around Dublin Zoo, the year the safari park part opened, on a very hot Sunday with loads of families about. It just happened to be feeding time when we were walking by the seal

area, and people had begun to gather around to watch the feeding.

A large crane landed on one of the boulders in the middle of the pool and a small boy pointed to the crane and asked his mother, 'What's tha'?'

The mother says with a big smile on her face, 'Oh tha', tha's a boird!'

God love the yout!

Overheard by Kate, Dublin Zoo
Posted on Wednesday, 21 June 2006

Space Knickers

I started working in Dublin Airport recently. While talking to my supervisor, a group of Ryanair air hostesses passed by. I enquired if the airport staff mingled with the airline's hostesses. His reply was,

'Ah yeah, the Ryanair girls are sound, but the Aer Lingus girls must have space knickers on 'cos they think their fanny is out of this world.'

Overheard by Dav, Dublin Airport
Posted on Friday, 16 June 2006

The Fashion

Two old dears talking on the no. 19A bus last night:

Old dear #1: 'Do you see the kids in the runners these days?'

Old dear #2: 'I do, yeah.'

Old dear #1: 'The thing they do now is they put the laces into the runners.'

Old dear #2: 'They don't?'

Old dear #1: 'They do!'

Old dear #2: 'Do they?'

Old dear #1: 'They do. It's the fashion.'

Old dear #2: 'They don't tie them?'

Old dear #1: 'They don't. Just put the laces into the runners.'

Old dear #2: 'That's the fashion, I suppose.'

Overheard by Shango, on the no. 19A bus
Posted on Friday, 16 June 2006

That's not HELP!

When I was waiting for the train in Connolly Station, my insanely bushy-haired friend had his bag stolen. He anxiously runs to the help desk:

'I'm sorry but my bag has been stolen.'

The person behind the desk smirks and replies,

'Did it contain a hairbrush?'

My friend stares at her, not amused.

Overheard by Donal, Connolly Station
Posted on Friday, 16 June 2006

Attention to detail

Was watching the start of the Italy versus Ghana match, when my Mum walks into the room. One or two of the Ghana players had tops with 'Germany '06' written on the front. Mum spots this and pipes up:

'Isn't that great, look at the German team, they're all black.'

Overheard by Richie, at home while watching the World Cup

Posted on Thursday, 15 June 2006

Religious bankers

While walking behind three office types toward the Green, I overheard them talking about the office:

Banker #1: 'How's work these days?'

Banker #2: 'You know the story in the Bible about the man who was being constantly annoyed at home? He went to a wise man for advice and was told to get a goat and to keep it in the house. The goat made a load of noise and a major mess so things got worse. The man went back to the wise man to complain, and was told to get rid of the goat. Once the goat was gone things didn't seem so bad. Well, the goat's on holidays.'

I think we've all been there …

Overheard by Mike, Baggot Street

Posted on Thursday, 15 June 2006

She's lovely

I was in a petrol station one day when a bunch of students came in. There was a bit of a queue forming as we were all waiting for the cashier to reappear from the back.

Anyway, I overheard one of the students boasting to his mates: 'You should see the one who works in here, she is f**kin' lovely.'

Just then the cashier comes into the front of the shop. He is fat, bald and in his 50s. The other students turn around and say,

'Oh yeah, she's a f**king stunner.'

Overheard by John, Bray
Posted on Thursday, 15 June 2006

Romance lives

One night, watching a movie with Brad Pitt in it.

My mother says, 'Ooh, I wouldn't throw him out of bed for eating nuts,' to which my dad replies,

'If he was in bed with you, he *would* be nuts!'

Romance lives!

Overheard by Lorraine, at home
Posted on Wednesday, 14 June 2006

Patience of a prisoner

My friend worked as an electrician in Mountjoy Prison and heard this one morning. There is a shop in there which is open to the prisoners. One morning the shop was late opening, and as the shopkeeper came along to open it, a prisoner shouts from his jail cell,

'About f**kin' time, I've been waiting ages!'

Overheard by Derek, Mountjoy
Posted on Wednesday, 14 June 2006

No sugar coating required

In Swords, two women bump into each other. One says,

'Jaysus, you're like our John — you're gone HUGE!'

Overheard by Bridie, Swords
Posted on Tuesday, 13 June 2006

A solution to Africa's problems

While watching an ad for Concern, the voiceover says, 'These people have to walk for three miles every day just to get water,' to which my five-year-old nephew replied,

'Why don't they just move closer to the water?'

Overheard by Derek, while watching TV at home
Posted on Monday, 12 June 2006

Miniature euros

I was getting fags in our local Spar for myself and my pal Eve, when I decided to get a box of chocolates for the pair of us. The chocs are behind the counter so I asked the young cashier for 'the big box of Miniature Heroes'.

She asked me what I wanted and I repeated, pointing out where they were to the mystified girl.

She walked over to the shelf, stared at it for a few moments and mumbled something to the other cashier, who kindly pointed them out to her.

She returned red-faced, announcing:

'Ah, jaysus, I thought you asked for Miniature Euros, and I was sayin' to meself "What the f**k does she want them for?!"'

Overheard by Lainey, Spar, SCR
Posted on Thursday, 8 June 2006

Women's Mini Marathon

'Ow! I'm never doing that to anyone again!'

Man on having his bra strap pinged during the Women's Mini Marathon.

Overheard by Ann, 2006 Women's Mini Marathon
Posted on Tuesday, 6 June 2006

B and Queue

Standing in the queue for the till in B&Q last Saturday, buying a step-ladder. There's only three people in front of me, but it's taking the hapless cashier about ten minutes to deal with each customer, what with a dodgy scanner and barcodes not in the system.

As she left the till for the third or fourth time to ask a colleague what to do next, the bloke behind me looks at the one item I'm getting and says to me,

'Bet you wish you'd just stood on a f**kin' chair now!'

Overheard by Gary, B&Q, Liffey Valley
Posted on Tuesday, 6 June 2006

Ah yes, the charms of the Dublin taxi driver

I was standing outside Bewley's Hotel in Ballsbridge. There were three women nearby. A taxi pulled up and the driver got out. One of the women said to him, 'Are you a taxi?' to which he replied, pointing to his car,

'That's a taxi, luv, I'm a human being!'

Overheard by Áine, Bewley's Hotel, Ballsbridge
Posted on Monday, 5 June 2006

Excuse me, love ...

I was downstairs on the no. 78 bus a couple of months ago and spotted a young one talking happily away to herself. I thought, 'Ah, God love her,' until I realised she was using a hands-free phone.

Just then an oul' one leaned over to her and said,

'Excuse me, love, but yeh look like a feckin' eejit!'

The young one appeared mystified and slightly startled as the rest of us sniggered. She began to talk again to whoever was still on the phone, when the oul' one leaned over again and said,

'Excuse me, love, yeh didn't hear me. Yeh look like a feckin' eejit!'

Howls of laughter!

Overheard by Dave, on the no. 78 bus
Posted on Sunday, 4 June 2006

Shortage of smarts in ICU

A woman was talking vehemently to her friend about nurses in intensive care units:

'They just don't have the brain cells to know who's wellest.'

THEY are short on brain cells?!

Overheard by Anonymous, in a café in Glasnevin
Posted on Saturday, 3 June 2006

The lights are on but nobody's at home

My boss was assisting one of the shop-floor girls with the Christmas lights for the window, and they were having problems with the electrics. My boss went in the back to the fuse box, and called out to the girl,

'Well, are they workin' now?'

To which she replied,

'Oh, yeah! They're on now! … Oh … wait, off again … Oh, back on again!'

My boss could barely get out the words to explain to her the purpose of 'twinkling fairylights' …

Overheard by Alison, at work in Swords
Posted on Saturday, 3 June 2006

No sign of the directions

Came back to Dublin in January this year after many years away. Anyway, I couldn't find the DART station on Amiens Street (access is now different). I asked this guy working there for directions. I mention to him there are not many signs, to which he replies,

'Sure, we don't bother with signs as most people know where it is.'

Overheard by Anonymous, Amiens Street
Posted on Friday, 2 June 2006

The bouncer scale

One of a group of young-looking lads to the bouncers outside a lap-dancing club:

'So, on a scale of one to ten, how much am I not allowed in?'

Overheard by David O'C, outside Club Lapello on Dame Street
Posted on Friday, 2 June 2006

Dog's abuse

Dublin man to his dog, after it did a huge poo at the entrance of Trinity College:

'What are ya? … That's right, a fecking eejit!'

Overheard by Robin, outside Trinity College
Posted on Thursday, 1 June 2006

The singer

An ould drunk on the DART on Saturday evening, trying to convince some Dutch tourists to sing with him:

'I'm a singer,

Sure my whole family were singers,

My mother was a singer,

My father was a singer,

Even the sewing machine was a Singer ...'

Overheard by Ruairi, on the DART
Posted on Tuesday, 30 May 2006

Wha's up?!?

In HMV Henry Street yesterday and there were two very white lads, about sixteen or seventeen years old, in the middle of doing an unnecessarily complicated handshake. As I walked by them, they finished and one said to the other,

'Right! Now we're black.'

Overheard by NM, HMV on Henry Street
Posted on Tuesday, 30 May 2006

You don't rip off an old lady

I was standing outside Clery's, waiting for a bus. Beside me was an oul' one (in her 70s) with one of them shopping bags on wheels. She was staring into Clery's window and shaking her head. She looked up at me and pointed at a hat in the window.

'Who the feck would pay tha' much for a jaysus haah?'

Overheard by Anonymous, under Clery's clock
Posted on Tuesday, 30 May 2006

High-pressure job?

In a busy furniture shop in Liffey Valley the other day. One of the sales guys was rushing past me when I said to him, 'Under pressure, yeah?'

To which he replied, with a smile on his face,

'Son, pressure is only for tyres!'

Overheard by Adrian, Liffey Valley
Posted on Tuesday, 30 May 2006

Decent boss

We have quite a 'hands on' boss — Pat. He has no problem taking over from a worker if they need a break etc.

One day the phone rang, and it was a customer looking for the boss. I put them on hold and asked a few of the factory boys who were in my office, 'Any sign of Pat?'

They told me he was out in the factory giving

one of the lads a break. So I pick up the phone and said (still can't believe I said this!),

'I'm afraid he's out on the floor, relieving one of the Polish boys!'

Overheard by Anonymous, at work
Posted on Thursday, 25 May 2006

Child protection services, anyone?

A guy at work asking one of the office cleaners about her Spanish holiday:

'So was it any good?'

'Oh yeah, it was brilliant, out on the piss every night until five, and English breakfasts every morning.'

'And did you get a babysitter?'

'Ah no — the child was out with us too — she wouldn't go home!'

Overheard by Anonymous, at work
Posted on Thursday, 25 May 2006

There's always some Anto in the crowd

I was at a Celtic supporters' club meeting a couple of years ago and the Chairman warned us not to leave our belongings on the buses outside Parkhead, because recently the buses were getting robbed during the game.

A couple of issues later the Chairman announced, 'The little nuns of Glasgow are no longer making charitable fund-raisers at Parkhead.'

Some headcase in the crowd called Anto shouts out,

'They don't have to — they're robbing the f**kin' buses!'

Overheard by B, Fraziers, O'Connell Street
Posted on Thursday, 25 May 2006

Give up the day job!

Getting a taxi from Dublin Airport one night and I was half-listening to something on the radio about fighting between India and Pakistan over Kashmir.

The cabbie looks back at me and goes, 'The Indians are on the warpath again, wha?'

Comedy genius!

Overheard by Johnno, cab from the airport
Posted on Sunday, 21 May 2006

What sport is that?

On the DART through Sandymount one day and there is a group of girls playing hockey in the grounds there. An American boy behind me asks,

Boy: 'Mommy, what sport is that?'

Mom: 'I dunno, Sweety, it looks kinda like ice-hockey outside.'

Dad: 'It's called Gaelic soccer …'

Overheard by Liam, on the DART
Posted on Saturday, 20 May 2006

How does milk come out of those?

Little boy, approx. seven years old, in the women's changing rooms in the gym, says to his mother, 'How does milk come out of those?'

To which the mother replies, 'Oh, it's when you have a baby,' and leaves it at that.

The child then laughs and says out very loud, 'I used to suck on them, haha!'

Overheard by Aoife, Westpoint Gym
Posted on Thursday, 11 May 2006

The cry of the common man

Charity mugger (with the usual dreadlocks): 'Excuse me, sir, do you have a second to talk about Oxfam?'

Guy: 'Leave me alone and get a haircut, you hippy!'

Overheard by Jason, Aungier Street
Posted on Thursday, 11 May 2006

Top priority

Speaking of charity muggers …

Chugger: 'Excuse me, could I just ask you for a minute of your time please to talk to you about …'

Guy: 'I'm sorry but I really need to do a poo.'

Chugger just stands there, speechless …

Overheard by Andy, outside Stephen's Green Shopping Centre
Posted on Thursday, 11 May 2006

Vegetarian friendly?

I was in a chipper with my friend, both of us being vegetarians, and she asks the Chinese guy behind the counter,

'Are spice burgers suitable for vegetarians?' and the guy goes,

'Well, there's not MUCH meat in them, it's mainly fat and other shite, so they're kind of vegetarian!'

Overheard by voodoogirl, chipper in Bray
Posted on Thursday, 11 May 2006

Chelsea who?

On the no. 46A bus recently surrounded by noisy D4 boys and girls. I overhear a guy slagging his friend (who was obviously a Man United fan).

Guy: 'Ha ha! Chelsea won!'

On hearing this one of the girls says, 'What, the X Factor?'

Overheard by Anonymous, on the no. 46A bus
Posted on Thursday, 11 May 2006

Excuse me

I was on the Luas the other day, getting off at Heuston Station, very busy, rush hour. Anyway I was making my way through the packed-out Luas, saying 'Excuse me please' etc., when this 'howya' girl shouts all over the place,

'Will yis move outta da f**kin' way, da young

one is tryin to get da hell outta here, now
F**KING MOVE!'

Well, I was 'scarlet'.

Overheard by Kayla, on the Luas
Posted on Wednesday, 10 May 2006

The eccentrics

Upstairs on the no. 150 bus home from town
one evening about seven o'clock, and these two
lads in overalls, half-pissed on the back seat,
were quite loudly fighting over a can of Bud.
Finally they settled down and still quite audibly
began leafing through the *Star* newspaper
together, when one of them pipes up,

'What's this bleedin' word here? Egg-sentrick?'

His mate replies, 'Eccentric, ye bleedin' dope ye,
it's eccentric ... (dramatic, pensive pause) well it
kinda means you're a bit strange and ye do all
sortsa mad stuff. Like yerman Richard Branson
going around the world in a bleedin' balloon
and all that shite. He'd be an eccentric. Ye have
to be rich to be an eccentric, though. If I went
around like that they'd just say I was a mad eejit
and I was crazy ... (further philosophical pause
for effect). Yeah, that's it. If you're rich you're
eccentric, if you're poor — you're just crazy ...'

Overheard by Shane, on the no. 150 bus
Posted on Monday, 8 May 2006

A Dub in a London college

A professor to student, explaining the double
negative:

'… and nowhere in the English language does a double positive mean a negative …'

To which a Dub voice at the back of the lecture room pipes up,

'Yea … right …'

Overheard by BC, a Dub in a London college
Posted on Monday, 8 May 2006

Free Fanta

Me and a few friends were walking around Dun Laoghaire recently. We heard rumours that there were free bottles of Fanta being given out as part of a promotion, but we didn't know where.

While searching for the free Fanta around the streets of Dun Laoghaire, a typical auld fella runs across the road towards us, grabs me by the arm and says,

'Do yez want free drink?' (opens a Superquinn bag with about 30 bottles of Fanta) 'They're given dem out down there.'

Overheard by Hoop, Dun Laoghaire
Posted on Saturday, 6 May 2006

Gambling problem?

I was walking home from the pub one night when a mother ran to catch up with her teenage daughter.

Mother: 'Mary, I've got your jacket here, why the f**k are there betting slips in the pocket, you stupid cow, you must be spending a grand a week in that f**king bookies!'

Mary (not missing a beat and screaming): 'That's not me f**king jacket, ya eijit, you f**king lost me bleeding coat!'

Overheard by Antoinette, in town
Posted on Thursday, 4 May 2006

Mackerel-economics

Before I started college, I got a letter from the college with a list of the subjects I would be studying, one of which was Macroeconomics. I was in the kitchen talking to my Mom and said, 'What's Macroeconomics?'

At which point my Dad came in, a wee bit drunk from the pub and shouts,

'Sure mackerel's a bleedin' fish.'

Right so, Dad.

Overheard by Voodoogirl, in my kitchen
Posted on Tuesday, 2 May 2006

Tongue-tied

Standing at a bus stop on the South Circular, I happened to notice a young couple kissing with

a degree of passion, but not what you'd call X-rated by any means, when a guy cycles past with a friendly,

'Get your f**king tongue out of her mouth!'

And they say romance is dead?

Overheard by Deebs, South Circular Road
Posted on Sunday, 30 April 2006

Gender bending in Inchicore

I used to get my hair cut in this very old-fashioned barber shop in Inchicore. I'm in there one afternoon — there's only me, the barber, a couple of auld fellas and a young mother with two sons. The black and white movie that was on telly finishes up, and Shirley Temple Bar comes on screen with the bingo numbers.

This causes a certain amount of discomfort with the auld fellas. They mutter a bit but the TV stays on. Then one of the young kids asks his Mammy, 'Mammy, is that a man or a woman on TV?'

His mother replies, 'It's a f**kin' eejit is what it is.'

Overheard by Baz, Inchicore
Posted on Saturday, 29 April 2006

Dancing sparks?

Seen this written in a toilet on a building site. Being a sparky myself, found it funny:

'Here come all the sparkys, dressed as ballroom dancers,

One in ten is qualified, the rest are f**in' chancers!'

Overheard by Ric, building site, Dublin
Posted on Tuesday, 25 April 2006

More than he bargained for!

In Busaras the other day, in one of the shops. A young guy queuing in front of me had ordered a cup of tea with milk and no sugar. The foreign girl behind the counter asked him,

'Would you like your bag squeezed?'

The guy replies,

'No, I'll just have the tea.'

He managed to keep a straight face — unlike myself who had to leave the shop!

Overheard by Stephen, shop in Busaras
Posted on Monday, 24 April 2006

Oh, suits you!

I overheard two gay guys on Georges Street (where else?). One was admiring the other's jacket.

Gay guy #1: 'I love your jacket, what make is it?'

Gay guy #2: 'Gucci.'

Gay guy #1: 'Oh! Gucci, Gucci, Goo!'

Overheard by Anonymous, Georges Street
Posted on Monday, 24 April 2006

Health health health!

In a Spar in the Liberties, mum with screaming brat:

Child: 'Ma, Ma, I want crisps … crisps, Ma … I want some crisps … crisps … crisps, Ma!'

Mother: 'No! You're not getting crisps, they're bad for you.'

Shopkeeper: 'Can I help you?'

Mother: 'Ten Marlboro Lights, please.'

Overheard by Paul, Spar
Posted on Friday, 21 April 2006

Leinster fans …

I was queuing last Friday at Donnybrook for tickets for the Leinster versus Munster match. My friend came over to keep me company, and the guy behind me asked my friend if he was going to the match.

He said no, he wasn't all that interested in rugby, and if he went he'd probably spend the time reading the newspaper, listening to his i-Pod and texting his mates. The guy behind said,

'Ah, you'd fit right in, so.'

Overheard by Anonymous, Donnybrook
Posted on Thursday, 20 April 2006

Inappropriate!

At a 5-a-side soccer tournament in UCD a few weeks ago, great craic. Afterwards, the referee declares, 'That was great, lads, I haven't had as much fun since I buried the mother-in-law ...'

Overheard by Louise, UCD
Posted on Thursday, 20 April 2006

Senior Cup

I was on the no. 46A bus on the way out of town. A bunch of lads from Blackrock get on at RTÉ. They started talking about their school rugby team and how they were playing in the middle of the mocks.

Jock #1: 'It's so unfair that they're expected to play in the middle of their mocks.'

Jock #2: 'I know, you'd think they'd move the mocks. You can always repeat the Leaving — you only get one shot at the Senior Cup.'

Overheard by Mick, on the no. 46A bus
Posted on Thursday, 20 April 2006

Interracial bonding

About 2 a.m. at the late-night window of a Texaco garage in Blackrock. Scumbag gets out of a van and waddles up to the window. There is an Asian man working there. The scumbag then roars aggressively at him in his best Asian accent,

'CHING BA PHAN DOO WAH' ... followed by ... 'DOES DAT MEAN ANYTIN' TO YOU, DUZ IH?'

Overheard by Rob, Texaco garage, Blackrock
Posted on Thursday, 20 April 2006

In the chipper

Standing in a chipper waiting for my order and a bloke walks in and orders the following:

'Will ye give us a bag of chips and two sausages and will you batter the f**k out of them for me, cheers?'

Overheard by Rob, chipper in Palmerstown
Posted on Thursday, 20 April 2006

All tracksuits are the same

Woman holds up two Reebok tracksuit tops and goes to her husband, 'Which one do you prefer?'

He says back to her, 'Don't take offence, love, but they all look the f**king same when they're on ya.'

So true. So true.

Overheard by Alan, Lifestyle Sports, Ilac Centre
Posted on Thursday, 20 April 2006

Brave eejit

Sitting on the no. 13A bus to Ballymun on Thursday surrounded by snivelling junkies and wreathed in clouds of hash smoke. Well-dressed gent beside me answers mobile phone and wife asks where he is:

'I'm on the skanger ride from hell,' he says, without batting an eyelid.

Overheard by a 13A victim, on the no. 13A bus
Posted on Wednesday, 19 April 2006

Confused?!

I was working at the information desk when a little boy about age three came up to my work colleague, looking lost, and asked her,

'Have you seen a woman going around without a boy that looks like me?'

Overheard by Beth, Shankill Shopping Centre
Posted on Wednesday, 19 April 2006

Music to watch the girls go by

Picture this. It's Tallaght, da boyz are in their car, blaring the tunes, rippin' around the estate like a dog on fire, shades on (even though it's nearing dark), equipped with those reflective blue light thingys that racer boys have under their set of wheels, beeping at anything in a skirt, about six fellas roaring, 'Wahey, luv, show us yer tits,' to every passing girl under the age of 30.

But there's something not right. Whilst I was waiting for my bus, they circled the estate several times, blaring one tune on repeat. It's not Scooter, it's not DJ Quicksilver … it's …

Shania Twain, 'Man, I feel like a woman' …

Overheard by M, Tallaght
Posted on Tuesday, 18 April 2006

You'd either love it or hate it

Was at the UCI Cinema in Coolock with a few mates last weekend and we asked the cashier guy about the films that had just started. We asked about one film in particular, to see if it was worth watching, and his reply was …

'I actually just saw it last night, it's a film you either love or hate. I thought it was alright.'

Overheard by ILLB, UCI Cinema Coolock
Posted on Tuesday, 18 April 2006

Hot stuff

Was in the Northside Shopping Centre looking for a present for my brother when I heard two oul' ones talking about a lava lamp:

Lady #1: 'Look at da, wharisit?'

Lady #2: 'It's a lava lamp.'

Lady #1 (touching it): 'It's very warm!'

Lady #2: 'Course it is, there's lava in it!'

Overheard by Kevin K, Northside Shopping Centre
Posted on Tuesday, 18 April 2006

Like mother, like son

My friend accompanies his father on a shopping trip for his Mum's birthday. While in a lingerie shop, the assistant asks the father if she can help. After some general questions, the assistant asks the father what size he is buying for. The father turns to his son (my pal) and loudly asks,

'Colin, what size are you?'

Overheard by Pocket Rocket, from my friend
Posted on Monday, 17 April 2006

Yes, no, Coke ...

Standing behind a woman in line for KFC. She orders (along with other stuff) a 'Coke'. The young Asian clerk behind the counter replies, 'I am sorry, we have no Coke.'

Woman: 'You have no Coke?'

Asian clerk: 'Yes.'

Woman: 'So you've got Coke?'

Asian clerk: 'No, we have no Coke.'

Woman: 'You have no Coke?'

Asian clerk: 'Yes.'

Woman: 'So you've got Coke?'

Overheard by Lamont, KFC at Clare Hall
Posted on Monday, 17 April 2006

The beautiful accent

Behind a group of French kids in McDonald's on Grafton Street. They pool their money together, and the best English-speaker is chosen to go to the counter and put the order in.

'Three Big Mac meals and two McChicken sandwiches, please,' says the chosen kid.

'Is dah ih?' replies the girl on the counter.

The French kid looks confused.

'Three Big Mac meals and two Mc ...'

'Yeah, I've got dat. Is dah it? Anyting else?'

After some chattering amongst themselves, they

just hand her a bunch of money and stare at her, bemused.

Overheard by Rory, McDonald's, Grafton Street
Posted on Monday, 17 April 2006

Colours, sizes, locations ... all too much!

Staff guy at Tan.ie serving some girl.

Guy: 'OK, nine minutes. You're in room no. 2, just press the blue button on the wall when you're ready to start the sunbed.'

Gal: 'Wha?'

Guy: 'When you're ready to start the sunbed, just press the blue button on the wall.'

Gal: 'Awwwwwww, right.'

Few minutes later she emerges from the tanning rooms:

Gal (shouting): 'It didn't come on!'

Guy goes in and checks while Gal stands in shop, bitching about why it's all a scam.

Guy emerges from rooms:

'It didn't start 'cos instead of pressing the Small Blue Button on the wall labelled "Start", you pressed the Large Red Button on the inside of the bed labelled "Emergency Stop".'

Overheard by Justin, Tan.ie (Chartbusters) in Clare Hall
Posted on Sunday, 16 April 2006

Rear 'em right

An auld granny pushing the young wan's baby in the pram. Granny leans over and goo-es at the baby and says, 'Giv us a luv!'

Baby gurgles. Encouraged, Granny leans in again and with a little more enthusiasm says, 'Ah gwan, giv us a luv!'

Baby beams responsively, Granny gets into the moment, leans over again, tickles baby and says, 'Ah, gwan, giv' us a f**kin' luv!'

Overheard by Wu, Irish Life Mall off Talbot Street
Posted on Sunday, 16 April 2006

Politically incorrect

Late 1990s and a few mates of mine were working as security guards on the door of shops on Grafton Street, watching out for shop-lifters. As you know, security guards have their own lingo for most things.

My mate on radio: 'Jim, there's a few knackers gone into Monsoon.'

Controller to all units: 'For the last time, lads, don't be calling them knackers, we could get into trouble for that.'

My mate: 'Right, Bud. Jim, there's a few cream crackers gone into Monsoon.'

Overheard by John, Grafton Street
Posted on Sunday, 16 April 2006

Has it all except Irish Times

A guy goes up to the newsagent counter and the girl behind it asks, 'What do you want?'

He replies, 'Thanks to a good education and wealthy parents, I want for nothing, however I do require a copy of the *Irish Times*.'

Overheard by Derrick, at a shop beside the Four Courts
Posted on Saturday, 15 April 2006

The auld ones

Old Lady #1: 'Did you hear what happened to Bernie yesterday morning after mass?'

Old Lady #2: 'Someone told me she took sick ...'

Old Lady #1: 'Mmmm. Got up and ran straight to the vestry after the communion.'

Old Lady #2: 'My God, what was wrong with her?'

Old Lady #1: 'Coleslaw!' (followed by a knowing sniff)

Old Lady #2: 'Oh no! That happened to me before.'

Old Lady #1: 'Mmmm, yes.'

Old Lady# 2: 'Mmmm, coleslaw, yes. It's lethal.'

Overheard by Liz, on the DART passing through Killester
Posted on Saturday, 15 April 2006

If ignorance is bliss, then meet the happiest girl in the world

In school, one of my nearest and dearest friends was telling us about the Ireland match she and her boyfriend had been to see the night before. We all asked her how it was and did she have a good time, to which she replied,

'I enjoyed it an' all but I was lost in the second half.'

I asked her why? Her answer was,

'Well, the gobshites changed sides.'

Overheard by Toni, Dublin school
Posted on Friday, 14 April 2006

Paying for a good education

While observing a case in the Four Courts last year. The girl in question was a past pupil of a well-known large south-Dublin fee-paying school.

Defence barrister: 'Is this where you were residing at the time?'

Girl: 'Sorry, what do you mean by residing?'

Her parents must be so proud — that was money well spent!

Overheard by observer, Court 24, the Four Courts
Posted on Friday, 14 April 2006

Buttered up by an Asian girl

I asked the Asian-looking girl behind the deli counter for a roll with sausages, rashers and tomato ketchup. As the girl replied too quickly and loudly for my ears to discern what she was saying, I asked her to repeat herself again and again and again.

Still unable to make out what she was asking me after her third attempt to communicate with me, I thought she was going to flip when she took a few deep breaths, composed herself and said:

'BUH ER? D'ya want Buh er on yar roll?' in the thickest Dublin accent imaginable. I said yes and thanked her very much. I left smiling to myself — completely forgetting to pay for the roll!

Overheard by Aidan, Spar
Posted on Thursday, 13 April 2006

Maxin' relaxin'

I was in a hospital the other day when I heard this guy from the next room shouting for ages. He then screamed, 'Oh God, somebody help me!'

I told a nurse that was walking by and she just said, 'He's crazy.'

Two minutes later a doctor went in to calm the man down.

Doctor: 'Would you relax?'

Patient: 'I'm gonna f**king relax your head against the wall in a minute.'

Overheard by Sean, St James's Hospital
Posted on Wednesday, 12 April 2006

Multi-talented George Foreman

I was watching the film *Ali* with my girlfriend and it came to the 'Rumble in the Jungle' between Muhammad Ali and George Foreman. Bear in mind this was a documentary of Ali's life.

Ring announcer: 'In the left corner we have George Foreman!'

Girlfriend: 'Oh my God, I can't believe he is an actor *and* a chef!'

Overheard by Niall, Star Century
Posted on Wednesday, 12 April 2006

Kids in the pub

We were just after leaving a pub on Paddy's Day that was full of kids watching their parents getting rubbered. So we got talking about how much of a waste of a day it was to have the kids locked up in a pub.

Heading home we jumped in a taxi. The taxi driver was full of chat and was asking about what we'd done for the day.

One of the lads — for the craic — says, 'Ah, nothing better then bringing the kids to the pub and having a few pints on Paddy's Day,' and the taxi driver goes,

'Ah God yeah, you're right, sure I was there this morning with them.'

Overheard by Deco, in a Dublin taxi
Posted on Tuesday, 11 April 2006

Half price!

Walking down the road, man on push bike with Tesco bags. The man just cycling, minding his own business, when a car slows down by him, window rolls down, and girl with a doll in her hands holds the doll out, screams out, 'HALF PRICE AT TESCO ...'

Only in Dublin!

Overheard by Anonymous, city centre
Posted on Tuesday, 11 April 2006

Wear them and die?

Old dear (dealer) on Henry Street: 'Get the last of the Terminal underwear!'

Overheard by Wally, Henry Street
Posted on Tuesday, 11 April 2006

Not the sharpest tool in the box

In Superquinn in Walkinstown last night. I was at the checkout and the checkout girl says, 'If any of you have less than five items you can go to the checkout at the off-licence.'

A woman behind me with one item in her hand (big piece of meat) says to me,

'I have less than five items, don't I?'

Overheard by Mossy, Superquinn, Walkinstown
Posted on Monday, 10 April 2006

Politically unaware

On the no. 42 bus to Malahide, couple of young ones. Passing by a house:

Young one #1: 'That's Charlie Haughey's house.'

Young one #2: 'Who's he?'

Young one #1: 'You're a bleedin' thick, sure wasn't he the President of Ireland.'

Overheard by Barry, on the no. 42 bus
Posted on Monday, 10 April 2006

Skangers versus D4s

Was coming out of Dundrum Shopping Centre on Saturday, three D4 head girls walking towards me (with the quiffed hairs and the UGG boots).

There was a gang of skangers sitting on the wall at the fountain, and one of them wolf-whistled over at the girls. They giggled and turned around to soak up the praise, but to their obvious dismay, the whistling skanger shouted,

'Wasn't wistlin' at yous, yiz uglee bitches!'

All the skangers fell about the place laughing … class.

Overheard by David, Dundrum Shopping Centre
Posted on Monday, 10 April 2006

Coming off bread

Two sales assistants discussing what to get for their lunch. The first girl says to her mate, 'I'm trying to give up bread, it's bad for me.'

The second girl replies, 'Yer dead right, I was reading the ingredients on a packet of bread the other day, it's full of bleeding addictives!'

Overheard by Sinéad, clothes shop
Posted on Sunday, 9 April 2006

I had to ask!

I was waiting for the bus from Busáras to go to the airport, but the CityLink bus which is supposed to be very regular hadn't appeared in over 30 minutes. When I eventually got on the bus I raised my voice over the traffic to ask the bus driver,

'How regular are you?' — no sooner had I said it I knew it came out wrong — to which he replied,

'At least once a day!'

Overheard by KL, Busáras
Posted on Sunday, 9 April 2006

Hail to the bus driver

Getting on the no. 46A bus heading towards town. Pulling change out of my pocket for fare. I had €1.10 and a €2 coin. The fare was €1.05. I popped the €2 coin into the machine. The driver looks at me and says,

'This isn't a savin' scheme I'm running here!'

Overheard by Stebag, on the no. 46A bus
Posted on Sunday, 9 April 2006

Begging techniques

Was walking towards Grafton Street when this old homeless lad shouts out, 'Here! Give us some money or I'll give ya a box!'

I turned round to see him standing there with a cardboard box in his hand — and a big smile on his face. Had to give him some cash after that …

Overheard by Kev, St Stephen's Green
Posted on Saturday, 8 April 2006

Classy

Couple in their 40s get on the bus and she goes upstairs. He asks the driver for change of €20, and then holds up the whole bus, arguing with the driver that he hasn't any more money.

From upstairs you hear her shouting, 'Darren, will ye hurry up!'

Next she shouts, 'If I hafta come downstayers there is gonna be some amount of trouble.'

Then you hear her stomping downstairs, screaming at the bus driver, 'I'm f**kin' disabled. I'm f**kin' disabled. What's your problem, it's not coming out of your bleedin' pockeh!'

She then grabs the man and storms back upstairs, still shouting at the driver.

At Cork Street she screams again, 'Get your bleedin' hands off me,' stomps downstairs again, smoking a smoke, gets off — and lies down by the railings!

Overheard by Sarah, on the no. 77A bus
Posted on Saturday, 8 April 2006

Erectile dysfunction

A good-looking girl was walking ahead of me through town. We were passing a building covered with scaffolding. One of the workers was leaning against the scaffold near the path. He winks at the girl as she passes, sweeps out a dramatic hand gesture towards the scaffold and says,

'Wha de ye tink o' me massive erection, love?'

Nice!

Overheard by Anonymous, Mercer Street
Posted on Saturday, 8 April 2006

Spare change

I was queuing for the ATM on Grafton Street one night, and as per usual there was a beggar, sitting in between both machines, sure to get some attention.

Beggar: 'Hey mista, any spare change, pleeaaasss?'

Me: 'Sorry man, all I have is a fifty.'

Beggar: 'No worries, I'll give ya change!'

Overheard by Peter, Grafton Street
Posted on Friday, 7 April 2006

Prazky: crazy-old-drunk-approved

At Ranelagh Luas stop there was this old drunk sort of talking to himself. I was carrying a six-pack of Prazky. Suddenly the old drunk shouts at me, with much enthusiasm,

'Prazky! By God, that's the way to do it, boy!'

Overheard by Dan, Ranelagh Luas stop
Posted on Friday, 7 April 2006

ALLIGATOR

Walking through Temple Bar last Saturday, I noticed a bit of a commotion and headed towards it. Two lads appeared to be in a bit of a scrap and the Garda asks one of the lads, 'What are the allegations you are making?'

To which the man replies, 'No, he's the alligator (pointing toward other lad) …'

FACT!

Overheard by Andy, Temple Bar
Posted on Friday, 7 April 2006

Telling it as it is

On the Luas last night just before the stop for Heuston Station, all of a sudden the driver slams the brakes and we screech to a halt, cue shrieks and general confusion as everyone thought we had crashed. The driver then switches on the intercom and announces ever so politely,

'Sorry about that, ladies and gents, some GOBSHITE just ran a red light right in front of us!'

Overheard by Ciara, Luas Red Line
Posted on Friday, 7 April 2006

Who's driving who?

On the no. 4 bus to Ballymun.

Bus stops at the top of Parnell Square, driver sticks his head out and shouts down the bus at the passengers,

'Any a youz use dis route regular? How do I get to Phibsboro from here?'

Everyone just laughs and wonders if they'll make it home at all!

Overheard by Anonymous, no. 4 bus to Ballymun
Posted on Friday, 7 April 2006

Discourage them while they're young

I was in the Ilac Centre Library and there was a mother in there with her young child. The child picks up a book and starts looking at it. The mum yells,

'PUT THAT BOOK DOWN, YOU KNOW YOU CAN'T READ!

What encouragement …

Overheard by Anna, Ilac Centre Central Library
Posted on Thursday, 6 April 2006

Blondie & Blondie

Two quite pretty blonde girls (around 19) sitting in the ground floor café in the Jervis Centre, talking (I thought) about the Iraq war. One (the one wearing a pink hoody amazingly) says, 'It's so terrible about Iraq,' to which the other replies,

'Oh my God, I know, the dust storms are awful there, women have to cover their heads so their hair doesn't get ruined …'

Overheard by Rick, in the ground floor café of the Jervis Centre
Posted on Thursday, 6 April 2006

Disgusting!

I was in Barcode on Paddy's Night and my friend and I went to use the ladies. As we made our way to the toilets we passed a group of lads playing pool. On our way back from the ladies one of the lads yells,

'I would have loved to be the toilet seat you two sat on!'

Overheard by K, Barcode
Posted on Thursday, 6 April 2006

Sound advice

While standing in a queue in a shop on South Circular Road I overheard a D4 girl ask for a cylinder of gas. She then asked,

'Like, how long will this bottle of gas last?' to which the shopkeeper quickly answered,

'Well, darling, if you never turn the cooker on it will last forever!'

Overheard by Gerry, shop, South Circular Road
Posted on Thursday, 6 April 2006

Shamrock shake

I was near Christ Church with my friends from America who were sampling a Shamrock Shake, which of course comes out around Paddy's Day every year.

A courier is cycling by quite fast and somehow spots the milkshake in my hand. As he cycles off into the distance he shouts back in a thick Dublin accent,

'Here, Bud, is that a Shamrock Shake?', to which I shout back, 'Yeah.' Courier shouts back enthusiastically from the distance, 'NICE ONE!'

Overheard by Dara, Christ Church
Posted on Wednesday, 5 April 2006

Paddy's Night mayhem

'I've lost the will to live.'

A clearly fed-up Garda expressing his feelings to another Garda.

Overheard by Fiona, in Temple Bar on Paddy's Night
Posted on Wednesday, 5 April 2006

Thick as thieves

Two blokes outside Paddy Powers having a smoke; one was asking the other if he knew 'John', to which the other replied,

'Of course I do, I've done loads of robberies with him.'

Overheard by Anonymous, outside Paddy Powers in Rathmines
Posted on Wednesday, 5 April 2006

Zero tolerance

Stressed out Posh Mother to misbehaving child (about five years old): 'Right, okay, right, that's it, that's final, that's absolutely final. You're getting no new toys and no McDonald's for a WHOLE WEEK.'

Overheard by DB, Tesco, Nutgrove Shopping Centre
Posted on Wednesday, 5 April 2006

Taxi humour

In a taxi with my boyfriend going out to DCU. We're chatting away to the taxi driver and he asks me what I'm studying. So I tell him about my course and he says, 'Ah, dat's great.'

Next thing he turns around, looks at my boyfriend and says, 'Jaysus, what are you studying to be — a heart-throb?'

We were both in hysterics. Yet another example of razor-sharp Dublin taxi driver wit!

Overheard by Dom, taxi
Posted on Wednesday, 5 April 2006

English lessons needed

Walking down Camden Street past two vegetable stalls. At the same time a man in his 20s was walking a bike with a flat tyre past the stalls.

Woman behind stall shouts out: 'Mister, yur chain is flaa!'

Man replies in French accent: 'Excuse me?'

Woman replies: 'I said, yur chain is flaa!'

French man replies: 'I do not understand.'

Woman behind stall replies: 'Ahh, come back to me when you learn English.'

Overheard by Anonymous, Camden Street
Posted on Tuesday, 4 April 2006

Banguard

I was out for lunch with a girl from work. She is not the brightest spark. She was telling me about a mutual friend who had gotten engaged.

I said, 'Oh yeah, she's marrying a guard, isn't she?'

The dope said, 'No, she's actually marrying a *banguard*.'

Confused, I said, 'Sorry?'

She replied, 'Yeah, he is in the Garda Band —
banguard, see …?'

Overheard by Nicola, Blanchardstown
Posted on Tuesday, 4 April 2006

A culchie thing to do

I was on the Luas Green Line going from St
Stephen's Green, and suddenly this old man
reeking of gin pushes in beside me on the seat.
As soon as he did this, he turned to me, scanned
me with his eyes and goes, 'You a culchie?'

I just said no, and started listening to some
music.

When the Luas stopped in Beechwood, a black
man tried to bring a bicycle onto the Luas, and
immediately the driver announces that he wasn't
allowed to bring a bike on the Luas. The old
man looks back, tuts at the black man, then
turns to me and goes,

'A bike on the Luas … that's a real culchie thing
to do.'

Overheard by Cian, on the Luas, Beechwood Station.
Posted on Tuesday, 4 April 2006

Fashion statement

Nice-looking girl wearing a t-shirt with a pair of
eyes printed across the chest, walks by a group
of road workers in yellow jackets.

On cue, one of them says, 'Nice eyes!'

Overheard by Robbo, Pearse Street
Posted on Monday, 3 April 2006

Dangerous woman

My brother had a bit of heartburn and was asking some people at work if they had anything for it. A nice older woman kindly assists, looking through her handbag of drugs saying, 'I have some of that semtex in here.'

Think she meant Zantac …

Overheard by Anonymous, workplace

Posted on Monday, 3 April 2006

In touch with his inner self

Some years ago, I was walking along near Stephen's Green on a gorgeous, sunny summer morning. It seemed that everyone was out enjoying the day. The street was fairly crowded with women pushing prams, school-kids, a bit of everything.

To one side of the path, there was a huge pile of Bord Gáis, bright, canary-yellow PVC pipes, piled in a pyramid about 6 foot high, about to be installed somewhere nearby. There must have been over a hundred of them, and they really were striking in their 'yellowness'.

Of course, a crowded Dublin street would not be complete without the friendly neighbourhood nutter, and sure enough, one came bouncing along, talking to himself.

When he came within view of the pipes, he froze and suddenly started shouting at the top of his lungs,

'YELLOW! YELLOW! YELLOW!'

Overheard by Heather, near St Stephen's Green
Posted on Sunday, 2 April 2006

He's right!

An old drunk, sitting singing on the bus, glared out at a billboard for 7 Up Free and shouted, 'F**king sham — 7 Up's not free!'

We were all in stitches ...

Overheard by Paul, the no. 130 bus coming home from town
Posted on Sunday, 2 April 2006

Getting out

Was out in the Red Cow Hotel playing a poker tournament recently, and during a break I had the following conversation with a true Dub:

Me: 'I've seen you at every poker tournament I've been at lately, do you ever not play, you know take a break?'

Guy: 'Do you ever wonder why I play so much?'

Me: 'You're making money!?'

Guy: 'No it's not that, but if you saw the mutt I had waiting for me at home you'd get out of the house as often as you could too.'

Overheard by Patrick, Red Cow Hotel
Posted on Saturday, 1 April 2006

Immaculate contraception

At the no. 77 bus stop, two youngish girls, maybe sixteen years old, discussing the contraceptive implant:

'It's like a match stick, goes under your skin, don't protect you from dem STDs though.'

'Wha abou' STIs?'

'What's dem then?'

'You know, a sexually transmitted injury?'

Overheard by Anonymous, at the no. 77 bus stop
Posted on Saturday, 1 April 2006

Where'll I meet ya so?

Walking out from Irish Life on Abbey Street for my lunch break and pass by a young yobbo with a phone glued to his ear, yammering away, trying to meet up with his friend. It went something like this:

Yob: 'Yeah, I'm outside Irish … eh? … Roight I'm on Abbey … F**k! Roight! You know the Spire? Grand, cause I'm nowhere near tha!'

Overheard by John, Abbey Street
Posted on Saturday, 1 April 2006

The invisible car

After leaving the Dew Drop in Kill slightly worse for wear, we walked down the road towards my sister's boyfriend's house. After a few minutes a Garda car pulls up beside them. The window rolls down.

Garda: 'Are you driving?'

Well …

Overheard by Ian, Kill (near Dublin)
Posted on Saturday, 1 April 2006

Good observation

While walking through the Square in Tallaght, I noticed two Tallaghites standing at the top of an escalator which wasn't moving. They were staring in bemusement at the motionless stairway, when after a good few minutes one looked up and said,

'I think we're going to have to walk.'

Overheard by Pete, Tallaght Square
Posted on Wednesday, 29 March 2006

From the mouths of babes ...

We all know how small children can REALLY embarrass adults, but this to me took the biscuit.

Little girl in the checkout queue was throwing a mega tantrum because Mammy wouldn't buy her sweets. When screaming, shouting, crying, lying on the floor and kicking didn't achieve the desired result, she stood, drew herself up to her full height, and yelled at the top of her voice,

'I saw you kissing Daddy's willie!'

I needn't tell you that one VERY embarrassed mother dropped her shopping and fled! I'm still laughing about it a year later!

Overheard by Anonymous, Tesco, The Square, Tallaght
Posted on Wednesday, 29 March 2006

Hmmm bop! or bus?!?

On the no. 16 to Rathfarnham when the bus pulls up at a stop. Three D4 young rugger heads that look like Hanson (remember them?) wannabes are standing half on/half off the bus debating something, when the bus driver vents his rage at them:

'Come on, girls, will ye?!'

The Hanson boys started blushing and the bus started laughing …

Overheard by Chops, on the no. 16 bus
Posted on Wednesday, 29 March 2006

Fag area?

Was at a gay night out a few years ago with a male friend. We decided to go out for a smoke, and my friend (who is wearing a dress, stilettos, wig and makeup) asks the bouncer,

'D'ya know where the fag area is?'

Poor bouncer was still laughing when we passed him ten minutes later …

Overheard by Annette, the Ambassador
Posted on Wednesday, 29 March 2006

Canal rescue

Along the canal at Baggot Street, a guy running past had managed to fall in. A large crowd gathered to watch the rescue operation which involved about 30 policemen, an ambulance, a rescue unit and two fire brigades.

The attempt to get him out using a rope had failed because he had pulled it in on top of himself, so they lowered a ladder. For some reason the (stoned or drunk) guy in the water swam around the back of the ladder and was screaming, 'Ouch me legs, me legs are freezing!'

At this stage the fireman lost his temper and shouted down, 'Shut up moanin' and climb up the ladder, ya f**kin' eejit!'

We were all thinking it!

Overheard by Stacy, Grand Canal at Baggot Street
Posted on Tuesday, 28 March 2006

A1 maths student?

On the bus home from work and a trio of secondary students pile on to an already packed bus. Their conversation is about their impending Leaving Cert exams this summer and one of the girls exclaims, 'I sooo need to get an A1 in maths to get my course.'

The conversation continues and then leads to talk of their mocks in April which prompts one of the girls to wonder how long they had 'til then. The A1 student pipes up,

'Don't worry that's, like, 20 weeks away.'

Overheard by AMB, on the no. 41 bus
Posted on Tuesday, 28 March 2006

Jim Apple

In Dubray Books in Dun Laoghaire I overheard a secondary school student enquiring about a school book at the desk. 'Do you have Jim Apple?'

'Jim Apple?' the confused clerk replied.

'Yeah, Jim Apple, it's a French book,' answered the teen.

'Oh, *Je m'appelle*,' the clerk replied, holding back a smirk. 'I'll just get it for you now.'

Let's hope there's a chapter in that book on pronunciation.

Overheard by Jack, Dubray Bookshop, Dun Laoghaire
Posted on Tuesday, 28 March 2006

Who needs the FBI

A while ago I was watching *Crimeline* on RTÉ and one of our finest was going through the details of a robbery that took place. He picks up a small green petrol tank and the rest goes like this.

Presenter: 'What's that you've got there?'

Garda: 'It's a green petrol container found at the crime scene and we believe it was used to carry petrol.'

I know you're thinking: 'Made up.'

I wish it was …

Overheard by Jimmy, *Crimeline*, RTÉ TV (Donnybrook)
Posted on Monday, 27 March 2006

Bulimic ... classic Dublin!

While out walking my dog a couple of months ago I passed a group of early teens talking about and getting ready for the upcoming night's merriments. One lad in particular was at one of the girls to come out and get trolleyed with them.

He pestered her until she got annoyed and gave the definitive answer:

'I told ye no! If me Ma catches me drinking again she'll go bulimic!'

Overheard by Will, Dundrum
Posted on Monday, 27 March 2006

Fashion police

I was in a sports shop last week in my civies when some aul' one taps me on the shoulder. As I turn around she barks, 'Size five, love, I'm in a rush,' to which I reply, 'Sorry I don't work here.'

Instead of her walking away rather sheepishly, she shouts, 'What, you mean they're your normal clothes? You're mad!'

Overheard by Roger Le Mont, The Square
Posted on Monday, 27 March 2006

Irish v. Germans

Guy on the bus asks for the fare *as Gaeilge*.

Bus driver (in a thick Dub accent): 'Nie sprecken de Irish.'

Overheard by Tom, on the no. 46A bus
Posted on Monday, 27 March 2006

Urinal traffic management

In the cinema a few months back. Movie ended and the scramble to the gents began. The toilets were crowded, as a number of films ended together, and there was a queue of two or three lads behind each urinal.

Then from the back of the queue, a random man in his best Dublin authoritarian voice shouts:

'Right, lads, have 'em out and ready when approaching the urinal!'

The guys didn't know whether to laugh, or pretend they couldn't hear!

Overheard by P, Savoy Cinema
Posted on Sunday, 26 March 2006

When the customer is a 13-year-old boy

I was at the local Spar, and this 13-year-old was at the counter buying a bottle of Pepsi.

He was counting one, two and five cents out, really slowly, just to annoy the girl behind the counter. When he finally got to the right amount, he threw the rest of the change down, grabbed his bottle and said,

'Keep the change, get yourself a decent haircut.'

He walked out — leaving me and the poor girl speechless!

Overheard by Katelynn, local Spar
Posted on Sunday, 26 March 2006

Good enough excuse as any

Walking along the street I noticed a young man being searched by a guard. Garda said to him,

'I'm arresting you for being a dickhead!'

Only in Ireland …

Overheard by Shauna, beside St Stephen's Green Shopping Centre

Posted on Sunday, 26 March 2006

Beer goggles

My brother and his mate sitting at the bar in their local, where the people within earshot heard the following conversation.

Brother: 'Mick, you're drunk.'

Mick: 'Feck off. What do you mean?'

Brother: 'You're pissed, I can tell when you've had too much.'

Mick: 'Ah stop messing and keep your voice down, you're very loud.'

Brother: 'I'm just telling you the facts, just ask anyone.'

Mick: 'How are you so sure that I'm drunk?'

Brother: 'You're gone all blurred …'

Overheard by Higgs, The Royal Oak

Posted on Saturday, 25 March 2006

Tasty

I was in the queue for breakfast in Jurys Ballsbridge last summer, when these two Yanks came back up for seconds.

'Scuse me, waiter,' she says, 'What are those black things? They were really delicious. We got nothing like that back home. What is it?'

Waiter: 'It's black pudding, very nice.'

'What's it made from?' she asks.

'Pig's blood,' comes the forthright reply.

American gent: 'I think we'll just have the eggs …'

Overheard by Shamo, Jurys Ballsbridge
Posted on Saturday, 25 March 2006

Patriotic pub customer

Elderly patriotic gentleman goes into his local pub much later than usual on a Sunday night about four years ago. He has obviously been drinking.

The barman says, 'Well, Johnny, we've been missing you. Where were you at all?'

'I was at a funeral,' declares Johnny.

'Who's funeral?' asks the barman.

'Kevin Barry's!' shouts Johnny.

'Jaze, I didn't even know he was sick,' replies the barman.

Overheard by Anonymous, Leeson Lounge
Posted on Saturday, 25 March 2006

Medical help

Young girl at bus stop on mobile phone:

Girl: 'I'm in town. Will you meet me?'

'Where are you?'

Girl: 'I'm opposite a shop. It's "The V ..., V ..."'

(Interrupted by man next to her) Man: 'It's the "VHI", love!'

Overheard by Anonymous, it happened to a friend of my daughter
Posted on Friday, 24 March 2006

Blondes

Two young wans sitting behind me on the no. 43 bus, discussing the merits of dyed hair, when one says to the other,

'If I had me hair dyed blonde and I was pregnant, would the baby be blonde too?'

Overheard by Anonymous, on the no. 43 bus
Posted on Friday, 24 March 2006

Surely there was a better place to make this call ...

Picture it: no. 10 bus going home from work the other evening. Young Dublin boy in front of me decides to call some girl that he had obviously only met the previous weekend. Conversation goes something like this:

Dublin Boy: 'Hi, Joanne, it's Danny!'

Girl: 'Danny who?'

Dublin Boy: 'Danny ... remember? The guy from last weekend?'

There's a couple of seconds of a pause:

Dublin Boy: 'Hello? Hello ...?'

She had hung up on him.

Everyone on the bus was in fits of laughter and the red-faced young fella got off at the next stop.

Overheard by Jonathan, on the no. 10 bus
Posted on Friday, 24 March 2006